# SHATTERED
# FATE
## —AND THE—
# LAWS OF
# EXISTENCE

BILLY MORRIS

Copyright © 2022 Billy Morris.

All rights reserved. No part of this book may be reproduced, stored, or transmitted by any means—whether auditory, graphic, mechanical, or electronic—without written permission of both publisher and author, except in the case of brief excerpts used in critical articles and reviews. Unauthorized reproduction of any part of this work is illegal and is punishable by law.

ISBN: 979-8-88640-606-1 (sc)
ISBN: 979-8-88640-607-8 (hc)
ISBN: 979-8-88640-608-5 (e)

Because of the dynamic nature of the Internet, any web addresses or links contained in this book may have changed since publication and may no longer be valid. The views expressed in this work are solely those of the author and do not necessarily reflect the views of the publisher, and the publisher hereby disclaims any responsibility for them.

One Galleria Blvd., Suite 1900, Metairie, LA 70001
1-888-421-2397

# CONTENTS

Introduction ..................................................................................... v
Chapter 1   The First Days of the Campaign ........................... 1
Chapter 2   The Venture Out of Hela ...................................... 10
Chapter 3   The Pangaea Prophecy ......................................... 18
Chapter 4   The Lost Awakening ............................................. 28
Chapter 5   The Charge of the Giant ....................................... 36
Chapter 6   The Dragon Master and the Death Stalker ......... 45
Chapter 7   The Dragon Guild's Prize ..................................... 54
Chapter 8   The Two-faced Witch ........................................... 62
Chapter 9   The Witch of Hela ................................................. 70
Chapter 10  A New Companion ............................................... 78
Chapter 11  The Forsaken Wench ............................................ 86
Chapter 12  Nowhere to Go ..................................................... 94
Chapter 13  Union of Dragon Guilds ..................................... 101
Chapter 14  A Whisper of the Truth ...................................... 110
Chapter 15  The Deception of Hela ....................................... 119
Chapter 16  The Collection of Information .......................... 127
Chapter 17  The Influence of the Two-faced Witch ............. 134
Chapter 18  Lost in the Light ................................................. 141
Chapter 19  The Sacrifice for the Dragon ............................. 149
Chapter 20  The Lost Companion .......................................... 156

| Chapter 21 | The First Contact | 163 |
| Chapter 22 | Stuck Between the Lights | 170 |
| Chapter 23 | The Meeting of Lost Souls | 177 |
| Chapter 24 | The Second Meeting | 184 |
| Chapter 25 | Two Halves of a Whole | 192 |
| Chapter 26 | The Giant and the Spellcaster | 199 |
| Chapter 27 | The Witch and the Warmonger | 207 |
| Chapter 28 | Rise of the Dragon Master | 215 |
| Chapter 29 | The Dragon Pursuit | 224 |
| Chapter 30 | The Day of Nightmares | 232 |
| Chapter 31 | In the Way of Dreams | 239 |
| Chapter 32 | Fading Hope | 246 |
| Chapter 33 | The Gathering of Forces | 254 |
| Chapter 34 | The End Game | 262 |
| Chapter 35 | The New Prophecy | 272 |

# INTRODUCTION

As anyone with half a mind will tell you, every civilization must come to the same conclusion about the universe and the laws that govern all things, living or otherwise. The people of the planets Eden and Metro once thought they understood the laws of existence, but as fate would have it, they only understood about half from their perspective.

Now, with their very existence hanging in the balance, they must figure out if these laws can save them before their world is lost and their fate shattered.

This story begins in a time long before the need to record history or long after history mattered, depending on your perspective. In this time, most people believed that no two objects could occupy the same space at the same time. Technically, this is true today, the same as it was then. Although Eden and Metro did occupy the same space, the two planets were at different ends of the time spectrum - if such things matter - but that did not stop them from colliding. It is quite easy to see how the collision could be misinterpreted as a breakdown in the physical laws of the universe or the laws of existence as they were known.

Metro, by all accounts, was an advanced planet that orbited a young yellow sun and was at the height of its technology just moments before the collision. Eden, on the other hand, was a garden world that circled an ancient red giant sun and was at the top of its evolutionary cycle just moments before the collision. According to the laws of existence, two opposing forces will always be drawn toward each other, regardless of the amount of space and time between them. Unknown to those of either world but consistent with the laws of existence, these two planets were opposite forces that had been pulled toward each other since the beginning of time itself. According to the fundamental laws, force is always equal to the mass of an object times the acceleration of the object, but most people believe the laws failed here.

When two objects of equal mass and velocity collide in the same way that Eden and Metro did, there should have been a massive explosion. When Eden and Metro smashed into each other, however, they were not destroyed as the laws might have predicted, but they were nevertheless devastated and would never be the same again. Except for a small landmass in Eden's northern hemisphere that was ejected during the collision, the two planets did not explode or implode as one might have expected.

This small landmass known as Selene now orbits this new world every twenty-eight days, and as the old language was forgotten, so was the name of this lost land. However, this moon was the only way to keep track of time as the new planet no longer rotated around either sun. The world that remained was twice as large as either Eden or Metro individually, and it seemed to be stuck somewhere in time between the old red giant sun of Eden and the young yellow sun of Metro. This planet had one large landmass that covered most of one side of the planet while a vast ocean covered the rest.

Magic had held this new world together in the moments after the collision, and now every time someone was born with this gift, there was less magic to hold the world together. Only a small group of scientists realized the force that held their world together needed to be returned if they had any chance of saving themselves.

Not everyone in this new world was born with this gift of magic, but anyone with the gift born within a certain region would show similarities in their abilities. The people born in the region of the world where only the yellow sun shone were blessed with the magic of the four elements of earth, wind, fire, and water. The people who were born on the other side of the world, where only the red sun shone, were blessed with the magic of change. The people born in the region between the two suns received the light from both, and they were blessed with the magic of sight, or will. When the people of these regions learned to take the gifts from each other, magic began to mix and allowed people to use it to cast spells. The people born in the region called the Dark Lands (or the land without sunlight) were not born with the gift of magic and had to find other ways to survive.

According to the laws of existence, anything and everyone had another half that could be their opposite or the love of their life. Most scholars of the day believed that Eden and Metro had been halves that were meant to be together since the beginning of time.

The people adopted the word *halves* to identify people who were lucky—or cursed, depending on the perspective—enough to find their other half. Halves were typically extremely powerful masters of magic who could share or take the magic from their other half at will.

By most accounts, the new world had not seen the dawn of a new day in a thousand years. The uncontrolled vegetation of Eden had consumed the new world, and the once-magnificent cities of Metro had all but crumbled to the ground.

What remained of civilization divided the lands into kingdoms. Most of these kingdoms were under constant attack from warmongers who would use their armies to control the people and the magic.

At first, most kingdoms, except those in the Dark Lands, only had a few people who processed the gift of magic. With the emergence of more people born in the light, however, magic became more commonplace with every cycle of the moon. Within the first fifty years after the two worlds collided, people born with the gift of magic started to lose control of their abilities.

As the years passed, most disciplines of magic formed guilds to teach and control those born with this gift. Guilds soon became the only way to protect kingdoms from the warmongers who continued to try to control the people and the magic.

Within the first hundred years after the collision, every kingdom had a dozen magic guilds to protect their citizens. Weaker kingdoms, though, fell to those with more powerful guilds and became slaves.

Within three hundred years, the magic guilds were not only protecting the kingdoms but also ruling them.

The people in the region known as the Dark Lands were not born with the gift of magic. The only weapon they had to defend themselves with was the dying technology of the planet Metro. All magic worked in the Dark Lands, but anyone or anything born without the light of one of the suns was not born with the gift of magic.

Technology, of course, was no match for those with the gift of magic. Soon, those who wanted to get away had to go deeper into the Dark Lands.

The biggest problem was that not much grew in the Dark Lands, so people still had to stay close to the light so they could grow food.

To protect their citizens from these warmongers who would use their magic guilds to destroy entire cities, the kingdoms of the Dark Lands genetically created creatures they called dragons.

These dragons had to be trained from the time they were hatched, but they were the most feared creatures on the planet. When the dragons were ten years old, they could be ridden and would serve as the best protection against warmongers and magic guilds. By the time the dragons turn thirty years old, neither magic guilds nor mighty armies had any chance against them.

These dragons had to be hatched in the dark, or they would become unstable and far more dangerous than magic. All dragons could fly, but only the ones hatched in the light of either sun could breathe fire. For hundreds of years, dragon riders protected the Dark Lands from magic guilds and warmongers. Eventually, the light regions discovered the weakness of dragons—if they controlled or killed the rider, then they could control these creatures.

When a rider was killed, the dragons would search for a new rider. If they did not find a new rider, they would wander aimlessly until they became wild. The longer the dragons went without a rider, the more dangerous they would become. Even if the dragon could not be turned against the Dark Lands, they were far easier to kill without the rider.

To make matters worse, the wild dragons would breed, and those hatched in the light would grow up without a rider or training. These dragons were the most dangerous creatures on the planet because they did not care for people.

Dragon guilds were formed with the sole purpose of hunting down the light dragons and driving them back into the Dark Lands.

After a hundred years passed, the dragon riders moved deeper into the Dark Lands where they would be safer. Therefore, the only dragons most people saw were the light dragons. As powerful as magic was, most people feared these creatures above all else, and they did not believe there were such things as blameless dragons.

When the light dragons were all hunted down and killed, the dragon guilds turned to bounty hunting, assassination, and anything else they could think of to make money.

Little grew in the Dark Lands, and there was no real reason for anyone to invade. However, what the people of the Dark Lands feared the most was an invasion that included the use of dragons. Dragons were the most powerful weapons on the planet, so it was a standing order that anyone who found one in the light had to return it to the Dark Lands.

Eight hundred and fifty years after the two worlds had collided, magic had almost grown out of control, and even the magic guilds had trouble controlling those with the gift. The scholars in the Dark Lands believed that every person born with this gift took away from the energy that held the world together.

One in every ten people who were born in the light had some manner of magical power. Most of them were taken by the magic guilds so that they could learn to control their ability and become functioning members of the community. Not everyone with the gift of magic would learn to control their power. These people typically found themselves serving in a dragon guild, which meant they served a warmonger.

Hundreds of kingdoms were formed with one primary purpose, which was to protect their citizens and resources from those who would enslave them. For every guild that wanted to protect their citizens, there were two warmongers who wanted to control their resources. Most kingdoms also built massive stone walls around their cities to keep the warmongers from conquering their magic guilds and enslaving their people.

As time passed, the new world became a free-for-all war zone in which only the strongest survived. In the East, West, and Center Regions—the three light regions of the world—magic was king, and whoever controlled this power controlled everything else. All conquerors were called warmongers and, just after dragon riders, were the most feared people on the planet. Most warmongers were masters of magic who would do anything to gain more power and control.

In the Dark Lands, there were few resources and even fewer reasons for outsiders to wander into the darkness other than to escape the wars or magic. The scholars of the Kingdom of Acoma had one last plan to save the world from magic before it destroyed what remained of both worlds.

They used all their resources, including their remaining ancient technology, to combine the DNA of a dragon with that of a human. A dragon master was created to restore power to the planet before the world was pulled apart and all was lost.

Although born without the power of magic, the dragon master Nedah soon became very powerful. With every victory, he learned to take more power from the warmongers, and once again, there was hope that the world might be saved.

However, the warmongers set a trap for Nedah, which ended all hope of stopping magic from destroying the world.

It was thought—although no one knows for sure what actually happened—that a powerful young warmonger named Lord Haden managed to kill the dragon master. He was able to claim all the power the dragon master had taken from the other warmongers. Not only was Haden now an extremely powerful master of magic, but he also controlled Nedah's four master dragons.

The dragons were two sets of halve dragons named Nereus, Eostre, Suntos, and Vesta. Their presence alone caused many kingdoms to surrender to Lord Haden and his ever-growing army long before they were anywhere near the city walls.

For the last 150 years, the most powerful regime was led by the ruthless warmonger Lord Haden, who conquered kingdom after kingdom in his endless quest for power. Lord Haden was a master of magic who controlled many witches, sorcerers, and wizards. His most powerful weapons, however, continued to be the two sets of halve dragons.

Haden had many wives who bore many children, most of whom possessed enormous power. Almost all his children were evil beyond comprehension and were some of the most ruthless warmongers on the planet. Although each of his children wanted the throne, all of them feared Haden because he ruled with an iron fist.

Many thought the warmonger was immortal, and few could remember a world without him.

Every kingdom in the region, where the yellow sun shone, felt his wrath. This story picks up as this warmonger was starting to turn his efforts toward the central kingdoms.

No one understood Lord Haden's interest in the small central kingdom of Utopia when there were so many other resources that were much easier to take. However, no one had the courage to question his orders to march upon the Kingdom of Utopia.

For years, a prophecy had predicted Lord Haden's arrival to this peaceful kingdom, and although he had never lost a war, it was foretold that he would never enter a single city in the kingdom. Although Utopia had its walls and magic guilds to protect themselves, Lord Haden had more soldiers in his armies than they had people.

It was not the warriors or the magic guilds he controlled that most people feared, but the four master dragons in his command.

# CHAPTER 1

# THE FIRST DAYS OF THE CAMPAIGN

It had been weeks since he had seen anything other than this ridiculous forest, but he knew his master, Lord Haden, wanted to be in the Kingdom of Utopia before the moon completed another cycle.

As commanding general of this campaign, Airus knew it was his job to make sure the legions kept moving. He had not heard anything from his master in over a week, but he knew this did not mean he could stop the movement without permission. To make matters worse, he was soaked through from the rain that had been falling for days.

He shook off the water the best he could and thought, *If Haden were to ask, it would be almost impossible to see if they were on schedule.* He had ordered the chief horologist to be ready to calculate the time the moment the sky cleared up enough to see the moon.

He reached up to adjust his hood as he watched the cutting foreman start walking toward him, but he already knew what the man wanted.

The foreman walked up and set his broad ax on the ground so that he could speak to the general. He asked, "Boss, any word from Lord Haden as to when we can take a break?"

Airus shook his head and replied, "You know the rules. We move until we are told to stop, but I can probably get you a few more men from the back lines."

After a few moments, the foreman picked up his ax, shook his head, and replied, "Boss, I guess that is what we have to do." He then swung the outsized ax over his shoulder and started walking back toward his crew to inform them of the news.

As he watched the foreman walk back toward his men, Airus also shook his head. He had moved enough people to understand that there was no easy way to move sixty thousand warriors across four hundred leagues. On the other hand, he knew there had to be a better way to get where they were going without traveling through this rainforest.

He had no doubt that his master was the most brilliant strategist he had ever met. However, there was one thing he did not understand, and that was why his master was driving this army so hard toward the small kingdom of Utopia.

Airus knew that going through the forest had reduced the time it took to get to Utopia, but it had also cost them hundreds of decent warriors. He could not help but wonder what tactical advantage his master saw in this insignificant kingdom because he had not yet figured it out.

In the thirty years since he had surrendered to Lord Haden, more people than he cared to remember had tried to kill the warmonger. In all that time, he had never known his master to use so many resources for one small kingdom or be so determined to seek retribution.

Airus had been told that for the last 150 years, his master had been conquering kingdoms in the West Region, where only the yellow sun could be seen in the sky.

Most people believed it was only a matter of time before his master turned his armies and dragons on the Center Region.

He shook his head once again and concluded that this was the reason for such a massive campaign on such a small kingdom. He knew the Center Region had light from both suns and many resources, which would make it an attractive stronghold for his master.

Lord Haden had ordered no less than ten of his twenty legions to march toward the small central kingdom of Utopia. According to his master's orders, seven legions would march north and then east, toward the western boundary of this kingdom, so that everyone knew they were coming.

At the same time, his master had decided to lead the other three legions through the rainforest on the southern tip of this kingdom in hopes of catching these people unprepared for an attack from the south.

Airus believed that this simple division of forces would confuse the people of Utopia and catch them unprepared between Lord Haden's armies. He had no doubt his master's plan would break this small kingdom's defenses, but he also knew that this campaign could have been done with an army half the size. Once the magic guilds and dragons started to break down their defenses, the people would begin to retreat north. Those that were not captured or killed would run to the safety of their stone walls, where they would be easy targets for Lord Haden's dragons and raiding parties. Then, he would lead the ground forces to isolate each city so that they could start to pick them off one by one.

~*~

Once again, it had been days since they had stopped to rest, but at least the rain had finally stopped. Despite being so close to Utopia, all Airus wanted to do was to loosen his armor. He pulled at the straps, but there was nothing he could do to get more comfortable.

When his underling had helped to put his armor on a few days ago, he had pulled the straps a little tighter than Airus would have liked. He looked up to see if he could find someone to loosen his armor when he noticed a tall man standing at the edge of the woods. Even at this distance, he could see the man was carrying Haden's banner. It was not unusual for his master to send a messenger forward to relay his orders.

He looked at the man in the distance for a few moments. He hesitated because he really wanted to find someone to loosen his armor, but he finally decided that there was no reason to delay. He pulled the reins to guide his horse toward the edge of the woods where the strange man was waiting for him. As he rode up, he asked, "Do you have orders from Lord Haden?"

The tall man pointed his long, skinny fingers toward a distant hill and replied, "The master demands that you make camp there and await his orders."

Airus thought, "At last, the order to stop has been given, and I can find someone to loosen this damn armor." He nodded to the messenger and then turned so that he could inform the foreman that he needed to cut toward the distant hilltop.

Within a few hours, rumors began spreading through the camp that Lord Haden and his select were approaching. Airus had seen this tactic many times, and as he watched the word spread, he knew the three legions would stay here for a while.

Lord Haden controlled more than twenty legions, two dozen magic guilds, and the four most powerful dragons that ever lived. As far as Airus was concerned, his master did not even have to be here, but as always, he demanded to be the first to step foot on an adversary's land.

His master normally traveled two or three days behind the frontlines until he was ready to begin the attack. Eventually, he would bring his dragons forward so that the enemy could see these giant creatures. By the time the enemy knew where the dragons were, it would be too late for them to set up anything to stop them.

Airus knew this sudden shift in Lord Haden's position meant that the legions were within a few days' travel of Utopia's southern border. He also knew this would be the last stop before the conquest of this kingdom began.

Regardless of what people thought of his master, there was one thing no one ever said about him, and that was that he was a coward. Unlike most so-called warmongers, Lord Haden would lead from the front lines and was almost as feared as his dragons. Airus and everyone who had ever served under Lord Haden knew he would lead the first attack and last attack from the front lines.

Airus understood that dragons of any size were the last thing you wanted to see an enemy force send toward your armies and cities, but Lord Haden's four dragons were not ordinary monsters. These four dragons were the mothers of all nightmares. They were massive and unusually well trained, and they could carry out highly complex operations with or without a rider. Few people knew it, but these dragons were two sets of halve dragons named Nereus, Eostre, Suntos, and Vesta. Airus knew their presence alone had caused many kingdoms to surrender to Lord Haden long before these monsters were anywhere near their city walls.

Because they were fire breathers, most people feared the two light dragons more than the two dark dragons. Over the years, he had learned just enough about the dragons to know that it was the dark dragons that were the alpha male and female. No one, including his closest advisors, understood how Lord Haden controlled the dragons, especially the light dragons, but most people believed it had something to do with the pairing of the two halves.

Although no one would know which creature he would choose until moments before the battle began, Lord Haden would personally ride one of the massive beasts into battle. He would lead the dragon strikes to weaken Utopia's magic guilds. He would then use his magic guilds to break down the walls and barriers to allow his army access to anywhere he wanted to be.

As the dragons were immune to all types of magic, there was not much chance the magic guilds would have any defense against them. Airus knew it would not take long before the armies of Utopia would pull back to defend their magic guilds.

As the guilds were trying to protect themselves against the dragon's strikes, Lord Haden's legions and magic guilds would take the opportunity to strike. Airus knew because people feared the dragons more than anything else, most of the time, they would never realize they were being attacked by land forces until it was too late.

Airus believed that his master did not have any reason to destroy opposing armies because once he broke them, he would own them. He also knew that if his master wanted the people of Utopia dead, then they would be dead.

Although he had seen a dozen kingdoms surrender once they saw these dragons, he also understood that this kingdom was not some broken territory, barely able to defend their people. As he looked into the distant land, he knew they would probably take a while to break. Airus also knew that even if it took a full year to break them, they would fall the same as everyone else who ever faced Lord Haden.

The horses had been saddled, and the first wave of ground troops had been given their orders to be ready to commence the fight at a moment's notice. Airus had been preparing his troops for days, just waiting to be given the order to start the conquest of Utopia. However, he still had not received his orders, and as far as he knew, neither had the other generals, so he waited.

Although Airus was reasonably good at keeping his troops busy, he wanted the ground war to begin before he had to deal with the problems that came with waiting.

Suddenly one of his captains reported, "Sir, a messenger from Lord Haden is requesting to speak to you."

He quickly told the captain, "See that this man is brought to me immediately so that we can know what Lord Haden wants us to do."

As the tall man walked into the camp, Airus was reasonably sure that it was the same messenger who had stopped the legions a week ago.

The messenger raised his long arms and replied, "The master demands that you prepare his forces but wait until he feels that the time is right."

Although he knew the other generals would not be happy, Airus nodded his head and told the messenger, "I will ensure that no one acts without receiving orders from Lord Haden."

He shook his head because he did not like the idea of waiting around with nothing to do and asked, "Did the master say how long he wanted me to wait?"

The tall man stood without any expression on his face and then finally replied, "No."

Airus already knew the answer, but still he asked, "So Lord Haden pushed us through this dense forest, and now, with the battle at hand, he has chosen to wait?"

The pale messenger had grown tired of Airus's complaining and did not make any effort to answer this time.

Airus knew Lord Haden wanted to let the people become overwhelmed with the fear of having his four dragons less than ten thousand cubits from their main camp. This tactic was one of Lord Haden's favorite tactics, and he could play this game for weeks or months if it pleased him.

He shook his head as he looked toward the men preparing for the battle not yet coming. He already understood he would need to find something else for his armies to do, or it would not take long before they were at each other's throats.

Airus looked around and realized that when the legions were moving through the forest, hunting parties could gather enough food and water for everyone as they went.

He turned toward the messenger and asked, "Would Lord Haden mind if I resupply the camps to keep everyone busy for a while?"

Once again, the messenger stood silent.

Airus could see that this man knew he was Haden's messenger and that he would not dare harm him no matter how much he was tempted to do so.

Within a few hours, Airus had a dozen groups ready to comb the countryside for supplies and information about the kingdom. He knew that with most of the people in the camps on the far side of the ridge, most of the countryside would be abandoned, and small groups could go unnoticed.

The tall messenger stood next to him and had only said a few words in the last few hours.

Airus could only guess that the man was hanging around to make sure he followed Lord Haden's instructions. He was not sure if this tall, thin man was listening, but he explained, "I need to keep everyone busy until Lord Haden is ready for them." When the man did not respond, he added, "I don't care much for dragon guilds, but anything that will get these people out of the camp is a good thing for everyone. These dragon guilds are nothing more than thieves and scavengers who don't deserve a place among the disciplined magic guilds."

The messenger nodded his head and replied, "Lord Haden is extremely fond of the dragon guilds. Therefore, everyone tolerates them."

Airus had to admit that no matter how much trouble the dragon guilds seemed to be, they were valued scavengers and gatherers in situations like this one.

Once the scouting parties were out, he knew it would only take a few hours before fresh supplies started coming in, not that they needed anything. Although he had sent a hundred people out of the camp, there were still twenty thousand other people in the encampment with whom he had to deal.

The messenger smiled and added, "The people of Utopia can see your campsites and Lord Haden's dragons."

Airus was not sure whether the messenger was gathering information, so he explained, "I have the dirt masters working to fortify our position, and they should be done within an hour." He did not want to say anything, but Airus knew the dirt masters would soon run out of things to do. He thought to himself, *No one cares to listen to the dirt masters brag about all the battles they have been in as they drank all the wine.*

The messenger then asked, "What about the fire benders?"

Airus quickly replied, "The fire benders are ready to conquer Utopia on their own and will probably lead the ground attacks once Lord Haden gives the command." He added, "For now, I have to figure out how to keep them from burning down the camps."

~*~

Lord Haden and his dragons had been hitting the distant camps for days, and it probably would not be long before the ground forces began their part of the battle.

Finally, the messenger told Airus, "Lord Haden is ready for you now," and then he walked out of the camp the same way he had walked into it.

It was clear that the Kingdom of Utopia had rushed to set up their defenses. Although there were many thousands of people in the distant camps, they would not come any closer to the dragons.

Every day that passed meant the other seven legions were getting closer, and the enemy campsites would get farther away. The raiding parties had already started going through the abandoned campsites to see whether there was anything left that would be of value.

Airus had made sure the ground forces were ready, but despite his warnings, once again, his armor was on too tight.

The sighting guilds all told the same story, which was that the southern defenses of Utopia had fallen back so that they could wait for reinforcements from the north. According to the sight master, five legions from the north were heading toward the city of Hela. Airus had also been told by the sight master that Lord Haden's other seven legions would arrive in less than two weeks.

Just looking at the distant camps, he knew that ten legions from Utopia still meant that Lord Haden's armies would outnumber them by at least four to one. If he knew anything about strategy and what his master wanted, then he knew that this situation was the best thing that could happen. He understood Hela would not fall without difficulty, but once the strongholds were destroyed, there would not be fractured armies trying to hold parts of this kingdom for themselves.

By now, Airus believed it would only take a few months to destroy the famous walls of Hela and to break the people of this kingdom.

## CHAPTER 2

# THE VENTURE OUT OF HELA

Angelina liked the quiet and peacefulness of the upper rooms of the temples and often went there to practice her chants and motions. It had only been thirty seconds, but she knew she had to concentrate if she was going to maintain control. If she could just balance the stone for a few more seconds, then she knew she would be able to make the stupid thing do anything she wanted.

As with every time she tried to do this exercise, the stone started coming toward her. It scrapped the side of her face when it whizzed by her head. She turned away from the center of the room before kicking a chair across it. Seconds later, she screamed, "I hate this! I don't know why I even try because I am never going to figure it out."

The young witch was not of noble blood, and the wielding guild only took her in because it was the law. She was now twenty years old and had studied for more years than she cared to remember in the stone temples. However, there was still nothing she could do to control her magic for more than a few seconds. Angelina knew the ancient scrolls by heart and could recite every word of the control chants. She could also perform the hand motions that were supposed to help her focus as well as any of the wielding masters, but nothing helped her control the magic.

She wiped away the small trickle of blood from the side of her face and decided that it had been adequate practice for one day. She knew she was not going to figure this out today, and her teacher had asked that she report to him when she was through practicing.

Angelina made her way down the long hall to the senior training room to meet with a man who had been her master for the last six years.

As she entered the chamber, the man meditating on the far side of the room turned around. He looked at her for a second and then said, "My child, thank you for coming." He then asked, "How are you today?" She could tell he was not genuinely interested in how she was doing because she could see he was watching her play with her hands.

She had been scolded for playing with her hands many times, so she quickly put them behind her so that her instructor would not say anything. She then replied, "Master Eric, I am doing okay. How are you?"

As her instructor walked closer to her, he placed his hand just below the fresh cut on her face and replied "Child, I need your help."

She quickly answered, "Master, anything you want. I am here to serve you, this temple, and the Kingdom of Utopia."

He looked at her for a few moments and replied, "There is a great evil in the south, and our guild is going to head there to see if we can help."

She knew what her master was hinting at but asked, "How would you like me to help?"

Master Eric realized she had already figured out what he was going to ask. After a few seconds, he responded, "We intend to fight this evil. However, someone needs to stay behind to keep the knowledge of this temple safe and to help the people of this city."

Angelina nodded her head and replied, "I will do as I am told. I will stay behind so that I can protect the ancient scrolls."

Angelina had been told most of her life that she most certainly had the gift of magic, but she was not surprised when she was asked to stay behind. She also knew Master Eric was just politely saying that it was best for everyone if she stayed in the temple where she cannot hurt anyone or herself.

She knew that in the known history of Utopia, no army had ever made it past their defenses or to the city of Hela. In her wildest dreams, she could not see how it would be possible for Haden's armies to defeat their defense in the south.

Angelina understood why everyone could not just leave the city to fight Haden's armies and why some people needed to stay to defend the city. She just wished there were something she could do to help protect her home. She did not need to be told no one in the temple trusted her because of her uncontrollable power, nor did she blame them. She just longed for something else she could do, even if it did not have anything to do with magic. She kicked the small oak cabinet as she walked into the area of the temple, she had called home for so many years. After a moment, she wiped away her tears and started to straighten her cabinet.

She could not remember a time when she did not have this gift of magic, as the temple elders called it, or remember controlling this power for more than a few seconds. It had been more than sixteen years since Angelina had been taken from her family. In all that time, her power had grown, but she still did not have any control. Thinking back, she knew that even all those years ago, people thought she was a danger to herself and everyone around her.

As she sat on her sleeping mat, she could still remember the first time she started to realize she was a danger to the world around her. Angelina could still see herself playing in her mother's garden when she realized she could make the rocks dance. It did not take long before she had persuaded what seemed like every rock on her family's farm to come to her. Within a few seconds, she had lost all control of the rocks that had once come at her call. She started running to get away from them, but that did little to keep the stones from following her and piling up around her.

Her father tried to knock the rocks away as they came into the house while her mother attempted to secure the openings to keep them out. Her parents fought the rocks and screamed for her to stop, but there was nothing anyone could do because they just would not stop coming. Within minutes, the rocks were coming through the walls in an attempt to please their little blue-eyed, blonde-haired master. For twenty minutes, there was nothing anyone could do to help her or to get her to stop wielding the rocks.

By the time the local wielding guild arrived, there was a pile of rocks a cubit high in the middle of her family's home. The guild elder was able to stop the rocks, but everyone in the house was beaten and battered.

She had destroyed her family's farmhouse, and although no one was seriously hurt, it was a clear indication of what the future held for her and her inability to control her power. The local wielding guild demanded that she be turned over to them for her safety. She did not believe her family wanted the guild to take her, but she knew then that they were afraid of her.

Although Angelina had many teachers and mentors over the years, she still could not control her power. For the last few years, even the masters had trouble helping her, and so she tried not to use her power unless she was alone in the upper temple rooms.

The lack of control did not stop the magic from wanting to be used. It seemed that her power got stronger every day and harder to ignore. Not that she meant anyone any harm, but she had hurt many students and even a few masters over the years.

Although she had spent almost every waking hour studying the ancient scrolls, Angelina did not believe that she would ever learn to control her power. She also had to wonder how long the wielding guild would let her stay if she never learned to control her power. Her worst fear was that, at some point, she would end up in a dragon guild or a slave for a warmonger.

As if having an uncontrollable ability to bring objects to life was not dangerous enough, the dreams had returned, just as dark and confusing as they were when she was extremely young. These dreams, which kept her from sleeping, also made it harder to control her magic. The less she slept, the more the magic beckoned to be used to control anyone and anything around her.

A thousand years ago, when the planets Eden and Metro collided, the new world that remained had two suns that gave light to three of the four regions on the planet. Where both stars shone was known for producing those with the gift of sight or the gift of will, but few people had the power to use both.

Angelina wanted to ask the elders to help her with the dreams but was afraid to because no one trusted her as it was. She did not want to find out what they would think of her if they knew she also had what she considered the curse of sight. She also did not know which of her powers scared her more. The young witch had destroyed more than her share of things in her life and now had the ability to see the destruction before it happened. As with most of the people of Hela, the sight guild masters were preparing to head south to help protect the kingdom from Haden. Even if she could find the courage to ask for help, she understood no one would take the time to help her with the dreams, so she just did not sleep.

From her history lessons, Angelina knew that the ancient stone temples in the center of Hela had been given to the wielding and sight guilds to train those with the gift of magic. The stone temples had been her home for the past sixteen years, but never had they been so empty or lonely. Now that no one was in the temples, she decided to go out into the city to determine whether there was anything she could do to help.

Everyone had heard the stories how the warmonger Haden had never been defeated. Although no one had ever breached Utopia's defenses, the city of Hela was full of people who were afraid to stay on their farms south of the city. The city was the capital of the southern region and was currently overrun with old women and children from the surrounding countryside.

The young witch had never been a prisoner of the wielding guild and could come and go as she pleased. However, she had spent most of the last sixteen years in the temples and away from other people because she did not trust herself around them.

Angelina found herself wandering the streets and looking for something to do. Although there were people everywhere who appeared to need help, she did not know what to do.

Suddenly, an old man walked up to her and asked, "Can you help me to find some food for my family?"

She looked at the man for a few moments and then replied, "Of course, I have some food that you can have." She reached into her bag and handed the man the food she had taken from the temple. The man took the food and then thanked her before hurrying off to share with his family.

Before she made it around the next corner, there was another person asking for help. Soon Angelina realized that there were too many people in the city and that she had too few resources to assist them in all.

Haden's army had moved through the dense forest much quicker than anyone could have expected. Now, instead of having months to prepare the kingdom, the people of Utopia only had a few weeks. As her kingdom had many rich farmlands, Angelina knew there were vast provisions just outside the city walls if people were just willing to go get them. If everyone had left Hela so quickly, they could have stocked up for six months or more. Instead, there was not enough food for all the additional refugees. The city elders had asked for anyone who could help to gather more rations.

It had been a long time since she had been outside the city walls, but Angelina needed to find something to do. Since there was no one to stop her, she decided to volunteer to help gather more supplies before she bored herself to death.

Angelina understood why the city elders had decided it was safer if people stayed in groups of at least ten. However, she could not remember how she became part of a group with ten old women. They decided to gather some more provisions in the area outside the south gate.

Although she did not understand how the leadership was determined, the smallest and oldest woman she had ever seen was in charge of the group.

The old woman barely stood three cubits high and could not weigh more than seven stones. Despite her small size, she had no problem ordering the rest of the group to do what she wanted because no one else seemed to know what needed to be done.

The group had been walking for about an hour before they found a large farm. There were lots of supplies here that could be collected and several old mules that had probably been left for a good reason. They managed to find a beat-up old wagon to attach to the mules so that they could haul supplies back to the city.

Angelina had been assigned the task of getting these animals attached to the wagon while the rest of the group gathered the provisions. Although she could make half of the farm do her bidding with a few words and a wave of her hands, there was nothing she could do to get one stupid mule to move toward the wagon.

She had managed to put the harnesses on larger of the two mules as an old woman had shown her. Although she had attempted to get the animal to move, she did not have the strength or the know-how to get the beast to take one step toward the wagon. First, she tried to pull it using the leather reins, and when that did not work, she tried to push it to no avail. She yelled and threatened to kill the creature if it did not move, but it just stood there looking at her as if it did not understand what she wanted.

After being bitten several times and having the mule stand on her sandal for several minutes, she began to get angry and decided she could will the animal to do anything she wanted.

She had been in her chant for several minutes when suddenly the leader of the group walked up behind her and smacked her in the back of the head.

Instantly, she lost her concentration, and without warning, objects began to fall all around them. She had not been able to persuade the mule to move a single cubit but had managed to convince almost everything else within a hundred cubits to come toward her.

The young witch quickly realized why the old woman had smacked her in the back of her head and turned so that she could thank her. Suddenly, the little old woman hit her again and replied, "Dumb girl, what are you doing? You are going to kill us all."

Angelina was shocked by the old woman's actions and tried to stumble through a comeback, but she just could not find the words.

The old woman grabbed the middle of the reins, made a few kissing sounds, and then swung the long end of the leather straps, which snapped as it reached the back end of the mule.

Without any hesitation, the stubborn mule began to move toward the wagon as if it somehow now knew what she wanted.

The young witch shook her head as she stood unable to move forward. She was not sure if she should be happy that the woman knew how to get the mule move or outraged that the woman had just hit her twice. After a few moments, she ran to catch up to the old woman so that she could prove that she was not just some dumb girl and to finish her assigned task.

She had planned to take the reins from the old woman, but to her surprise, the old woman handed her a one-cubit dagger. After a moment, the old woman said, "You will need this to get something to secure the supplies to the wagon."

Angelina wanted nothing more than to use the well-crafted dagger to teach the old woman a lesson. She thought, *No one can talk to me like this*, but for some odd reason, the dagger distracted her. She liked the feel of the blade and decided it would be easier to go find some rope for the wagon.

By the time, she found some rope and returned, the old woman had the mules harnessed to the wagon. To her surprise, no one wanted to drive the wagon, so when the old woman told her, "Hop up and grab the reins," she did not hesitate.

As she started to pick up the reins, she replied, "I don't mind driving, but I don't know what I am doing."

The old woman sat down next to her and responded, "Don't worry, child, I will walk you through it."

# CHAPTER 3

# THE PANGAEA PROPHECY

There was not much that still needed to be done, but Anna lingered in the stables. She loosened the straps that held the extra supplies and then started her inspection even though she knew a full one had just been completed a week ago.

She had been born and raised in the Dark Lands, but lately, she could not stop thinking about what it must be like in the light to the east. She had never been beyond the great glow because she was not yet old enough to ride her dragon beyond the wall of darkness into the kingdoms of light. Although she was only seventeen years old, for as long as she could remember, she had been on the back of one dragon or another even before her dragon was old enough to fly.

The masses had long since left the large cities of the Dark Lands to make a better life in the light regions of the world, and the Kingdom of Acoma was no exception. Although the once magnificent cities of Metro had all but fallen, there were still dozens of small communities in the Dark Lands where the people refused to give up and leave.

Piasa was one of the last large cities that was close to the light region. From what her friend had told her and according to legend, this was the birthplace of dragons.

Anna did not know how many dragon communities were left, but she knew there were far less than there were just 150 years ago. Even the warmongers to the east had no real reason to venture into the darkness other than to look for dragon eggs.

She was still pretending to do an inventory when her father came into the stable to check on her. He acted as if he had something to do with one of the dragons. Finally, he told her, "You know, if you stall too long, your mother will figure it out."

She nodded her head and replied, "I am almost done."

Her father was the regional captain of the guard and a master dragon rider, while her mother was a master dragon handler. Anna knew she had delayed as long as she dared, and although she would miss her dragon, at least she would get to see her friend and great-grandmother.

Her parents had told her she was the great-granddaughter of Gaho-Meda or the Mother Prophet, as she was known throughout the Dark Lands. Since everyone called this old woman grandmother, Anna was not sure she was related to this woman.

She watched her father leave and knew he was right. Though there was no one she cared about as much as Gaho-Meda, she still did not want to leave her dragon.

Gaho-Meda did not process the gift of magic, but instead, she was an interpreter of the laws of existence and teacher of the ancient ways. Anna knew it was an enormous honor that Gaho-Meda had chosen her as an apprentice because she had not taken one in many years. She also believed there was much she could learn from her friend, but it was dragons that were her real love, not an ancient religion that few people still followed.

Anna was still too young to join the dragon rider guild of Acoma, but she knew as much about dragons as any of the master handlers. She had just spent last two days with her father's border guard and had even managed to see the glow of the light kingdoms. No matter how much she wanted to stay, she knew if she did not get cleaned up soon, her mother was likely to smack her in the back of the head again.

~*~

Anna had gotten cleaned up as her mother had instructed and was ready for another lesson with Gaho-Meda. She stood quietly waiting as her mother and the old woman exchanged a few words. As always, she had to wait until her parents left before she could be herself and tell the old woman about her weekend.

As soon as her parents left, the old woman put her cane on the table and asked, "So, child, tell me, how far did you make it this time?" She had been waiting for this chance for a long time and quickly jumped up to hug the old woman.

As she released her from the embrace, she replied, "You should have seen it. I thought I could see the forest in the great glow."

The young dragon rider continued to tell the old woman about the wonders she saw until the old woman once again picked up her cane. Anna could not remember the old woman needing her cane to stand which, of course, meant that she was having trouble with her leg.

She stopped speaking for a moment to watch as the old woman hobbled across the room and then replied, "I am sorry, Gaho-Meda. I should have asked sooner, but how is your leg?"

The old woman mumbled something to herself that the young girl could not quite hear and then replied, "Child, I am afraid that I need this damn stick more every day." She hobbled further across the room and then told Anna, "Please continue. I have not seen a forest in many years."

The old woman smiled as she listened to Anna talk about the edge of the great glow. When she finally stopped for a few seconds, the old woman asked, "If you have never seen a forest, how do you know that what you saw was a forest?"

She smiled because she loved the way the old woman could use her excitement about her weekend to start a lesson. Anna had flown near the glow before, and it was only a week ago that the old woman had explained what a forest was. Therefore, she replied, "Because you told me what a forest looked like, Gaho-Meda."

The woman smiled and replied, "You have flown near the great glow many times, and yet you had not noticed the forest before this weekend." After a few moments, she asked, "So why did you not see the forest before I explained what a forest looked like?"

The young girl began to wonder why she had not seen the forest before but did not know the answer. The old woman laughed and replied, "Maybe the forest was not there before, or maybe you just imagined that you saw a forest."

As Anna took a moment to think about the question, she knew there was always a lesson in the old woman's questions. However, all she could think about was how long it took a forest to grow.

After nearly two minutes, it was clear she was not going to be able to provide an answer.

The old woman laughed again and then added, "It makes the mind wonder, does it not? I believe the forest was there, but you just could not see it because you did not understand what a forest was."

~*~

It had been a few hours and Gaho-Meda could see that Anna was getting tired of the lesson. The old woman said, "Your father tells me that your dragon is near maturity now and one of the finest dragons he has ever seen."

Without so much as a second thought about the lesson, Anna replied, "He is the best dragon anyone has ever seen. He is faster, stronger, and wiser than even the dragons twice his age."

The old woman smiled again as she listened to the young girl talk about her dragon. After a few moments, she asked, "Has he shown any signs of being born in the light or the desire to return to the light?"

Anna had always tried to convince herself that her parents were somehow wrong about her dragon. However, she somehow always knew the truth even if she attempted to pretend that it could not happen to her dragon. She did not know how the old woman knew about her dragon or how she knew so much about anything. She quickly replied, "He wants to fly into the glow, and I can see the difference in his eyes when we get close to the light." She then added, "He has not shown any sign of being able to breathe fire, but only time will tell if he will become a full light dragon."

The old woman smiled again and replied, "Spoken like someone much older and wiser, but I believe all will turn out well."

After a brief pause, the old woman declared, "Well, I guess it is time to start a new lesson." She then asked Anna, "Do you know why Eden and Metro were not destroyed when they collided a thousand years ago?"

Anna immediately replied, "When the two objects collided, according to the laws of existence, there should have been an equal and opposite reaction that ripped both planets apart." She took a moment to make sure she remembered correctly and then added, "Energy that we now call magic held the two worlds together to create this world in which we now live."

The old woman nodded her head. "Yes, my child, you are correct. The scholars of this world also believe that if too many people possess this power, then there will not be enough magic to keep the world together; therefore, dragons were created."

She took a deep breath and added, "Our people thought they had found a way to save the world with the creation of dragons that were not affected by magic."

The young girl watched as the old woman appeared as though she was trying to remember something from her past. Gaho-Meda looked up and then offered, "The scholars did not even consider what would happen when a dragon was born in the light."

Anna knew that when it came to dragons, being born in the light meant being born with the magic of fire. Suddenly—she did not know why—she remembered the wall in the city center and asked, "What about the prophecy of the one who would return the magic to the ground?"

The old woman replied, "Yes, child, but of course. There is the prophecy that a man would be born that could control the dragons and who would return the magic to the ground."

Anna knew this story all too well because her mother had told her it many times as a little girl, and it was on the wall in the center of the city of Piasa.

The old woman looked at the young girl and then continued "The scholars thought once again that they had found a way to save the world." She paused as though she was trying to remember the story, but Anna knew better and quickly pleaded for her to continue. Gaho-Meda smiled and continued. "They thought they could use the code of the dragons and the code of mankind to create the one who could return magic to the ground." Once again, she shook her head before adding, "Again, they did not understand."

Anna knew this story all to well. However, she waited eagerly for teacher and friend to continue.

The old woman laid her cane on the table again. "For many years, this man called Nedah defeated the warmongers of the east and stripped them of their power. Yes," continued the old woman, "they thought they had saved the world with this dragon master. What they did not foresee was the one day when this man would be defeated and that the warmongers would learn to take the magic from each other."

For some reason, the old woman's version of the story seemed more real than anything her mother had ever told her. After seeing the old woman had trouble standing, Anna asked, "Can I help you to one of the chairs?"

The old woman stared at Anna for a few moments as if she had forgotten where she was. She replied, "No, my dear Pangaea." But after a few moments, she corrected herself and added, "But, of course, you are not Pangaea."

Anna did not know who Pangaea was. She was not sure if this was another lesson or if, for a moment, the old woman had believed she was this Pangaea.

Before she could ask who, Pangaea was, the old woman smiled and replied, "My child, do not be shy. Pangaea was my youngest daughter." As memories of her child came back to her, she said, "She was the one who helped me to see the wisdom that comes from the laws of existence."

Gaho-Meda gestured to Anna. "Come closer, child, and I will tell you a story." She softly continued. "Even before Pangaea was as old as you are now, people for hundreds of leagues came to ask for her assistance." The old woman nodded her head and went on, "She may have been our greatest hope to save the world." After a long pause, the old woman took a deep breath and continued. "And may have also been our greatest failure."

Anna could not remember her mother telling her the story of Pangaea, so she asked, "Grandmother, what happen to your daughter?"

Gaho-Meda smiled again and mumbled, "When she was years younger than you are now, she lay down and asked if I would mark the top of her head and the bottom of her feet."

Anna, as almost every child before her, had been to the place where marks were made. As a little girl, her mother had taken her. It had been many years since she had been to the place where marks were made, and soon she began to wonder if the marks her mother had created so long ago were still there.

The old woman, still smiling, shook her head. "Yes, every child goes there at one time or another, but very few adults go back to realize what the marks mean." The old woman took a deep breath and continued. "If you ever go back, you too will understand why the marks are so significant. However, since you asked, I need to explain what happened to my daughter."

The old woman offered, "Pangaea had a child of her own, and that child had enormous potential, but he was lost in the war with the warmongers of the east." The old woman put down her cane. "My child never recovered from the loss of her child and just could not believe he was gone. "Finally, the time came when she could not stay here any longer. She claimed that she could still hear him and that he called for her." The old woman put her hand on the girl and added, "This is the part that pertains to you, my child."

Anna, with tears in her eyes, replied, "Gaho-Meda, I do not understand what this has to do with me." The old woman wiped away the young girl's tears and replied, "You, my dear, are a chosen one. However, you are not my chosen one, and as Pangaea had to follow her heart, so will you."

The two talked for hours about the few lessons the old woman still needed to teach the young girl before fate pulled them in different directions. Finally, Anna gathered her belongings, and with tears in her eyes, she said, "I will be back. There is still so much that I need to learn."

As she was leaving, the old woman smiled. "Soon, you will be pulled toward your destiny, and there is nothing that can stop that, my child."

Once again, the young girl said, "I will be back as soon as I can, and you need to take care of yourself."

Still smiling, the old woman said, "When you find the one that will replace me, please send them my way because I am getting old and cannot wait forever."

It had been several hours since Anna had left, but the old woman could not stop thinking about Pangaea. Finally, she decided to walk to the place where her daughter's marks were made so many years ago. It only took a couple of minutes before she found the first set of marks. She kneeled down and cleaned out the mark where Pangaea's feet had been so many years ago.

When the old woman was finished cleaning the marks, she looked around at dozens of other marks until she found the one, she was sure was Anna's marks.

The old woman cleaned out those marks also and made certain that Anna's name could still be read before she started to look for the other set of marks from Pangaea.

As she continued to walk, from time to time, she would come across a name scratched in the dirt, which, of course, she would clean. It had been years she had cleaned the markers, and her memory was not what it used to be, but she soon found where Pangaea had laid her head. From where she now stood, she could see it was at least fifty cubits to where she had marked Pangaea's feet.

The old woman stood, looking back at where she had started, but she could not remember the marks being so far apart. Even as she struggled to see that far, she understood there were only two reasons she did not remember the marks being that distant. The first reason, of course, was that although she did not want to admit it, her memory was not what it used to be. The second reason was what worried the old woman the most because it meant that the world was pulling apart faster than ever.

It had been almost a week since Anna had been on a real ride with her dragon. She had completed all her chores so that her mother would not have a reason to keep her from going. As she waited for her mother to respond, she began to wonder if there was something else, she should have done.

However, after a few moments, her mother answered, "Yes, you can go, but do not go beyond the great glow. You need to be back in time for your lesson with Gaho-Meda."

She knew the rules, but she smiled and replied, "Of course, I know that I am not allowed to go into the light."

It had been all she had thought about since her last lesson with Gaho-Meda, and she wanted to determine whether it was a forest that she had seen a week ago.

~*~

Anna had been able to see the great glow for the last hour, but her dragon was starting to act strangely. She had noticed before that he always acted different as they got closer to the glow, but this was not the same.

After a few seconds, the squad leader pointed out a group of twenty to thirty people sneaking across the plains below.

Anna knew that the people who were born in the Dark Lands could find their way around without so many torches; she was sure that the strangers below were up to no good.

The lead rider soon extended his left arm in the direction they had just come from and demanded that Anna return to Piasa until they dealt with these intruders.

Although she did not want to go back so early, she understood that the people below could be anyone from scavengers to dragon hunters. She watched as the other four riders began to descend into the darkness. Within a few seconds, she could no longer see the other riders but was sure that her dragon could still see them.

As she started to turn to return home, for some reason, she decided she still want to get a better look at the forest before she went home. She could see the glow in the distance and hear the light beckoning her to come see the wonders of the light world.

# CHAPTER 4

# THE LOST AWAKENING

Everything was dark, but the man was slowly beginning to awaken. However, he soon realized that he was trapped beneath something. As his vision gradually started to return, a foul odor filled the air that made it hard for him to breath.

After several minutes, he figured out that he was buried beneath rocks and dead animals. To make matters worse, the man's head hurt as if someone had tightened a vise on it. He was not sure if it was the numbing pain in his head or the weight on top of him, but he did not know who he was. It took a few moments, but he realized that he was still somewhat able to move his right arm just enough that he might be able to pull it loose. After several minutes, he wiggled his arm enough to free it from beneath the debris. He took a deep breath and, with all his strength, started trying to free the rest of himself.

He pulled himself loose for a little while but, when he grew tired of struggling, he attempted to push the horses off. Although he was making some progress, it was taking a lot of time and effort to get free. As he started to break through, he gasped for air while trying to find the strength to continue. He told himself, "You just have to keep going, it is the only thing that you have."

~*~

After an hour and a half, the man was tired and sore but had somehow managed to free himself from beneath the dead animals and rocks. Once he was free, he fell to the ground where he tried to catch his breath. A few moments later, he sat up. Still attempting to catch his breath and gain his composure, he soon realized he was on the battlefield. He continued to look around for several minutes, but there was nothing that seemed remotely familiar to him. He did not have any way of knowing how long he had been beneath the debris, but from the decaying smell that filled the air, it had to be several days.

He looked down at his armor, but it was an ordinary leather set and did not have any rank or name markings on it. He knew the armor meant he was a warrior, but because it lacked any markings other than a strange symbol, it did little to explain who he was.

As he once again looked over the battlefield, he suddenly noticed what he believed to be the movement of another person. Even from this distance, he could see the man was dressed in nearly the same armor, except with steel plates. After another thirty seconds, the man lying on the ground moved again, and it was clear he was still alive.

Without so much as a moment's hesitation, he got up and started walking toward the man to see whether there was anything that could be done to help him. It did not take long before he was standing over the wounded man, watching him gasp for every breath he took. He looked around to see if there was anyone else who could help, but there were no other living beings among the dead. He knew he needed to help this man, but he also understood that he probably needed to take him somewhere safer.

He looked toward the distant horizon and could see vultures circling in the sky above. Although there was plenty for these creatures to eat, there was no reason for them to stay here, leaving them vulnerable to anything lurking on the field.

He stooped down to grab the man lying on the ground and, in one motion, slung the man across his shoulders. Once he was able to regain his balance, he began walking away from the battlefield. He did not know where he was going but knew it would be safer for him to treat the man away from the battlefield.

As he began to walk, he noticed a small figure hidden in some rubble not far from where he had been buried. He did not believe this person was a threat, so he acted as though he did not see the child. He had other things he needed to do and continued to walk away from the battlefield.

He had only gone a few hundred cubits when he stopped to look around, but he could not see the child's parents or anyone else on the battlefield. He still did not want to take any chances because he could only guess that scavengers were skulking around and had sent children into the battlefield to determine whether it was safe for them. Every time he looked back, he would see the child dart behind a tree or a rock and was never able to get a good look at him.

After about ten minutes, the man stopped to adjust the other man lying across his shoulder. When he looked back to see how far he had traveled, he realized the child was still following him. He did not believe he had anything of value and began to wonder why the child was still following them.

He stopped and yelled, "Go back to your parents! I have nothing for you!" He knew the child was not a threat, but he did not know how many other people were following the child. He could only hope the boy would soon get tired and return to his parents.

Every time the man looked back, he would catch a glimpse of this person, who was trying not to be seen. He did not have the time to chase the child away or any desire to hurt the boy. In hopes of frightening the child away, he stopped once again and yelled, "Go back to your parents before you get hurt or get so far away that they cannot find you!"

The child did not answer but continued to hide just outside the range of being seen clearly.

He continued to yell for a few more minutes, "Go home before you get hurt!" but again, the child did not answer. He did not like the idea of stopping since he did not know how many people were following him, so he decided to see if he could walk fast enough to leave this child behind.

~*~

The man had walked for at least another twenty minutes before he felt it was safe enough to take a break. After looking around, he decided to see whether there was anything that could be done for his brother-in-arms. He took care to set the wounded man on the ground while trying not to hurt him more. He then began trying to see whether or not the person could be helped.

After a couple of minutes, he determined that the man did not have any visible life-threatening wounds that could be treated. Although he could not tell what was wrong, the man was barely breathing but was still alive.

He noticed a sizeable dent in the wounded man's armor that was clearly not helping him. He decided if he could get this man's armor off, then maybe he would be able to breathe a little easier. As he tried to get the wounded man's armor off, he realized this man was of high stature. He wore shiny armor with many markings etched into it, unlike his plain leather armor. As far as he could tell from the etching in the man's armor, his name was Suria or something to that effect. Although the symbols of rank seemed to be in the wrong order, he was also fairly sure that this man was a general or a high-ranking person. He also understood that regardless of the man's rank, what mattered for the moment was that the armor needed to come off if he had any chance of living.

Once the armor was removed, it was clear from the blueness of the man's chest that he had been hit and that the impact had compressed his armor. His armor was keeping him from breathing, and the impact had broken at least five ribs. However, with just the armor removed, Suria could already breathe easier and was starting to regain some of his color. Removing the armor did nothing to stop his internal bleeding, if he had any, but at least it was something.

As he inspected the man for additional cuts or something he could help with, he realized that his entire chest and lower neck region was blue. He was not sure whether the blue was a sign of internal bleeding or just bruises caused by his armor. He then used Suria's brightly colored clothes to wrap his chest. He took care to hold the man's ribs in place without tightening the bandage to a point where it was hard for him to breathe again. After a few moments, he moved the man to a position that appeared to be more comfortable so he could get some rest.

He looked around the clearing and determined that the area was safe, so he decided to see if he could find something to keep Suria warm. As he was leaving, he thought to himself, *If I have any luck, then I should be able to find something to eat or drink in this valley.*

Although there were plenty of trees, he was not sure it was safe to build a fire because he did not know who else might be in the area.

For nearly twenty minutes, he continued to look for a farmhouse or somewhere he could find some supplies, but he soon found himself back on the battlefield. As far as he could tell, no one had been through the battlefield yet to scavenge the belongings of the dead. He knew it would be relatively easy to find some water and blankets for the wounded man. After another thirty minutes, he returned with some horse blankets and a few days' supply of water for his injured friend.

By this time, the man was semiconscious and was trying to get up. He quickly attempted to get Suria to calm down by giving him some of the water and getting him to lie back down before he passed out again. As the barely conscious man started to relax again, he covered him with the wool blankets and tried to make him as comfortable as possible. Suria used what strength he had left to whisper, "We cannot stay for too long. The death stalkers will be scavenging the area soon. If you help me up, I think I can walk."

He told the general, "Sir, just relax for now," and pulled the blanket up to keep him warm. After a short pause, he added, "We are safe here for a while. You need to rest while I try to figure out what to do next."

Soon Suria was fading off to sleep, but with his last waking breath, he replied, "Yes, sir," before he fell unconscious beneath the blankets again. As the wounded man fell asleep, the other man looked down at his armor once more to make sure he had read his rank correctly. He started shaking his head because he was a bit confused. He knew they could not stay where they were for long. He also knew Suria needed to rest if he had any chance of living.

While Suria slept, the other man sat wondering what to do next when he noticed a branded symbol on each of his forearms. The symbols resembled dragon wings attached to a small sphere set upon a tower with two reptiles intertwined up the sides. The symbol did not have any meaning to him, but when he looked up a distant hill, there was a banner resembling the symbols on his arms.

He knew the best thing he could do for the wounded man was to locate the army that left the banners. He had no doubt that if he could find this army, they would have a healing witch or two. The symbols on Suria's armor meant he was a prominent person and maybe even a general thought to be lost. He believed that if he could find the remains of this army, he could get help for Suria. He also thought he might even be able to figure out who he was; after all, he wore their marks. He decided that the distant hill was abandoned and the best place to see if the army was close.

It took twenty minutes to carry Suria to the top of the hill where the army had left the banner. As he had expected, the site had long been abandoned, but at least he could see a lot farther in every direction. He looked north and could not believe that a beaten army did not seem to care who knew which direction they were going. They had marked their path with a banner every thousand cubits or so for anyone to see.

He looked around and felt safe here because the hilltop held no value to the death stalkers and was quite a distance from the decaying corpses of the battlefield. He could clearly see from the peak that the sky was far darker in the north, which was a sign that Suria's army had moved in that direction. As far as he could tell, the army was at least a day's and maybe even two days' travel north if he had to carry his wounded comrade.

After a few seconds, he noticed the same small figure that had been following them had also followed him to the top of this little hill. He began to wonder how long the boy had been hiding behind just beyond his sight.

He sat down beside his wounded comrade and told him, "Suria, we will be safe here for a little while. However, in a few hours, when we have had a chance to rest, we will head north."

Suddenly, the ground began to shake beneath them, and he knew that he had felt this before as he watched the trees sway in the distance. He did not understand why, but he somehow knew that the death stalkers would not risk climbing to the top of this small mound especially with the ground shaking. He again looked at the wounded man lying on the ground and repeated, "We will be safe here for a little while." He was not sure whether Suria could hear him, but it made him feel better just to talk to someone.

It had been well over an hour since he had carried his wounded friend to the top of this small mound and at least twenty minutes since the ground had stopped shaking. He had all but forgotten about the child until he noticed the boy about two hundred cubits down the ridge of the hill. He decided that if he pretended to sleep, the child might choose to come closer. He did not have any desire to harm a child. However, he realized that if he could keep the child from reporting back to his parents for a little while, they would be able to stay here for a bit longer.

After several hours, he awoke to find his companion was awake and was requesting some water. As he gave Suria some water, he could see the child was still hiding in the rocks. The wounded man drank some of the water and softly said, "You were wrong about my name. You had it reversed. My name is Airus, not Suria." After a few moments, Airus continued. "You were correct about the direction that my army went. We needed to go north, but if you can wait a few more hours, I might be able to walk on my own."

He looked around, and although the child was still hiding in the rocks, there was no reason for anyone to make the effort to climb the small lookout point. After a few moments, he replied, "We can wait a few hours. However, any longer than that and someone is bound to come on top of this hill, if for no other reason than to look around."

He then looked at Airus and asked, "Do you know who I am? I do not remember my name or where we are."

Airus did not say anything for well over a minute and then replied, "I thought I knew who you were, but apparently I was mistaken," and then fell back to sleep.

# CHAPTER 5

# THE CHARGE OF THE GIANT

He could be heard throughout the palace, but no one was foolish enough to be anywhere close to the giant when he was like this.

The training drills were just a matter of procedure at this point, and most people knew it. Everyone, including the giant, was hoping the new recruits would start to show up sooner rather than later. Half the kingdom knew that Taron the Destroyer was bored, and only the lowest-ranking people and those mentioned by name had any business near the palace.

According to the last message he received a couple weeks ago, his father's campaign in the east had finally started. However, the giant understood that this meant it would still be some time before the new recruits began to arrive. Most of the current recruits were in their final training stage and did not require as much supervision. With his sergeants doing most of the day-to-day training, there was not much for him to do and no reason to believe things would change any time soon.

Taron had little patience for sitting around waiting for news or being isolated in the forgotten kingdom of Epson was not doing anything to help his boredom. It took all his self-control to keep from taking his father's four legions of recruits east to join his father in whatever he was doing there.

His father was Lord Haden and demanded that he train the new recruits to be capable warriors. For 150 years, his father had conquered kingdom after kingdom in the West Region, and now he was turning his attention to the Center Region.

Taron was Haden's youngest son and second youngest child and had a bad reputation for breaking everything around him. He believed that this was the reason his father no longer allowed him to lead his armies into battles. Instead, he had helped train his father's legions and mine ore from the western mines for the last ten years.

Although few people had the courage to call him this to his face, it was easy to see why most people referred to him as Taron the Destroyer.

He stood well over five cubits high and weighed more than thirty-five stones, most of which was solid muscle. His weapon of choice was a large broadsword that took two grown men to carry when he was not using it. He also possessed enormous strength, which made him almost unstoppable once he was in motion.

As the chief horologist, Jayce Quinn knew it was only a matter of time before he was ordered to see the giant. When he entered his master's day quarters, he could see Taron the Destroyer standing with his back to the doorway. While he waited for his master to turn around and acknowledge him, he looked around the room, but as far as he could tell, nothing was broken.

Without turning around, the giant asked, "How long has it been since we received any word from my father's forces?"

Jayce quickly looked through his notes and then replied, "Sir, it has been three weeks since we have heard any new information about this campaign."

Taron had rarely known his father to go so long without sending a messenger, but he wanted to believe it had to do with the distance to the Center Region. As with most of his father's campaigns, he did not understand the ultimate objective of this war. He thought, *I don't care what my father's interests are because anything would be better than what I am doing now.*

Jayce was not sure if his commander had any other questions, but the truth of the matter was that he was not going anywhere until he was told to do so. As he waited for further instructions, he could feel the ground shake as he watched the giant pace back and forth across the stone floor.

With every step of his master's feet, the click of his boots echoed throughout the palace. He could see that Taron was trying to think of something he had not done a thousand times already.

Finally, the giant asked, "How long before the moon leaves the sky?"

Jayce looked at his notes once more before he replied, "Less than two days, sir."

Taron replied, "When the moon has left the sky, I want a messenger ready to go east." After a few moments, he added, "I would like to know what is going on in the real world."

The old horologist quickly replied, "Sir, I will make sure a messenger is ready to go." He could see the giant was just looking for something to do and probably did not care about the moon. He had known Taron long enough to know he would rather be helping his father break things or hurt people, but it was not his choice.

The giant did not have any love for this mediocre work although Jayce knew he was probably better at it than anyone in the world. The monster that people referred to as Taron the Destroyer only had one fear in the entire world, and that was the man he called father. His father demanded that he run the mines and train his legions. Therefore, Taron did as he was told and would continue to do so until he was told to do something else.

Suddenly, the giant asked, "Do you think that someday my father will let my sister Sabrina lead his armies the way I used to lead them?"

The timekeeper knew that Haden had taken the spellcaster Scorpion to join him on this campaign. Haden had also appointed Sabrina, who did not have any power, to be his successor. He could see that just the mere thought of his siblings made Taron angry.

Before he could answer, the giant turned his back to him again and started stomping away. He said, "I don't understand why I am here when I could do a better job than most of my siblings, especially Sabrina."

As with every time he thought about his inferior siblings, Taron started to become enraged and slammed his massive right hand down on the stone table in the center of the room.

However, this stone table was no match for Taron's massive right hand, and a corner section almost a cubit across dropped to the ground. Within a fraction of a second, rage overtook the giant. He grabbed the broken table and slung it across the room to the back wall. As the table fell to the ground, Taron screamed, "Damn it! I need to find something to do before I destroy this entire palace!"

As the crashing sound echoed throughout the palace, everyone held their breath as they waited to see whether or not the giant was coming out of his quarters.

Jayce had not been dismissed and knew better than to show any fear, so he stood his ground and waited for directions.

After pacing around for a few moments, Taron grabbed his broadsword from the wall and smiled as if he just realized some bit of information he had forgotten. Seconds later, he screamed, "I want my sergeants of arms to gather my father's recruits because it is time to do an inspection!"

Jayce nodded his head and waited until the giant dismissed him before leaving to spread the word that his master was ready to inspect the recruits.

Although no one was around when the giant first started screaming, when he demanded his sergeants of arms, everyone in the palace knew it. No one needed to be told twice, and long before the giant came out of his quarters, people were scrambling to make ready for the inspection.

Within a matter of seconds, orders were being dispatched to the legions of new warriors just beyond the palace gates. The word quickly spread that Taron the Destroyer was coming to inspect them, which, of course, meant everything had to be perfect. Everyone familiar with the giant knew that he was not a patient person and that he demanded perfection in everything he did, especially during his inspections.

Most of the four legions had been under his control for more than a year and a half now, but today they would truly understand what it meant to be in Lord Haden's army. Since the first day of their training, Taron had overseen their training from a distance, but that was about to change. Most of the people under his control understood that if they had any ambition to be anything other than a foot soldier, then this inspection might be their only chance.

A year and a half ago, most of the recruits were slaves or untouchables of some sort, but now they were well-trained warriors in Lord Haden's army. His father had realized many years ago that the slaves of a defeated enemy made excellent soldiers because they had nowhere else to go.

Although Lord Haden was a warmonger and at any given time could be in a dozen conflicts, it was never hard to find recruits because he always won. It did not take a genius to understand it was better to be a foot soldier to this warmonger than to be crushed beneath his massive armies.

Twelve of his senior sergeants were ready to assist with the inspection long before Taron darkened the entrance to the palace and demanded that someone bring his horse.

It was barely a fifteen-minute ride from the palace to the area that was set aside for the inspection. Well before Taron and his sergeants arrived, the recruits were being prepared for what might be the most important day of their meaningless lives. Forty thousand men and women from the far reaches of the known kingdoms stood in columns that extended for a thousand cubits in every direction.

As he looked at the columns of eager faces, Taron knew that this inspection was the right thing to do and just what he needed. He also understood that many of the recruits would be dead within a few years if he failed to train them or prepare them for leadership correctly. The giant and his sergeants of arms had pushed most of these recruits to their breaking point, but he knew that if someone did not, their fate was already written.

Before the inspection began, his sergeants began combing through the columns. They made sure that the columns stood straight and that every warrior carried a shield in their left hand and a blade in their right hand. Everyone who knew Taron understood that the one thing that mattered more to him than how to properly hold a weapon and shield was the formality of the procedures.

Throughout the inspection area, the sergeants of arms were prepping the new recruits for the inspection. Every sergeant on the field was yelling, "If you are approached by the inspector, you will stand your ground, and if you lose your composure, you are to make every effort to recover!"

By the time Taron dismounted his large horse, all but the most senior sergeants had moved far beyond his vision to make sure the recruits were ready before he began the inspection. He had long forgotten his boredom and could barely hide his excitement as he stepped forward to start the examination.

Seconds later, every sergeant of arms echoed the same order. "Prepare to be inspected."

Without any hesitation, the lines and columns snapped to attention and waited for this long-awaited inspection to begin.

Taron had waited about as long as he could and grabbed the first person he found and demanded that the young man report. The young man tried to speak, but when he found himself face-to-face with the giant, the words just would not come.

Taron opened his massive mouth and growled through his oversized teeth. By this time, the young man was just lucky he was able to stay conscious. The giant smiled and, without any further hesitation, tossed the young man a dozen cubits and yelled, "Next!"

Few had the courage to look at the giant as he screamed and tossed those who did not meet his approval. Most wet themselves or got sick long before Taron had a chance to complete his inspection.

There were a few, however, who wanted to be leaders and tried to stand their ground as the giant finished his inspection. Even if some had the courage to stand up to Taron, it was no guarantee that he would not toss them into the adjacent column or beyond. Even then, some people would get back up and return to their assigned spots.

For ten straight hours, Taron marched up and down the columns, looking for those who could not follow the simplest of instructions. Finally, he grew tired of the inspection, and when he looked around at his father's newest legions, he knew, as he always knew, that they were ready to serve his father.

Although the columns were no longer pretty and straight, there were those who still stood near their assigned spots. Most people who were still standing were waiting to see if they would be selected for a leadership role.

Taron took a deep breath. He felt alive again and began wondering why he had not done this sooner. He exhaled and yelled in a voice that echoed for hundreds of cubits in every direction, "Let the games begin! It is time this sorry bunch picked their leaders!"

Before he made his announcement, his sergeants had started going through the columns to find the people who were still standing in or near their assigned spots. As Taron looked back at the warriors who were still standing, he thought to himself, *Look at all these people who understood the formalities of the inspection. These games should be most entertaining.*

Although he was pleased with the number of people still standing, there were only ten or twelve people in a hundred-cubit radius.

Taron soon found his horse and started to make his way back to the palace, where he knew the games were already being set up.

Everyone who was conscious and still able to walk quickly started gathering his or her equipment. Even in their bruised and battered state, they were helping each other off the field because they knew that anyone who was left on the field would be sent to the mines.

~*~

The games had been going on for more than five hours, and Taron could not remember a time when he had so much fun.

From the early reports, only about four thousand people had not passed the inspection. By all accounts, this number was low compared to some years past when ten thousand had to be carried off the field and later transferred to the mines.

Some people in his inner circle thought little of those who were sent to the mines and even called them cowards. Taron, on the other hand, was glad there were people who did not pass the inspection because he needed people for the mines, and some people just were not cut out to be warriors.

Taron had seen the games last for up to fifteen hours, but if he had any say in the matter, he would make sure that the games lasted for a week. He also understood that no matter how well trained this group was, even he could not make them fight forever.

Several dozen people had already earned a promotion, and by this time, there were only a few lieutenant promotions left to be given out.

Taron had half a dozen women around him and had drunk more wine than he cared to recall. Suddenly, someone informed him that a messenger had arrived with news of his father's campaign. He quickly gestured for the man to be brought to the center courtyard so that news of his father's victory could add to the glory of the games.

Within a matter of moments, a single messenger was brought before the giant and his court. Taron wanted everyone to hear of his father's brilliant victory over whatever kingdom it was four hundred leagues to the northeast. He gestured for the games to pause as the messenger entered the courtyard. He then demanded, "Tell me of my father's victory in . . ." but could not remember the name of the backwoods kingdom where his father had gone.

After a few moments, someone yelled, "Utopia!"

The giant repeated, "Yes, Utopia." He took another drink and started laughing. He was so loud that it echoed throughout the courtyard. He turned toward the messenger and then demanded, "Well, how long are you going to keep us waiting?"

The messenger hesitated for a few second, but as he was more that forty cubits from the giant, he felt he was safe from his rage. The messenger loudly replied, "Your father, Lord Haden, has been defeated, but your brother asks that you—"

By this time, Taron had charged through the middle of the games, knocking the fighters to the ground, and he was looming over the messenger. He quickly demanded, "Tell me what my brother has asked and where my father is."

The messenger had not expected the giant to come across the courtyard so quickly and suddenly found it difficult to speak. He soon regained his composure because he knew that if he showed any fear, Taron the Destroyer would throw him across the room. The messenger quickly replied, "Lord Taron, your father was killed by a witch from Utopia, but your brother Scorpion has the situation under control."

The giant grabbed the messenger's head in his massive hands and lifted him off the ground. After a few moments, he screamed, "What do you mean my father is dead, but my brother has the situation under control?"

Under the pressure of the giant's hand, the messenger's face continued to turn red but could not speak until he was thrown to the ground. He gasped for air but quickly replied, "Lord Taron, I am sorry, but your father is dead." After a few moments, he added, "I am sure your brother would welcome your help to find his killer."

Taron stood over the messenger, wanting to stomp him into the ground, but at the same time, he could not see how that would help. He turned and, with his voice echoing throughout the palace, informed everyone, "I want my sword because we are marching toward Utopia."

As soon as his two squires brought his sword, he charged out of the palace with a dozen sergeants following him. He barely knew which way to head but had no doubt the navigators would soon catch up and direct him toward the Kingdom of Utopia. For the moment, only one thing mattered to him, and that was how he was going to avenge his father.

# CHAPTER 6

# THE DRAGON MASTER AND THE DEATH STALKER

Xio Ying and his dragon guild had been traveling for days just to see what they could scavenge from the abandoned city. Even through the smoke and dust, he could see the outline of the small capital city in the valley below. Most of the guild was lingering a few hundred cubits behind him and his master Yang Hon. It had been well over an hour since his master had spoken, but suddenly he asked, "I wonder what spoils await us?"

Xio looked up at the burning city and replied, "I hope that there is at least enough to get us some supplies." Although he was not sure if there would be anything left to scavenge, he had little doubt there would be anyone who would stop them from taking whatever they wanted. He only hoped there would be some metal left for him to make weapons, or at least some food left in the wake of the battle.

It had been two weeks since the warmonger Lord Ojak had ordered his army to destroy the city of Sal if they did not turn over their magic guilds.

The city of Sal thought they could stand on the high walls and hold off this warmonger. Of course, they were no match for even the small, poorly trained dragons Lord Ojak sent to attack the city. While the dragons picked off the people on the high walls, his armies smashed through the gates and set the city ablaze.

The magic guilds and walls of the city of Sal had protected the people for hundreds of years, but they were no match for even these juvenile dragons.

As they got closer to the burning city, Yang laughed and said, "I bet even as Ojak's armies smashed through their walls, they were probably still worried about the dragons."

Xio shook his head because he knew his master was probably right. There was nothing people feared more than a dragon even if it did not have a rider and was untrained. It had been many years since he had seen a dragon close up and was happy just to watch these hatchlings from a distance. However, he was sure that without riders, these dragons would never live up to their potential.

The East Region had never been a safe place for those born with the gift of magic, but now every warmonger within five hundred leagues was trying to prepare for Haden. Magic had been king for hundreds of years, and although dragons were fairly new to the region, the fear of them was not. Word had spread to the East Region, where the yellow sun could barely be seen, that the warmonger Lord Haden had started to conquer kingdoms in the Center Region.

Xio announced to his master, "If these fools fear these small, untrained dragons, wait until they see Haden's giant monsters and the destruction they can create."

Some in the East, such as Lord Ojak, saw the value of dragons a long time ago and had spent years trying to get their eggs. His dragons were small and untrained, but they could not be defeated by magic. Most people, however, still believed that magic was the key to defending against the slaughter of the warmongers.

It would be many years before Lord Haden and his vast armies made their way this far to the east, to where the red sun gave the gift of change. The warmongers of the region, though, were already fighting for control of the magic guilds although anyone with half a mind knew it would not be enough. The warmongers were destroying everything along the edge of the East Region fifty years before Lord Haden would even start to show any interest in the area.

If Haden and his dragons were as strong as the stories depicted them to be, then it would not matter how many magic guilds the warmongers of this region were able to control. He had no doubt the people of this region would bow down to this man when the time came.

Xio Ying knew that where warmongers went, the dragon guilds were sure to follow, and the guild he belonged to was no exception. It had not always been this way; he was born to a noble family and had once been part of a powerful guild. He had spent the last fifty years bound by blood and magic to this group of misfit scavengers, led by the ruthless death stalker named Yang Hon.

Xio had fought alongside the great dragon master Nedah to save the world, but he was the first to fall to Lord Haden. As far as he was concerned, the world had ended that day 150 years ago when his master was defeated and the world forsaken. In his youth, he was the youngest person ever to become a dragon master. Now, by right or attrition, he had worked his way up to second in command of the largest dragon guild within a hundred leagues. He was, for all practical purposes, the person who controlled the day-to-day operations of this dragon guild and the only person who could relay orders from Yang Hon. If the warmongers knew he was once a dragon master, they would kill everyone in the dragon guild to get to him. That life was behind him now, and he no longer had any interest in dragons.

For the last twenty years, his dragon guild had been following the area's most powerful warmonger. Lord Ojak had a large army and was in the process of taking control of the regional guilds. However, he demanded the dragon guild stayed close in case he needed a task performed, and he did not wish to risk his precious magic guilds. For the most part, however, Lord Ojak did not care what they did as long as they stayed out of his way.

Lord Ojak would also send members of his magic guilds who could not learn to control their power to his dragon guild. Most of them would only last a few years before someone sucked their power from their dying bodies. Xio had always been told that draining the life force or magic from a living being would drive you crazy. He believed this was just an old wives' tale because his master had done it for fifty years, and the bastard did not seem affected by the process.

~*~

Xio did not consider himself a violent man or someone to be feared, but as usual, someone was following him, waiting to be spoken to before he would speak. He knew from experience that the man needed to relay some message but would follow him for days if he was not given permission to speak. He could only assume that everyone was so afraid of him because they were afraid of his master, the death stalker, who was, by all accounts, a cold-blooded killer who fed on the weak.

He knew that Yang did whatever he felt like doing whenever he felt like doing it. Because it could be days before he showed up again to order everyone around, Xio motioned for the man to come forward.

As the man stepped closer with his head still bowed, Xio told him, "Yang is not in the camp. Please tell me whatever news it is that you have."

The man looked at him for a moment as if he was confused, and then he quickly replied "Master, there is a messenger from the West, who would like to speak to you."

He had not seen anyone from the West in a long time and could not even imagine why someone would come this far into the East. He could only assume that the messenger had been sent to see whether anyone was foolish enough to aid the Center Region in its efforts against Haden. He knew that Yang would not even entertain the idea of sending people to fight the warmonger, but he thought it might be amusing to hear the messenger beg for help.

After a few moments, he smiled and told the man, "Please show this messenger to our camp so that he can share his message with us and maybe entertain us for a while."

~*~

It was well over an hour before the young messenger was led to the center of the camp where Xio and a few other senior members of his dragon guild had been waiting. Although he knew that Yang had no interest in helping anyone but himself, Xio was looking forward to hearing what this messenger had to offer if they would help him.

Soon a young, skinny messenger approached, but he did not look as Xio expected. He thought to himself, *This messenger looks more like someone from a dragon guild rather than someone from a rich center kingdom. No wonder they were already sending people out to beg for help.*

The man approached as anyone from a dragon guild would, with his weapon in its sheath and his palms facing outward so that everyone could see his hands. As soon as the young man put his hands out, Xio stood up because he instantly knew this boy was a member of a dragon guild. He demanded, "Tell me why someone from a dragon guild is so far from where he belongs and what do you want from us?"

The young man continued to keep his hands facing out but quickly replied, "Lord, the dragon guilds of the western and central kingdoms are rebelling against their masters."

Xio shook his head and replied, "Many have rebelled against their masters, but few have lived to tell their stories." He wanted nothing to do with this nonsense and started to walk away.

The young man shouted, "This may be our only chance while they prepare to fight each other!"

Xio waved his hand for the man to go away. He then turned back around and said, "The warmongers of the West and Center Regions are no concern of ours." After a few moments, he added, "You are wasting your time and mine."

The young man politely added, "Lord, I mean no disrespect, but this may be our one and only chance to be free of the warmongers."

Xio replied, "They will hunt you down just to take your power from your dying body. You will find no help from any of the dragon guilds in the east."

Without thinking, the man put his hands down. He looked up and replied, "Several of our brother guilds have already joined the cause, and a river city has offered shelter to anyone who would help defend their city."

Xio started yelling at the young man. "You are a fool, and you will die without understanding why!"

Suddenly, Yang appeared out of nowhere and demanded, "Why should we help in your pathetic rebellion?"

The man was a bit confused but kept looking at Xio to see if he could figure out what was going on with this guild leader. After a moment, he replied, "With Haden dead, the warmongers will turn on each other, and they will not have time to worry about what the dragon guilds are doing."

Everyone's attention was clearly focused on Yang as he screamed, "What do you mean, Haden is dead?"

By this time, the young man was completely confused as to whom the leader of this guild was. Finally, he replied, "Lord, a very powerful witch from Utopia has killed him, and now his armies are turning on each other." After a few moments, he added, "Lord, if the dragon guilds have any chance of ever being free, then we must unite against the warmongers now."

Xio started walking toward the man, who had placed his palms out again so that everyone could tell he was not going to try anything. He extended his right hand to show the young man he accepted him into this dragon guild as an equal and a brother. The young man reached out and grabbed Xio's hand. When he leaned forward to embrace the old man, he was stabbed in the back by Yang's dagger.

Yang grabbed the man with both hands just before he fell to the ground and started slowly chanting in an ancient language. He dug his fingernails deep into the young man's skull and continued chanting louder and louder as the years were sucked from the dying man's body.

Within a few minutes, the young man had lost enough blood that Yang the Death Stalker could effortlessly drain the life from him. Xio watched helplessly as the years left the man until there was nearly nothing left to keep him alive. Yang dropped the now-old man on the ground, leaving him with what could only be hours left on his once-young life.

Yang turned and ordered his dragon guild to prepare to move out even though they had not had a chance to scavenge the city yet. No one had any doubt that the death stalker was in charge, and they were not going to say anything after that demonstration of his ability.

~*~

It had only been a couple of minutes, but Xio again had no idea where his master had disappeared to without saying a word. He could not help but feel sorry for the old man lying on the ground and dying more quickly of old age than he was from the loss of blood. He reached down to see if could help the man or at least ease some of his pain. He took a deep breath and told the messenger, "Hold still, or you will bleed to death."

The man now looked more like someone who was four or five times older than he was when he arrived. Although he was quickly dying of old age, he was still trying to figure out what had just happened to him. When he realized that it was Xio who was attempting to help him to his feet, he pulled away, but he was far too weak to hold himself up and fell back to the ground. Instead of trying to get up, the messenger started to crawl away before the rest of his life was taken.

Once again, Xio walked over to the man to help him to his feet. He ordered the first person he saw, "Bring this poor boy something to drink." He then turned to see if he could find a healer although he did not think there was anything that could be done for him now.

For several seconds, no one moved until Xio started to speak again, and then suddenly everyone started scrambling to do as they were told. He reached down to help the man up again, but the man used what strength he had left to pull away from him again.

The man did not get very far before Xio grabbed him and started lifting him to his feet yet again. As the man was lifted up, he begged, "Why did you do this to me? I am one of your kind."

Suddenly a young man showed up with a container of water, which he gave to Xio, and then stepped back so that he did not catch the attention of his master.

Xio tried to get the man to drink the water as he reassured him that everything was going to be okay, but the man did not want anything from him.

Again, the man begged, "Why did you do to this to me?" but Xio did not answer as he drove his dagger into the man's heart. As he let the man fall to the ground, he turned to the guild and replied, "The poor man had lost his mind, and there was nothing left to save."

It had only been a few days since Yang had ordered the dragon guild to abandon the city of Sal, but Xio could already see the difference in the landscape. The Center Region was a fertile farmland with powerful magic guilds. However, it was no place for a dragon guild.

He did not want to leave Sal without taking the time to gather supplies, and although he did not believe his master would harm him, he did as was told. It had been a long time since he had been this far to the West, but he knew they should be able to find food soon. He still did not understand what Yang thought he was going to do with just two hundred guild members against the vast armies of the West.

As usual, there was someone following him who needed to relay a message. Again, he knew the messenger would not speak until he was given permission. Xio did not understand why his people seemed so afraid of him because he had never even raised a hand toward any of them. He waved his hand for the man to come forward so that he could get on with his other responsibilities.

The man quickly stepped forward and replied, "Master, we have reason to believe that Lord Ojak is following us." He then explained,

"There is also a large army, about two days south of us, traveling in the same direction as we are."

Xio stopped for a moment to make sure he understood what the messenger was telling him and why he should care. Suddenly, he realized his master might have known that everyone would be heading west once the word spread that Haden was dead to see how much power they could claim for themselves.

He dismissed the messenger and started looking around to see if he could see his master, but as usual, he was nowhere to be found. He had known Yang for fifty years and could only hope that his master had a plan.

For as long as he had served his master, Xio had never known the death stalker to be kind or compassionate, but he had never seen him kill one of his own kind without a reason. He tried to think back to see if he could remember when his master had first started acting differently. Other than draining the life out of the young dragon guild member, he could not remember anything out of character.

Suddenly, he saw his reflection in a shield carry by a large shape-shifter. He was dressed exactly the same as he remembered Yang was the last time, he saw him. However, Xio could not remember changing into this armor. As he stood looking at his reflection, he could not help but wonder if Yang had cast a spell on him to make him dress the same and what purpose this game could serve.

# CHAPTER 7

# THE DRAGON GUILD'S PRIZE

It was hard to keep track of time, but as far as Angelina could tell, it had been at least two days since she had tried to kill herself. At least, that is what she believes most people would say about what she had attempted to do. Although she felt that her actions were the right thing to do at the time, now she was beginning to wonder whether she had made any difference in her efforts to save her kingdom.

The young witch tried to turn her body so that she would be a little more comfortable, but there was nothing she could do to ease her discomfort. She had not seen the old woman in at least two days, and now she feared that her only friend had been killed during the battle. Death was a fate she was willing to accept because she had brought this on herself, but she felt sorry for the old woman. The truth of the matter was that she might never know what happened to her friend because she was now a prisoner in a dragon guild somewhere behind Haden's forward lines.

Angelina had been bound and kept inside a tent since she first awoke days ago. Even though she had finally concluded that she was not dreaming, she still did not fully understand what had happened. From what she could remember, she was helping the old woman collect information when they ran into a small detachment from Haden's army.

Now every time she woke up, she was bounded and gagged, lying on a different dirt floor, and trying to figure out whether or not she was dreaming. She knew it was only a matter of time before the dragon guild killed her or started torturing her for information.

As far as she could recall, her turn of fate started when the retreating armies from her home began to return to the safety of the walls of Hela. As the fighting moved deeper into her kingdom, most of the gathering parties also returned.

She could still remember the old woman saying, "I want to see for myself why grown men cower before this one man." The old woman then asked, "Is there anyone brave enough to go with me?"

Angelina had only been out of the city a few times in her life, so, of course, she said yes. She had assumed the old woman probably just wanted to determine whether there was anything that could be scavenged. She just wanted to get out of the city and did not believe they would see anyone from Haden's army this far north. Despite the ground shaking most of the time, once outside the city, the old woman seemed determined to find the monster so many people feared.

Angelina had nothing to do except to think as she lay on the ground with her hands bound behind her. She could remember it was days before she realized the old woman was actually heading south to see the warmonger Haden. By the time she figured it out, her curiosity had gotten the best of her and her need to know how far this woman would go far outweighed her fear of finding Haden's army.

Even as the young witch thought back, she still did not understand how the old woman had been able to sneak past the enemies' forward lines. After a few days, they ran into several hundred people who caught the old woman's interest. Although she did not realize it at the time, she later remembered that the old woman seemed distracted that day. She was also sure this was the moment when she realized she needed to do something to help the people of Utopia.

The two women had been watching this group for several minutes when suddenly, an enormous dragon with a single rider landed in the middle of the camp. The group seemed confused by the sudden appearance of the dragon rider and did not appear to be ready to receive him.

The women watched while everyone in the group scrambled to figure out what was going on until another rider jumped on the dragon and took to the air again.

From everything she knew about the old woman, what happened next confused her more than anything else. Suddenly, the old woman was as white as the lilies that grew near the temples, and she still did not know why.

After a few seconds, the old woman turned toward her and exclaimed, "Don't do anything stupid, I will be right back!" The old woman turned back to her and added, "No matter how much you want to."

She remembered watching the old woman as long as she could, but it did not take long before she had navigated through the thick shrubs and disappeared. Soon she could no longer see the old woman, but she was sure she heard her say, "Child, I will be back in a minute." With the old woman gone, she was left to her own devices.

Even as Angelina tried to remember what happen, she could not believe the old woman had so much courage. She did remember thinking to herself, *We are in the middle of nowhere. What does she think I am going to do?*

Now, as she lay on the ground, she wished she had had the sense to listen to the old woman and her words of wisdom.

Angelina had never been particularly good at listening especially when it came to doing something that she was not supposed to be doing. She remembered trying to get to higher ground so she could see better. She genuinely believed she did not plan to do anything stupid and only wanted to get a better look at what had made the old woman so concerned. Suddenly, as she looked up and saw the enormous dragon flying toward Hela, she started to panic because she felt like she needed to help her people.

Before long and without realizing it, she had willed hundreds of rocks and other objects of various sizes toward the unsuspecting detachment of Haden's army. Even as the flying objects went past her, she knew that once she was discovered, she would probably be killed instantly. That did not matter by this time because at least she would have done her part to protect her kingdom.

Angelina had never been able to use her full power or had so much control, but for some reason, her power seemed to have no bounds. Before she knew it, there were large rocks and other objects flying all over the battlefield, smashing everything in their wake. Suddenly, people and horses were being knocked to the ground by the flying debris, and most were not getting back up.

She did not understand why, but as the minutes passed, there seemed to be more people entering the field, which only seemed to confuse the matter.

Several large birds flying overhead caused her to suddenly lose her focus. She tried to scare the birds away, but they were merely a diversion because someone had discovered what she was doing. Before she even realized what was happening, someone had grabbed her from behind and was using something to keep her from breathing. She fell unconscious to the ground. When she awoke, she found herself bound and gagged in the middle a tent.

Angelina had been lying on the cold ground for hours and was starting to think they had forgotten about her. Only once in the last two days had anyone given her something to drink or eat. She did not understand why, but she felt they were more afraid of her than she was of them. She could not imagine why anyone would be afraid of someone who could not even control her power for more than a few seconds.

She still did not understand how she was able to control her power or why she seemed so powerful before. Her actions, though, had to be the dumbest thing of all the stupid things she had done. She wished she had made a different choice, but it was done, and there was nothing she could do about it now.

Angelina once again began to wonder if the old woman could have escaped, but she had not seen any sign of her since the battle. The last thing she could remember was her friend telling her not to do anything stupid, and by all definitions, this was clearly something stupid.

She believed that the old woman would be quick to point this out, but still, she wished she were here to tell her what to do now. She thought, *At least if the old woman were here, she would find a way to get me something to eat or drink.*

It was very lonely in the tent because not many people came in other than a young man who checked on her every couple of hours.

She feared that the only reason she was being kept alive was that they planned to sacrifice her so that they could take her power.

The clerics and wielding masters at the Great Stone Temple in Hela had always told her that if she did not learn to use her power, it would cost her. She had heard the story of the warmongers who could drain the power from her dying body. However, she never thought she would be kept alive just to be sacrificed like a common farm animal.

She soon realized that thinking about it was not going to help her and that she needed to find a way to take her mind off what they might do to her.

Her hands had gone numb, so she tried to move her fingers to get the blood circulating again. She also attempted to turn to take the pressure off her face and stomach, but the ropes that bound her did not allow her to move enough to get comfortable.

As the hours passed, and she continued to lay on the ground, she thought to herself that maybe even Haden himself would take her power, not that it made her feel any better.

After a while, the only thing she could think of was that once she had been brutally murdered by Haden, they would feed her lifeless body to his dragons. She had never met Haden, but every time she closed her eyes, she was sure she could see his face looking back at her.

Suddenly, she could hear the rustling sound of other people coming into the tent. Before she knew it, there were at least twenty-five people standing around her, chanting something at her that she did not understand. She had no idea whether she should pretend to be unconscious or not.

She concluded that this was finally the end and that they had come to drain her power and take her life. She was tired from hunger, but she was going to make sure whatever bastard or wench tried to take her power would have to earn it. She thought, *I am not an animal, and I have no intention of just being a good little sacrifice.*

~*~

The guild leader had told him, "There would be no harm to the girl, but the guild could use a laugh or two." The crowd had already gathered around the young girl lying on the ground, but he still did not know what he was going to say or do.

He watched the guild members gather around the young woman and chant some kind of nonsense that was supposed to confuse her. When they were finished, he announced, "I am the son of Taico, the headmaster of the wielding guild and the newest member of this dragon guild." Seconds later, and as somewhat of an afterthought, he proclaimed, "I am Likos." He then announced, "I captured you. Therefore, you belong to me to do with as I like."

He reached down, grabbed her by what was left of her dress, and confidently started to lift her to her feet. Suddenly, with what seemed like the last ounce of strength she could muster, Angelina kicked him between the legs.

Likos quickly grabbed his groin and fell to his knees. As he fell, he lost his grip on her and dropped her. Her feet were barely touching the ground, but because her hands were bound behind her, she fell to the ground face first.

Although he could barely move, he could not help but wonder if she were still conscious as she lay on the ground without moving.

Understandably still in pain, Likos hastily jumped back to his feet and grabbed Angelina by her dress again to lift her to her feet. This time, he did not lift her completely off the ground. As he tried to help her to her feet, she attempted to head-butt him in the face, but this time, he did not fall or let her go. As he struggled to make sure she did not fall again, she tried to kick him.

Her element of surprise was long gone, and he quickly moved to one side as she started to fall to the ground, but this time, he was there to catch her.

By this time, everyone in the tent was laughing and yelling at the two young people. Although he was not sure whether the group was laughing at him or the girl, Likos started laughing too.

As he listened to everyone laughing, he began to wonder if this game had gone too far. He could see she had split open the side of her face when she fell and now appeared to be glowing.

Finally, an older man stepped forward and, with a wave of his hand, was able to get everyone to calm down. He then turned toward Likos and stated, "This woman is obviously a little more than you can handle today." After a few seconds, he added, "Maybe you should wait until you are a little wiser before you try again."

The crowd quickly started pointing at him and laughing, but once again, the man waved his hand, and the crowd began to settle down as they had done before.

Likos looked at the man and then at the young witch. He shook his head because he was glad to see this game was finally over. He laughed and replied, "This girl is a bit too beat up for me anyway." Once again, the crowd started laughing, but this time, they seemed to be laughing with him instead of at him.

The old man waved his hand once more and then signaled some of the women in the tent to come to the center. He told the oldest woman in the group, "Make sure that this wench is cleaned up and fed." He then turned to the rest of the guild. After a moment stated, "This witch will bring us enough money to live on for a year—we need to take care of her until we can get rid of her."

As he watched the young witch being led away, Likos began to wonder what fate had in store for the beautiful girl.

The women lifted the young witch up, and it took only a few moments before they started leading her out of the tent.

~*~

At first, Angelina was so happy to see the light that she did not notice anything else. When she looked around though, she could not believe the amount of destruction. She could see the city of Hela in the distance, and although it was still standing, the walls had been breached. As she continued to look around at the destruction, she began to wonder if she would be better off if this, in fact, had been the end.

She felt like she had failed in her efforts and was struggling to find any hope among the vast destruction. As she looked into the crowd of unfamiliar faces, only one face stood out—that of the young man who called himself Likos. As she looked at him, she was not sure if she should just give up or if she should be mad as hell. Either way, she could not see how anything was going to help her out of this situation or save her home.

There were four heavily armed men who were there to make sure she did not try anything during the few seconds she was untied. She could tell that even though they were willing to untie her so she could be bathed, they were reluctant to remove the gag for fear that she would speak and kill them all.

She was washed publicly but did not care that she now stood naked in front of at least a hundred people. For some reason, everyone around her seemed scared, and she doubted that anyone noticed the naked woman in the middle of their camp.

She was just as likely to harm herself if she tried to use her magic, but she liked the fact that everyone in the camp seemed afraid of her. Although there was nothing she could do, she was not going to correct them even if she could talk.

As her mind started to wander again, she felt the ground begin to tremble beneath her feet, but even this did not seem to draw their attention from her. As she looked up, no one appeared to notice the shaking as they refused to look away or find safer ground. Once again, the peering eyes of Likos caught her attention.

## CHAPTER 8

# THE TWO-FACED WITCH

The fat man had been at this for hours, and as far as Sabrina could tell, he had no intention of letting her take a break any time soon. Master Pythagoras had been her instructor for as long as she could remember, but not once had he done anything, she ordered him to do. She needed to find out if there was any information from her father. However, no matter what she wanted, her father had ordered him to teach, so he taught. She knew they had been through this lesson before, but that did not stop him from asking the same dumb questions. Once again, he smacked his hand on the desk and asked, "According to the laws of existence, which is greater, potential energy or stored energy?"

She knew that this was a trick question, but she could not resist the chance to have a little fun, so without any hesitation, she replied, "Potential."

He smiled and was about to teach her a lesson in manners when a guardsman came rushing into the room.

Despite Master Pythagoras's warnings, he walked past the fat man to get to the princess. He quickly bowed his head and waited for her to give him permission to speak.

She did not even look at her schoolmaster when she told the guardsman, "Tell me what news you have of my father."

He raised his head and replied, "The word is spreading across the region that your father has been defeated."

She waved her hand to dismiss the guardsman and then got up to walk out of the room.

Master Pythagoras demanded, "Young lady, sit back down. This lesson is not over yet." He stepped in front of her and added, "If you do not sit back down, these lessons are over forever, and I will leave the palace."

She had spent far more time with this fat man than she cared to, and without looking back, she stepped around him and walked out of the room. She knew that she no longer had to listen to anyone, especially this short, fat man. She was going to be queen, and she had better things to do than to listen to this nonsense any longer.

It had been well over a week, and Sabrina had done everything she could to take her mind off the fact that there just was not any more news about the war or her father. She was Haden's youngest child, and although she did not understand why, her father had appointed her to be his successor.

She was beginning to believe that the rumors of her father's demise were true. However, she needed to know the truth before she tried to take command of his armies because no one had taken anything from him in 150 years.

Just the thought of not having to deal with her overbearing and omnipotent father, the invincible warmonger Haden, ever again, almost made her giggle—not that she would giggle in public.

She had manipulated and slept with half the generals in her father's military for more than two years to turn Haden's army against itself. That was the easy part because it took almost twice that long to find a reason to get her father to go to Utopia.

In the last three hours, Sabrina had looked everywhere for her father's soothsayer—an ugly old sight witch named Jeannie—but as usual, the old hag was nowhere to be found. She believed the witch had long since lost her mind because she always spoke of herself in the third person. No matter how loyal the witch was to her father in public, she knew the woman hated him just as much as she did.

The two-faced witch always had two versions of her visions to tell, but few people knew her well enough to ask for both. There was the one version she would share with anyone who would listen to her. Although the prediction would be accurate, it was often misleading and dangerous. Then there was the second version, which was just as true but was far less misleading. Sabrina knew the witch only told this other version to a select few. She believed that her father, the arrogant bastard that he was, trusted every word the witch spoke, and now she believed he was paying the price.

She understood why most people did not trust the distorted words of this crazy old woman and why they called her the two-faced witch. Everyone assumed the witch was a close consultant to Haden and one of his most trusted advisors, but behind closed doors, she was just a nasty old witch who hated him.

It had been almost fifteen years since the witch had told her of the dangers that awaited her father in Utopia. The old hag told her that Haden's only weakness was in Utopia, but she could not have guessed what this entailed. She was starting to believe that it meant he would never return, and she would be the queen of the largest empire on the planet. She thought to herself, *I need answers, and the only way I will get them is to find my old friend Jeannie.*

Sabrina had been walking around the palace searching for the two-faced witch and was about to give up. Suddenly, out of nowhere, the ugly old hag stepped in front of her. She started to ask where she had been, but the witch began chanting some nonsense about Haden and the one who walks in his place. Sabrina shook her head because she had no idea what the old witch was trying to tell her. After the third time she was told the same thing, she replied, "I don't understand."

The old hag then repeated, "Jeannie believes that the one who walks in Haden's place is the same as Jeannie is to Jeannie." The witch then added, "You must find Jeannie so we can determine the fate of your father."

Sabrina shook her head again and replied "Okay, I am here."

The old witch repeated, "Jeannie believes that the one who walks in Haden's place is the same as Jeannie is to Jeannie."

Although the old hag was an exceptional sight witch, Sabrina could only guess that she had finally lost her mind. She did not understand what the witch was saying, but she believed that the woman probably knew the fate of her father.

As she listened to the two-faced witch babble nonsense, she was not sure if this sudden display was for her or if it was for everyone. Like most people, she was never entirely sure which facet of the witch she was dealing with, and the rumors that her father was dead only made matters worse. If she were going to get any information from the hag, she resigned herself to playing this game until she got some answers.

Sabrina tried to think about the words of the two-faced witch, but she did not understand what she was attempting to tell her. After a few seconds, she said aloud, "Jeannie believes that the one who walks in Haden's place is the same as Jeannie is to Jeannie," but the words had no meaning to her.

The witch laughed and replied, "Yes, the one who walks in Haden's place is the same as Jeannie is to Jeannie."

Sabrina started trying to walk closer to the old hag to ask if she would explain what she meant by this statement. Before she could get to the witch though, she disappeared around the corner just as suddenly as she had appeared. Suddenly, twenty cubits in front of her, the two-faced witch appeared once more.

Again, she declared, "Jeannie believes that the one who walks in Haden's place is the same as Jeannie is to Jeannie." A moment later, the old hag flashed her ugly teeth and added "Poor girl, I wonder what your sweet siblings are doing right now."

Sabrina ran to catch the old witch because she did not want to hear about her siblings. She only wanted information about her father.

Seconds later, before Sabrina could get to her, the old hag stepped around the corner of a building. When Sabrina turned the corner to look for the witch, it was a dead end with no one there.

As Sabrina thought about what the old hag had said, she began to realize her beloved siblings must also believe that their father was dead. She knew they were probably already plotting to see what they could steal from her.

Her father had conquered tens of dozens of kingdoms over last 150 years, and she understood that whoever controlled his resources would control most of the known world.

Sabrina had never understood why her father had taken so many resources to the small, meaningless kingdom of Utopia. Now, if she could be convinced that her father was dead, she knew she needed to go there. She had not thought about it before, but she did not even know how much of her father's army was left behind or how long it would take to get them moving.

Suddenly, she began to wonder whether or not anyone had thought about her father's dragons. Sabrina knew that whoever controlled the dragons would also rule everything else, including his armies. She now wanted to talk to the two-faced witch more than ever, but she also needed to prepare her forces to go to Utopia to recover the forgotten dragons.

If she thought she could get away with it, Sabrina would take the palace guards and all the forces she could find and head to Utopia. She needed to find the two-faced witch, however, because she believed that the witch was playing some game she did not understand.

She had known the witch for as long as she could remember and had never known her to refuse to tell her anything when she was asked directly. Sabrina shook her head because even if she found the witch, she had no doubt that the information would be twisted somehow, but at least it would be correct. She knew she needed to continue to look for the witch, but since she had looked everywhere, she could think of, she stopped to collect her thoughts.

Finally, she had enough of this nonsense and stomped off to find the captain of the guard. The guards quickly snapped to attention when she entered the guard station.

Apparently, the palace guards were doing some kind of inspection, but this was of no concern to her. Without any hesitation, she demanded, "I want the witch, Jeannie, found immediately."

The captain of the guard looked at the princess for a few seconds and then said to his men, "What are you people waiting for? I want the two-faced witch found within the hour."

Sabrina smiled because she had grown tired of the two-faced witch and her half-truths and was going to teach the old hag a lesson once and for all.

~*~

It took more than an hour for the palace guards to find her, but to everyone's surprise, there were two witches.

The nasty hags were in a cave they had dug out beneath the throne room floor. The two-faced witch apparently had a twin sister, a halve sister, which explained why she always told two different stories.

Sabrina now realized why the witch always seemed to be everywhere and nowhere at the same time. She had been taught that when it came to halve witches, there was always one that could be trusted and one that could not be trusted. As she looked at the two witches, she had no way of knowing which witch was which.

She did not know why, but for some reason, she began to wonder if her father knew that there were two witches. She shook her head as she realized why her father always seemed to take his time to think about what the witch said or, in this case, what the witches were saying.

The two nasty old hags had stripped off all their clothes and were sitting in the middle of an oddly shaped trench cut deep into the black dirt beneath the throne room. They were facing each other and chanting something, but Sabrina did not understand what they were saying to each other.

As far as she could tell, the old hags were identical to each other and seemed to know what the other one was going to say. With each word that came from their mouths, one would finish the words of the other, or both would speak at the same time. Each witch had five small stones with strange markings etched on each side. As they threw the flat stones into the air over and over again, they chanted in an unknown language.

Sabrina could only guess that the stones they were tossing into the air were wielding stones, which her short, fat teacher claimed were old when the previous worlds were still young. She had never believed the stones existed; however, according to Master Pythagoras, who tried to teach her about the old laws of existence, the rocks never lied. She laughed because he had also told her that truth was only relevant to the beholder.

She watched as the stones went into the air again and then thought to herself, *At least I learned something from my chubby little teacher.* After a few moments, she thought, *I must figure out how to get the stones from these old hags.*

Together both witches started waving their hands and repeating, "Come, sister, join Jeannie and me to see what fate awaits you, my dear."

She had never had a reason to fear the two-faced witch, but suddenly, chills ran down her back as they continued to beckon her to join them. Nonetheless, she needed to know if her father was alive and if she should travel to Utopia.

Sabrina looked around the room where there were at least twelve other people crowded into the small space. She did not believe the witches were planning to harm her but thought someone would prevent them from killing Haden's baby girl and their queen.

When she entered the oddly shaped ditch to join the witches, they began to strip off her clothes. At first, she refused to allow them to continue and pretended she was going to leave if they did not stop. After looking around the room though, she realized she had slept with most of these people and decided she did not have time to play these games. She removed her clothing and sat down between the old hags.

Once all three women were sitting down, the witches began to chant again as they once more started tossing the wielding stones into the air.

Sabrina understood the process because if her father had done nothing else, he had made sure she was highly educated in all the principal forms of magic and sciences of the day.

Suddenly, each of the two-faced witches grabbed one of her arms. While chanting, the witches forced Sabrina's hands open and then cut down the center of each of her palms until blood streamed down on the wielding stones.

Her fat teacher had said that the stones only noticed those with a part to play in destiny's game. She smiled ever so slightly because the witches had just confirmed she had a destiny.

The witches quickly let go of her hands and grabbed the blood-soaked stones before throwing them into the air. The stone spun high in the air and then fell scattered between the three women. As she watched, almost every stone landed with the same symbol facing up.

When the witches did not say anything, she demanded, "Is my father alive, and where do I find his dragons?"

The two old hags gasped and quickly replied, "Your Majesty, Lord Haden is gone,"

Sabrina smiled because they realized she was finally queen. After a few seconds, she began wondering, if they were truly halves, then why did they tell the same story?

As the witches reached for the stones, one of the stones rolled over, and the two witches squealed at each other.

Seconds later, the hag on her right said, "There is another that walks in his place who is far more dangerous than Haden." Before she could continue, the second hag squealed, flashed her nasty-looking teeth, and added, "Do not mention his name."

The witch on Sabrina's left then squealed "Haden's dragons are scattered north, east, south, and west." Both witches then turned toward Sabrina and together proclaimed, "My dear, you must take all the forces that you have at your control to avenge your father."

This was the information she wanted to hear. Sabrina stood up so that everyone could see her and ordered, "Prepare my forces. We are going to Utopia."

When she turned back toward the witches, they were also standing and smiling their ghastly smiles.

## CHAPTER 9

# THE WITCH OF HELA

It had been two days since her captors had decided to move her from a tent to the ancient stone temples. Still, Angelina did not know what they were planning to do with her, but for the moment, she would give almost anything to scratch her face. A few days ago, when she was dropped, a healing witch put something on her face to help heal the cut. Although the medicine helped, her face tingled like crazy.

She had tried to lean so that she could rub the side of her face on her shoulder, but the cut was just beyond her reach. She had stretched as far as she could when the old chair, she had been sitting on gave out, bringing her crashing to the ground.

She had barely hit the ground when the two guardsmen rushed to the center of the room and started pointing their weapons at her.

The large dirt master stomped his feet and shouted, "Don't move if you want to live, wench!"

She had been through this kind of treatment half a dozen times in the last few days, but at least she could rub her face on the ground before they threaten to kill her again.

The dirt master demanded that she stop now and poked her with his spear.

At that moment, Likos walked into the room and demanded that the dirt master stop before he killed them all.

The man stepped back and asked, "What about the witch? I think she is trying to escape."

Likos shook his head and replied, "She is not attempting to escape—her chair broke." He reached down and pulled the young witch to her feet. He turned toward the dirt master. "I have her. Can you go find a better chair?"

The man looked at the Angelina for a moment and then at Likos before turning to leave the room. After a few minutes, he returned with another chair.

He helped put the witch back on the new chair and then quickly walked to the other side of the room so that he did not have to be so close to her.

Angelina was starting to get used to these people being so scared of her, but she still did not understand why. Although she was back in the only place, she had ever called home, it did not feel like the same safe place it once was.

She was still being gagged and bound, but at least people were feeding her from time to time and were no longer playing games she did not understand. There was always someone in the room with her, but rarely would anyone talk to her.

A week ago, she had been able to use more of her power and control it better than she had ever been able to in her life. Thanks to the old woman, whom she could not stop thinking about, she had struck a mighty blow at the enemy, but that still did not explain why everyone was so afraid of her now.

She could hear the whispering and gasping each time she was paraded into another room or structure, which seemed to occur every few hours. As far as she could tell, the dragon guild somehow believed she was the grandmaster of the wielding guild of Hela. She also understood that the guild needed to keep her alive, at least until someone came to claim her.

Angelina also assumed she was being kept alive because Haden's generals wanted her to surrender the city. She found this idea amusing because, for the moment, no one trusted her enough to be ungagged for any longer than the time it took to shove some food into her mouth.

It had been at least a week since the dragon guild had captured her, and not once had they been brave enough to remove her gag and untie her at the same time.

The stone temples had long ago been abandoned by both the sight and wielding guilds, so it was easy enough for the dragon guild to take control of the temples. Of course, no one was left to tell them she did not belong in the grandmaster's chambers.

As one of the guards adjusted his weapon, Angelina slowly opened her eyes but had not yet concluded whether or not she was still dreaming. Since she was not allowed to do anything on her own, she often found herself falling asleep whenever the attention was not focused on her. To make matters worse, her nightmares had returned. Since she had never seen these two guards before, she was not convinced they were real. She struggled most of the time to determine whether she was dreaming or whether the dragon guild was doing something she did not understand. Either way, she found herself exceedingly restless and confused.

After a few moments, she realized the guards had not even noticed she was awake. She knew that if she started moving, she might scare the guards, but if she went back to sleep, the dreams would return.

This new nightmare frightened her more than all the other dreams she ever had, but there was nothing she could do about it. The nightmare always started with the arrival of the dragon rider that entered Haden's camp moments before she decided to attack. From the moment the dragon landed, a large man seemed to focus on her. When the dragon took to the air again, the man started toward her in an attempt to stop her.

Although it would only be seconds later when she began her attack, it seemed like an hour that the man spent charging toward her. She would lose sight of the man during the attack, which appeared to last only a few seconds. Once the attack was over and everyone was gone, she would find herself face-to-face with an enormous dragon. Before the dragon could eat her, she would awaken from her dream, only to realize she was still bound and gagged. She had this reoccurring dream almost every time she fell asleep.

~*~

When Angelina awoke from her nightmare once again, Likos was talking to the guards. She could see he was carrying what looked like a basket of rocks.

She thought, *I am in no mood to play these games*, and decided she was not going without a fight. As he approached, she tried to kick him and once again knocked her chair over.

Unlike the first time, he was not caught by surprise and quickly moved out of the way. Although he was never in any real danger, this time, no one was laughing.

The guards rushed toward her to make sure she did not try to escape.

Likos quickly put his hands up. "It is okay. I have food for the wench, and she will behave if she wants it." He then looked at Angelina to confirm she understood he was not going to hurt her.

She was not sure she could trust him but nodded her head so that the guards would back off a little. She thought, *I will let him have it the same as I did before if he tries anything*. By now, there were four guards in the room and not much she could do anyway, so she nodded her head again to let them know she was not going to try anything.

When guards realized she was not trying to escape, they backed away to give Likos more room.

She was fully awake now and could see he only had a basket of bread and meat in his hand and not a basket of rocks to bash in her skull.

She took a deep breath to calm down and waited for someone to help her up off the cold stone floor.

When Likos tried to return her chair to the upright position, the guards stepped back a little farther because they did not like being so close to the witch but kept their weapons drawn. "Put your weapons down. I don't think she is planning to kill everyone just yet."

Likos slowly explained to Angelina, "I am going to remove your gag, but you need to calm down just a little so that I can feed you."

She took another deep breath and nodded her head once again to indicate she was not going to try anything.

He looked at the guards for confirmation and then, after a few seconds, removed the gag so that she could be fed.

Angelina tried to stretch her jaw muscles by opening and closing her mouth before saying, "Thank you." Before she could say anything else, the guards started toward her with their spears again.

She instantly realized she was better off not to speak, even to say thank you.

Likos waved his hand once again, which was enough for the guards to step away from her.

Likos began to break the fresh bread into several smaller pieces so that he could feed them to her. He asked, "Would you like something to drink?"

She nodded her head. He turned and ordered one of the guards to get something from the wine cellar.

When the guards left to see if he could find some wine, the other three guards stepped even farther back so that Likos had the opportunity to feed the wench. It was clear they did not like being so close to the witch.

He turned to Angelina and said, "These guards will not hesitate to use their spears if you try anything."

She would have calm down if she could. However, it was not so simple with everyone on edge and ready to spear her every time she moved.

It had been several minutes since Angelina had finished her food, and she was already starting to feel much better. She could also tell that the guards were starting to settle down. Although she comprehended the consequences of saying something, she realized that this might be her one chance to get some answers. She needed to know why everyone was so afraid of her so, without any warning, she asked, "Why are you afraid of me?"

The room was silent for several seconds before the guards realized that she had spoken and that it had been their job to keep her from saying anything. They quickly rushed forward again with their spears to stop her before she killed everyone in the room.

She took a deep breath and closed her eyes as she prepared to be hit or stabbed.

Likos quickly stepped between the guards and the young witch. He put his hand out once more and demanded, "Stop! It was an accident, and she is not going to do that again."

The guards continued to come forward despite being told to stop until Likos shouted, "Enough! There is no harm because she was not trying to kill you!"

The guards lowered their weapons and slowly started backing away from the witch.

Realizing she had not been beaten or stabbed to death, Angelina slowly opened her eyes.

Likos turned to her and asked, "Honestly, you don't know why everyone is so afraid of you?"

She did not know what to do, but she dared not try to speak again. She just shook her head back and forth several times in the hope that he would figure it out.

He was not sure if he believed her or if he thought this was a trick. However, after looking at her and only seeing a scared young woman, he decided it could not hurt to tell her.

Likos began, "I believe that every warmonger on the planet will try to find the killer of the warmonger Haden."

Angelina shook her head because she did not have a clue about what Haden had to do with her current condition.

When he asked if she understood, she shook her head again in the hope that he would continue.

He was confused by her response to the statement but even more confused by the look in her eyes. After a few seconds, he asked, "You genuinely do not know, do you?" He looked at her for a moment and then shook his head because again, he was not certain whether he believed her or not.

Angelina was still not sure what he was talking about but did not want to miss her opportunity to get more information. She shook her head to indicate she did not know and then leaned forward as if she was trying to hear him better.

He did not understand what she could hope to gain from this act but decided he would play along. He explained, "A few days ago, this dragon guild did not know the whole story, or we probably would not have treated you the way we did." He thought to himself that if this woman believed she was fooling him, then maybe she would calm down. Likos continued. "The dragon riders told of how you drove Haden and his dragon from the sky so that you could face him on the ground."

Angelina was not certain if the young man was still talking about her or if he had switched to some other story, but either way, for some reason, she did not feel very well. If she were not afraid that one of the guards would stab her, she did not believe she would have been able to keep her food down.

Likos was even more perplexed as the girl looked more confused and sicker at the very mention of Haden's name. He shook his head and continued. "Once Haden was on the ground, you attacked his entire command section, killing most of the senior leadership before you turned on the warmonger." He stopped for a moment and added, "Most people thought that the whole Utopian army had attacked us."

Angelina started to say something, but the guards had failed their duties once, and she was sure they would not do so again.

He explained, "We thought that Haden would have called for his dragons, but the dragon riders later told us that the dragons would not land."

He thought, *The witch would like me to believe that Haden's dragons just refused to help their master.* As he watched her pull back in disbelief, he added, "It was not until a few days ago that we realized it was just you and Haden who caused so much damage."

Angelina quickly realized that Likos's story was remarkably similar to her dream and started feeling even sicker to her stomach.

He realized this information was upsetting the very person he was trying to keep calm. As he looked around the room, Likos was sure that if he did not do something soon, either the guards were going to kill the witch, or she was going to kill everyone.

He grabbed her, put his arms around her, and whispered in her ear, "You need to calm down, or the guards will kill you to protect this guild even if it means that they lose their bounty."

She was so scared, and she felt like everyone in the room could see her fear, but to her surprise, everyone in the room was in a panic and was screaming at each other. She just did not understand why everyone was so scared and did not know what to do.

Likos stood looking at the woman who was no older than he was, and he started wondering how she could be powerful enough to have killed Haden. He felt sorry for her until he stepped back and looked at her. He realized the witch would have killed them all if he had not stopped her.

He was not sure what he needed to do to get Angelina to calm down before someone tried to kill her or before she destroyed the temple and everyone in it. As he looked around, there were at least eight other people in the small room now, and all of them were in a panic.

Suddenly, he had an idea that might solve the problem if this witch really did not know why everyone was so afraid of her. He ordered one of the guards to find something that was shiny and large enough to see one's reflection.

A few minutes later, the guard returned with a silver-coated shield that he gave to Likos. When Likos made Angelina look into the shield, she suddenly realized why everyone was so scared of her.

As she looked at herself in the shield, she could not believe they had not killed her already. She took a few deep breaths as she had been taught to do. Angelina looked around and realized there were no other lights in this room because all the light came from her. She could not believe she had not been able to see this before without the shield, but she was glowing as brightly as any flame she had ever seen.

## CHAPTER 10

# A NEW COMPANION

It had been two days since he had removed Airus's smashed armor, but his friend was still having a hard time keeping up. It had also been two days since he had dug himself out from beneath the rocks and dead animals. His head was not pounding like it was, but he still was not any closer to figuring out who he was or what he was doing under the debris.

He looked back to see how his companion was doing and could see that Airus clearly needed to stop. After observing the surroundings, he decided they needed to get to higher ground before they took another break.

As he once again looked back to see if Airus could make it to the next ridge, he noticed the same small figure dart behind a large rock some fifty or so cubits back.

He looked forward again and could see a clearing on top of a ridge just north of where they were going. He believed that if his friend could hold out for just a little while longer, they could probably rest there for a while.

He looked back once more to see if the small figure was going to follow them to the top of the ridge. He thought, *I find it hard to believe that child could be so skilled or has continued to follow us for so long.* He shook his head because he did not believe the small figure would follow them up the ridge unless there were something else that drove the child. He looked back down the valley, but at least he could not see anyone else following them.

~*~

Airus tried to catch his breath, but it hurt too much for him to breathe, so he had to take short breaths. His feet hurt from walking, and he thought he was going to need to start pulling the bark from the trees if he did not get something to eat soon. He refused to say anything because he felt that the man had done more than enough to help him.

When they finally stepped into the clearing on top of the ridge, the man informed him, "We are going to rest here for a while." He almost smiled as he sat down.

He could see that the man had something else on his mind when he said, "I am going to check out the area to make sure it is safe."

It took a few seconds, but Airus stood back up and then asked, "Is there anything that you need me to do?"

The man replied, "No, I think I can handle this. You need to get some rest. I am not sure how long we will be able to stay here if there are other people following us."

Airus would have done anything that was asked of him, but he sat back down as the man turned around to check out the area.

When the man began to walk away, Airus said, "I saw a small farmhouse a few hundred cubits below the tree line."

The man nodded and replied, "I would bet that there is some food there if you are hungry."

He turned, smiled, and looked back toward the direction from which they had just come. He then loudly announced, "I am going to see if I can find some food and water. I will be gone for about an hour."

He watched the man abruptly stomp off in what appeared to be the wrong direction and could not grasp where he thought he was going. He whispered to himself, "I hope that he knows what he is doing because the small house is not in that direction."

When Airus looked back in the direction of the small house, he noticed the same small figure that had been following them for days. He watched as the child adjusted to the man's movement. He suddenly realized that the man's behavior was purely for the benefit of the child. He only hoped that the man still planned to get some food and water before he starved to death.

He watched for several minutes as the man would go for a while in one direction and then, for no apparent reason, change his mind. It was apparent that the man knew he was being followed and was trying to trap the child. Every time the man changed direction, the child would dart behind a rock or bush. From Airus's view, the small figure always appeared to be one step ahead of the man as they both disappeared over the ridge.

Airus had almost fallen asleep when he noticed the man coming back with an armful of supplies. As the man got closer, he quickly got to his feet to offer assistance.

As far as he could tell, the man had only been gone for about forty minutes. He had managed to find some fruit, dried meat, and enough water to last a couple of days.

He could not help but wonder if the man had caught the child because he did not appear to have been in a struggle of any kind and did not have the boy with him. To his relief, as he sat going through the supplies, Airus suddenly noticed that the child was again hiding in the bushes about forty cubits away.

As they sat eating some of the fruit, Airus conveyed, "I do not believe that you were able to capture the child because I can still see him hiding in the bushes." He then paused to see how the man would react before asking, "So what is your plan for catching the child, or have you spent enough time chasing him?"

The man smiled and responded, "That is not a child but an adult female who is following us for reasons that I do not understand." After a few seconds, he added, "The woman will need to eat the same as we do. If she wants to stay where she can see us, then she will have to come to us for food."

Airus looked at the small figure hiding in the bushes before he asked, "What makes you think that this is a woman and not a small child who wants to steal from us?"

The man laughed and replied, "The little wench does her business away from the trees, and she is far more patient than any child I have ever seen." He then looked toward the bushes where the small figure was hiding and added, "Mostly because she moves like a mother cat watching her kittens learning to hunt."

Airus tried to take a deep breath and looked once again at the small figure hiding in the bushes.

She did not lay flat in the bushes, like a male cat that did not want his prey to see him but was high so she could escape if anyone got too close. After a few seconds, he lost sight of her. He thought about the way the small figure had followed them and could not believe he had not come to the same conclusion sooner.

Airus had finished his food and was feeling a lot better. He would have liked to have stayed a bit longer, but he knew they needed to catch his army. Hesitantly, he asked, "Shouldn't we get started soon?"

The man looked toward the small figure hiding in the bushes and then loudly replied, "We will make camp here for a couple of hours because I need to get some sleep." He then laid out some of the fruit so that the woman could see them from where she was hiding. He stretched a bit before lying down so that he could pretend to sleep.

Airus could only guess that he wanted to see if the woman would come closer. It did not take long before he suspected that although the man was supposed to be pretending to sleep, he appeared to be fast asleep.

He watched the man for about twenty minutes and soon convinced himself that the woman was not coming. He thought to himself, *How could I have been so wrong about him?* Airus knew that the man had, for no apparent reason, taken the time to save him and was now working selflessly to help him get back to the army that had left him for dead.

As he lay there, he wondered if he should do something to thank the man and if he should tell him about what he knew.

Suddenly, a small figure appeared out of nowhere, just as his friend had predicted.

Airus held his breath as the woman inched her way closer to his companion because he did not want to scare her away. He watched as a very old woman stood staring at the sleeping man. He believed she was going to strike at any second now because she held a dagger with both hands, as if it were a large broadsword, and was edging ever closer to his sleeping friend.

Airus knew that his colleague had planned this, but unfortunately, he had fallen asleep before he was able to follow through. He had to do something before the woman tried to kill his friend. Airus was not sure what he could do in his current condition without startling her, which would mess up his friend's plan.

Despite the pain in his chest, he managed to make it to his feet. Fortunately, the old woman was so mesmerized by the sleeping man that she did not notice him. He believed that if he made any sudden movement, he would scare the old woman away before he could catch her.

The man had gone to a lot of effort to get the woman to come close enough so that she might be caught. Now all Airus had to do was grab her before she tried to kill his friend.

It was apparent that the woman knew this man because from the moment that she had appeared in their camp, she had not once taken her eyes off him.

Airus owed the man everything, including his life, and it did not matter what his friend had done to the woman. He slowly moved closer to the old woman and could not help but wonder why she hated this man so much.

She continued to face the sleeping man with her back to Airus. Luckily for him, she never took her eyes off his friend and did not hear him coming. It only took a few seconds to get close enough to grab her and confiscate the dagger from her small fragile hands.

Before he could do anything else, the man he thought was sleeping said, "Do not harm the old wench. She is not a threat to us."

Airus had not realized that the man was awake and did not understand why he did not want her harmed. Since he did not have any desire to do anything to anger the man or harm the old woman, he did as he was instructed.

As he held the old woman, Airus began to wonder if the man had been sleeping or if he was just pretending to sleep to draw the woman closer as he had planned. He knew that the man wanted him to let the woman go, but he was not sure if he trusted her.

After a few moments, the man realized that Airus did not want to let the woman go just yet, so he remarked, "Look at this old wench. What is it that you think that she could have done to me with such a weapon as the meat sticker that you now have in your hand?"

Airus looked down at the fragile old woman and quickly realized that the man was correct. He began to feel ridiculous because it was obvious that the old woman, even with the dagger, was not a threat to his friend. He had to be twice her height and three or four times her body weight. Now, while looking at the woman, he doubted she had the strength to push the dagger into the man.

He took a deep breath but wanted to show the old woman who was in charge before he let her go. He asked, "Are you sure that I should not just put her out of her misery? She must be well over a hundred years old and could probably use the rest."

The man smiled but said nothing as he continued to stare at Airus until he finally released the woman.

To Airus's astonishment, the old woman turned and jumped into the air so that she could slap him across his face. He stood motionless for a moment, but it did not take long for him to realize what had happened. He immediately tried to grab the old woman again, but she was long out of his reach by the time her feet hit the ground.

The man started laughing. "Maybe she is more dangerous than I thought." He continued to laugh for a few moments and then added, "Maybe I should have let you terminate the little wench before she kills us all."

Airus was a bit embarrassed that he had let the old woman hit him but was determined that he was not going to show it. He started laughing and replied, "Funny you should say that because you are the one that sleeps like a northern bear and the one that she wants to kill."

The man nodded his head and then said to the woman, "There is enough food for everyone if you are hungry." He turned toward Airus and asked, "Are you sure that you are going to be okay?"

Airus smiled and replied, "I think I will be okay, but it might take a while."

After a few moments, the man nodded his head, lay back down, and closed his eyes again so that he could get some sleep.

Airus stood for several minutes, watching his friend sleep, when suddenly he realized he still had the old woman's beautifully crafted dagger. Since they did not have any other weapons made of steel, he decided he would keep it. As he put the dagger in his bare sword case, he looked at the old woman, who now sat going through the food that was left for her. He thought, *If this old woman knows who the man is, then why in the hell does she stay anywhere near him?*

The old woman suddenly looked up and noticed that she was being watched. After a moment, she barked, "You think you are a mighty warrior now because you were able to catch a little old woman who was befuddled for a few moments?" After a couple of seconds, she added, "Oh, I am so afraid of the scary giant man."

He had no interest in what the old woman had to say and decided he needed to see if he could get some rest.

It only took a few minutes before the old woman was somehow able to sneak up on him and was standing above him, knocking on his skull with her little bony fist.

He had not been asleep, but he still had no idea how the she had been able to get so close without making a sound. He slowly opened his eyes and said, "Stop."

She stepped back just out of his reach and replied, "He does not know who he is."

Airus closed his eyes once again. "I know, but I am not sure what to tell him."

She then asked, "What do you plan to do next?"

He opened his eyes for a moment and replied, "Sleep." Before he could close his eyes, the old woman tried to get his attention again. This time, though, he was expecting her to try something, and he grabbed her bony little hand before she could hit him again. He demanded, "What do you want?"

She again asked, "What do you plan to do next?"

Airus replied, "We are going to head north to Hela to catch my forces, assuming that I can rest."

She quickly told him "Let me go," and when he did, she stepped back just out of his reach.

He looked at the old woman and added, "It is not safe for you to stay with us."

She looked at the sleeping man and then back at him, but she did not say a word.

Airus added, "You need to run as fast as you can and as far away from us as you can."

She turned and once again looked back at the man sleeping on the ground and asked, "Why?"

He asked, "Who do you think that man is?" as he pointed at the sleeping man.

She stopped looking at the sleeping man and asked, "Who do you think he is?"

Neither of them wanted to answer the other, so they just stared at each other for a while.

Finally, he looked at the old woman and said, "You need to leave. It is not safe here, and I cannot protect you."

She shook her head and replied, "No, you cannot make me." She turned away from him and continued to eat the fruit.

# CHAPTER 11

# THE FORSAKEN WENCH

Likos did not know how he had managed to find his way to this meeting or why no one was making any effort to remove him. There were a few dozen elders, most of whom he had seen before, but there were also several new faces. He did not know the name of the man who was speaking, but he recognized him as one of Haden's messengers

The tall skinny man explained, "Lord Scorpion has taken command of a large part of Haden's army and is using his newfound power to hunt down the scattered factions."

Many of the guild leaders began to shift about restlessly as each of them tried to be heard or to see if any of the other leaders had a plan.

The old man who served as the guild leader waved his hand, and the guild settled down as they waited for him to speak. After a few moments, he said, "We have some time to figure this out. Go back to your clans, and in an hour, we will all come together to decide what we will do next."

No one wanted to have to tell their people that Lord Scorpion was coming for them, but everyone knew that the old man was correct, so the group slowly started filtering out of the room.

The tall man nodded his head because he believed he already knew this dragon guild would not freely join Lord Scorpion or any warmonger. The man picked up the small bag he had brought with him and started leaving. As he walked out of the room, he looked at Likos as if he knew him but did not say anything as he walked past.

Likos knew the dragon guild could not stay in the devastated city of Hela for long now that the remnants of Haden's army were on the move. He had about an hour before the next meeting, so he decided to check on the witch they were holding captive. He laughed and thought, *Maybe she has calmed down enough so that I can feed her again.*

~*~

As he wiped the sweat away, Likos assumed that this witch would have gotten tired of kicking and fighting by now. She had been dropped several times, and it was taking everything he could do to keep her from being stabbed. He had hoped she would have given up by now, but it seemed as though she was just getting more frustrated and more dangerous by the minute.

To make matters worse, she now glowed like a rampant flame that was hell-bent on burning the city down around them. By the way people avoided the stone temple, he was sure they probably believed that if she exploded, she would take half of the city with her.

Finally, Likos demanded that everyone leave the room before the witch killed them all and took out the temple in the process. To his surprise, everyone was so afraid to be in the same room with her that no one hesitated to leave.

For some reason, he felt sorry for the witch and would help her if he could figure out how. Even if he felt sorry for her, he was not stupid enough to believe she was the poor, helpless girl she pretended to be. With just everyone else out of the room, she was finally starting to calm down a bit, but now Likos did not believe he had enough time to feed her. The guild leaders had called for everyone to attend the meeting except for those who were being made to guard her.

He told her, "You need to calm down. I will be back as soon as I can so that you can eat."

He had done all he could do to calm her down. He had also spent as much time with her as he dared, and now he had to get to the meeting.

~*~

Likos had planned to get to the meeting early, but now he was having trouble finding somewhere to sit. He could barely think with all the noise and people trying to get into the small auditorium.

Finally, the old man waved his hand and announced, "We are in danger if we stay here, and we, as a group, must make a choice."

Likos did not understand why they did not just leave if they were in that much danger, but he decided that it was not his place to tell the guild what to do.

The old man said nothing as he watched the guilds yell at each other. Eventually, though, he waved his hand again and said, "Most of you do not have a place to go, but you should know that we cannot stay here."

A large dirt master yelled, "Where would you have us go if we cannot stay here?"

Suddenly, a young fire bender whom Likos knew as Alexander stood up and yelled above the crowd, "We are not cowards that will run at the first sign of trouble!"

Someone in the back responded, "We cannot defend ourselves against an army of fifty thousand or more plus their magic guilds. This war is no longer our fight. There must be somewhere else that we can go."

Suddenly, the large dirt master stomped his foot, which made the ground shake all the way to where Likos was sitting. He demanded, "We need to rejoin Haden's army and pledge our allegiance to whoever is in control."

The old man was tired but once again spoke a few words and waved his hands to calm everyone down. He took a deep breath and then added, "According to our sight witches, the legions that we traveled with have been attacked by Lord Scorpion's army. We could join them, but it would be Lord Scorpion that we would be joining, and we have all heard the stories of what he thinks about dragon guilds. I, for one, am not willing to join this monster on his death crusades."

Likos did not know a lot about Haden's son, but he knew the warmonger took great pleasure in drawing the power from people. He looked around, and it did not appear that anyone else was eager to join this warmonger either.

The old man then asked, "If not Lord Scorpion, then which faction of Haden's army would you have us pledge our allegiance to?" When no one answered, he added, "We are in a foreign land, and we do not know who we can trust."

He took a deep breath and continued. "Most of you belong to this guild because you do not have a home of your own. With that said, your home is wherever this guild is. There are many power-hungry warmongers out there that would love the opportunity to take your life and your power."

Everyone quickly started to talk at once, but it only took a wave of the tired old man's hand to settle them down again.

He told the group, "Not all is lost. There is a city called Athena, which is on the banks of the river that marks the eastern border of Utopia."

Before the old man could finished, Alexander asked, "What does this have to do with us?"

Within a few seconds, half of the guild was asking the same question.

The old man hesitated but once again said a few words and waved his hands. He waited for everyone to settle down before he continued. "With so many warmongers on their way to this kingdom, they have sent messengers to ask for help to defend their people."

As the group turned toward each other to discuss the matter, he added, "In return, Athena has promised protection to anyone who will help defend their city walls."

A large dirt master stood up and asked, "Can we trust these people?"

The old man lifted his shoulders and replied, "Normally, I would say that we should not trust anyone who does not belong to our guild. Now, I do not know where else to go because Haden's army has turned on itself, and we cannot stay here."

The dirt master looked at the rest of his clan until he found the other leaders, who nodded their heads in agreement. He then replied,

"I agree that Athena is better than staying in this city to be slaughtered alongside the witch." At the mere mention of the witch, the ground started shaking.

The old man nodded his head and replied, "The sooner we get away from this witch, the better off we will be."

~*~

Likos had barely been listening to the conversation around him, but now that the ground had stopped shaking, he was very interested in what the guild was planning to do with the witch.

Everyone started to leave when he asked loudly enough to get their attention, "What are we going to do with this witch that we have as our prisoner? Is she not worth taking with us?"

Suddenly, Alexander and one of the healing witches began yelling and screaming at each other. After a few moments, the old man once again waved his hand, but this time, the group took longer to settle down.

The old man looked at Likos and asked, "What would you have us do with this powerful wench? As it is now, no one wants to go near her, and I cannot imagine that anyone wants to take her with us."

Likos thought for a few seconds and replied, "She has to be worth something. Therefore, I believe that we should put her in a box so that she cannot hurt anyone. If she cannot hurt anyone, then why not take the witch with us until someone is willing to pay for her?"

While slightly shaking his head from side to side, the old man smiled and said, "Spoken like a true member of a dragon guild." He started to add something else, but the group started talking all at once again.

Most people were so afraid of the woman that they could not even begin to accept the idea that they would take her with them. Moments later, most of the group was screaming at the old man or at Likos.

The old man wanted to wave his hands again to calm the group down, but he needed to rest before he could use his power.

It did not take long for Likos to get frustrated with everyone yelling at him, so he began yelling back at them, "What do you want to do with her?"

To his surprise, it only took a few seconds before most of the group was demanding that they kill this witch and take her power for themselves.

He was stunned because he would never have thought that the guild would be so quick to slaughter someone else for their power. He was about to yell back at the group that he would not allow them to harm the witch when suddenly, the old man found the strength to wave his hand again.

He did not know what power the old man had, but he was starting to realize that he was calming the group down every time he waved his hand. Soon, everyone stopped to see what the old man wanted to say.

The old man raised his hands as he asked, "Which of you have the courage to kill the wench and take her power?" After a brief pause, he added, "There are dozens—if not hundreds—of the world's most powerful warmongers on their way here. Surely, we could use such power to defend ourselves."

Suddenly the large dirt master spoke up. "I will kill the little wench myself. She does not mean anything to me or this guild." Almost as justification, he added, "Besides, if anyone deserves this, then she does."

The old man laughed and replied, "When you have killed this wench, will you then kill all the other warmongers who will come to claim the power of the one who killed Haden?"

It took almost a minute for the dirt master to realize that if he killed this witch and took her power, then he would be the target of every power-hungry warmonger out there.

The dirt master stammered, "I do not mean that I want to kill her but that someone should."

The old man shook his head. "If we are going kill her, then this is our one chance. Her power could do a lot to protect this guild."

The room was quiet as the old man waited to see whether anyone else was stupid enough to volunteer to kill the woman. As he expected, no one wanted anything to do with the power the wench could provide.

After several minutes, he announced, "I guess that it is decided then. We will leave the wench to her fate and head west toward the city of Athena."

As Likos sat listening to the old man, he did not understand why, but he was glad they had decided to spare her. He could not help but wonder what fate awaited her.

Likos knew that if the guild wanted to leave in the next couple of hours, then, as one of its youngest members, he had a dozen things he needed to do. He had to do his part because the guild would have a difficult journey even if there were some kind of safe haven waiting for them.

It only took about two hours to get all the supplies packed into the few wagons the guild had managed to save. With everything packed and ready for the trip, it looked as if they would be ready to leave in the next ten to fifteen minutes.

Likos did not know why, but he decided to stop and check on the witch before they left. When he entered the room, she was lying face first on the floor. She was still bound and gagged, but to his amazement, there was no one left to guard her.

He could not believe that someone had dropped her on her face again and then left her that way, so he decided to help her to get more comfortable before rejoining the guild. After helping her sit up, he cleaned her face. He explained, "The elders believe that this is the best thing we can do. We are going to leave you here for someone else to find, but believe me, it was the better of the two options." He could see the fear in her eyes and wanted to tell her that it was going to be all right, but at the same time, he did not want to lie to her.

He talked to her until Alexander came in and told him "The elders are ready to leave and have asked that you rejoin the guild."

He looked at her for a few seconds and then apologized again before he turned and walked out of the room to leave her alone and to her fate.

~*~

Angelina had sat alone for more than an hour, wondering whether she would starve to death before someone came to kill her.

Suddenly, Likos walked back into the room.

He smiled and told her, "It just did not feel right to leave you here to be slaughtered by the first warmonger to find you."

He told her he was going to remove her ropes if she promised not to kill him.

She was not sure she trusted him, but at this point, she did not have anything to lose, so she shook her head to indicate that she was not going to do anything.

He began to loosen the ropes, but all he could think about was that he hoped she did not kill him the moment she was unbound and ungagged.

# CHAPTER 12

# NOWHERE TO GO

Likos looked at the young witch and thought, *If I had to do this again, I would not hesitate to do the same thing.*

He was there the day Angelina killed the warmonger Haden and knew what she could do. He had no reason to trust this woman, but a few hours ago, he had untied her so that she could feed herself in the hope that she would be less stressed.

He had tried to keep some distance as she slept, but there was no place to go. As she turned over and began to sit up, he could see by the confusion in her eyes that she was not sure where she was or even who he was.

He took a step back, but since he could only move so far away from her, he put his hand on his bow. Finally, she stretched and smiled a little. The small distance helped him feel a bit safer, so he removed his hand from the bow.

Angelina introduced herself. After a moment, she added, "Thank you for not leaving me here to be slaughtered by the first warmonger to find me."

Likos was not sure what to say, but he replied, "I am sorry for everything that my people have done to you," but she was already starting to lie back down.

She turned her back to the young man and began wondering, *Why is this person willing to risk his life just to help me?* She shook her head because she did not care why he was staying; at least she was still alive and no longer alone.

Likos suddenly remembered that he needed to breathe and exhale, but he did not take his eyes off the young woman. He thought, *What am I doing?"*

~*~

Likos knew they needed to leave soon, but he was not sure if he should tell Angelina they needed to leave because she was finally starting to calm down a bit. He did not want to upset her again, but the truth was he did not know what he was going to do next or even how long they could stay in the temple. Above all else, he was just glad she had not tried to kill him.

He looked across the room again at the sleeping witch and thought, *I must be crazy to leave the safety of my guild for this woman.* He shook his head and wondered if she would kill him the first chance she got.

Likos did not realize it, but he had started to pace back and forth. He thought, *Everything will work out. I just need to figure out what I am going to do next.* He stopped and asked himself, "What am I even doing here?"

He suddenly realized his pacing was beginning to disturb Angelina. He tried to calm himself down so that he did not look like a scared little boy who did not have a plan of action.

Soon the young woman began to wake up, but once again, she did not seem fully aware of where she was. It took a few moments for her to come to her senses and to recognize the young man who had stopped in the middle of the room.

After a moment, she asked, "We cannot stay here any longer, can we?"

He hesitated because he did not want to upset her, but before he could answer, she asked, "How long do you think we have?"

He slowly shook his head and replied, "I do not think we would be safe here for long, and that is why my dragon guild left hours ago." After a few seconds, Likos asked, "Do you have any family or friends around Hela that we could stay with until we have a chance to figure this out?"

She thought about her childhood for a few moments but quickly realized she had no idea how to find her family, and she had never had any friends. She hesitated for a few moments and then replied, "I am not sure I would have any clue where to find them if they are still alive."

For several minutes, they stood looking at each other without saying a word. It was clear that neither one of them had a plan or anything to add to the conversation.

As they stood there saying nothing, all kinds of thoughts went through her head. Suddenly, Angelina remembered the dream she had been having for the last few days. She gasped, "We cannot stay here any longer because Haden is coming to get revenge."

Angelina was trembling and so terrified that she could not breathe, but when she finally caught her breath, she repeated, "Haden is coming for me. I have seen it because he knows what I did and where I am." For several minutes, she pleaded with Likos to save her in the hope that he did know what to do and where to go.

He felt a chill run down his back at the mere mention of the warmonger. He could only hope that this was some sort of trick. However, as far as he could tell, she looked as frightened as he felt.

He grabbed her and put his arms around her. He whispered, "Haden is dead, you killed him." After a few seconds, he continued. "I saw this with my own eyes."

She was still trembling and barely able to speak by this time, but she tried once again to make him understand. Finally, she cried, "We cannot stay here because Haden is coming for me, and he is almost here. Please help me."

Likos wanted to believe her, but he just could not see how it was possible that Haden was still alive or was any threat to this woman. He explained, "I watched the healing witches try to revive him, but they could not." He shook his head as he also started to shake a little.

After a moment, he said, "We buried him beneath everything we could find, and if he was not dead, he is now." He pulled her closer and began stroking the back of her head, but she was far too frightened to listen to anything he had to say. As he held her, he tried to remember that day, and he could not even imagine how Haden could still be alive.

Once again, Angelina pleaded, "Haden is coming for me, and I cannot stay here. Please help me."

After a few moments, she added, "If you want to help me, then we have to get out of here now, or I will find a way out by myself."

He was not sure what he could do or say to reassure her, but she was right about one thing—they needed to leave. However, he did not believe that Haden was alive or was on his way to Hela. What worried him, though, were all the other people who were on their way.

He thought for a minute and offered, "If nothing else, we could find an abandoned farmhouse somewhere in the countryside. That will give us some time to figure out what to do."

She smiled because she had been out of the city, and she knew there were hundreds of abandoned farms.

Angelina was finally becoming more composed so that they could leave when several small mice ran past them.

Likos watched the rodents scamper across the room and knew without any doubt that there were other people in the temple. He realized he would need to find another way out, but he also had to explain the situation so that Angelina would not panic.

He lifted her head and told her, "There are other people in the temple, and you need to remain calm so that I can figure out how to get us out of here."

She nodded to show that she understood, but at the same time, she was glowing as brightly as any fire Likos had ever seen.

There was no way they would be able to sneak out without been seen. Therefore, he looked around the room to see if there was anything to cover her. However, all he found were several old drapes. He knew these drapes were not comfortable, but he grabbed as many as he could find to cover her. It took a couple of minutes, but he covered her so that she did not light up the room.

Once again, the mice ran across the room. One of the mice stopped midway, turned toward Likos, and after a few seconds, continued its way out of the room.

He quickly whispered, "We need to be quiet. The mice do not believe these men know we are here, but I do not want to take any chances."

Angelina was so scared that she could not think, but she was sure that Likos had just said, "The mice do not believe these men know we are here." She did not know what else to do because she could hear the other people by this time, so she just tried to stay as close to Likos as possible.

It had been twenty minutes since Likos and Angelina had started to make their way through the temple. As far as they could tell, no one seemed to know they were there. According to the mice, the strangers were only looking for valuables that might have been left behind.

Several mice ran past them again, and as before, they stopped and turned toward Likos for a few seconds before continuing down the hallway.

He did not want to say anything to Angelina, but the mice were saying that there were at least a dozen other people in the temple. Likos hesitated because he knew that the mice could not count and were not always trustworthy. Still, it only made sense to keep moving away from the other people in the temple and find somewhere safer.

Angelina could not even open the cover enough to see where they were going without lighting up the corridors as if she were carrying a torch. Likos had to lead her slowly down the corridor.

Soon, Likos could not find any more mice and knew this part of the temple was probably abandoned. He was able to find a door with a window large enough he could see into the courtyard. He quickly realized they were not going to be able to escape this way because there were a dozen men a hundred cubits from the door.

Likos and Angelina had been so close to getting out of the temple, but now they had been stuck sitting near the door for the last few hours. Now that his guild had left, people were starting to move around the city again. To make matters worse, a small unit of guardsmen had returned and set up a command center just outside the temple.

It had been a while since he had checked on Angelina, so he lifted a small corner of the drapes so that she could see him. She looked a bit stressed, so he explained that they could not leave this way because there were still too many people in the courtyard, including some guardsmen from some army.

He then told her, "The good news is that I don't believe that they are looking for you."

She asked, "Why are they in the temple then? They do not belong in here."

He quickly replied, "They probably only want to see if my guild left anything of value."

She smiled slightly and asked, "Is it normal for dragon guilds to leave stuff behind?"

He laughed and replied, "There are many reasons to leave something behind, but I don't think that they did."

She tried to smile again, but she was shaking and trembling. "What are we going to do now? We cannot stay here, and we cannot go out there because, well, we just cannot."

Likos did not intend to walk out into the courtyard, especially with her glowing, but she was correct. They could not stay where they were.

After a few moments, she suggested, "We could hide in one of the meditation rooms. No one should have any reason to be in there now that my wielding guild has abandoned the temple."

Likos thought for a few moments and then explained to her that he did not know how to get to the meditation rooms. He told Angelina that if she could give him some directions, he would be glad to take her there.

As soon as she opened the drapes, she lit up the area. He had to pull the cloth back down to keep anyone from seeing them.

He looked at the drapes, shook his head, and decided he needed to climb under the drapes with her if he was going to talk to her. It only took a few seconds for her to give him some rudimentary directions to the meditation rooms, but by the time he came out, there were two guardsmen waiting for him.

As Likos drew his bow, he yelled to Angelina to get out of the temple even if she had to run through the courtyard.

She opened her cover to see what he was talking about and saw the guardsmen. She quickly dropped the drapes and decided she was going to do whatever it took to help the man who had come back for her.

## CHAPTER 13

# UNION OF DRAGON GUILDS

It had taken well over a week to get to Athena, which was supposed to be a haven for all dragon guilds. However, the city was not exactly what Alexander expected. It was true the city had welcomed them, but it was not without some shortcomings.

The problem was that every dragon guild for a thousand leagues had shown up looking for refuge, and the city was not equipped to handle so many people.

Life in a dragon guild was the only one Alexander had ever known. In spite of this, for the first time in his life, he had walls to protect his guild and clan. He thought, *With all the uncertainty in the world, this was as good a place as any to stay for a while.*

By the time his guild arrived, there were more people from a dragon guild than there were other people in the city.

The members of the guilds had risked everything to leave their masters behind in the hopes of finding freedom, and now they were not about to accept new masters in Athena.

The city leaders were almost powerless to control the guilds, and by last count, there were people from 147 different guilds seeking refuge, with more coming every day.

Alexander believed there were twenty to twenty-five thousand extra people in the city, and it seemed that none of them wanted to leave.

It seemed as if everyone in the city had a different idea on what needed to be done, and at this point, he did not know who was correct. To make matter worst, once they entered the city, most of his dragon guild scattered to rejoin their kind. He spent most of his time just trying to keep his clan members out of trouble and fed, which in itself was not very easy.

A few of the larger clans had somehow managed to form a coalition or council of elders. They were able to maintain the peace to some degree, but they lacked any real authority and could do little to enforce the rules they made.

Although he was still in his early twenties, Alexander had taken charge of his clan about a year ago when Haden defeated the warmonger who had enslaved his people. Now most of the clan looked to him for leadership.

His father had once belonged to a great fire guild until the warmongers of his time destroyed everything and scattered his people. Alexander's clan were fire benders, which made them frontline fighters, but it did little to help them provide for themselves. All he seemed to have time to do was try to negotiate his guild's services for food and basic supplies so that they could survive a while longer. He had sworn to his father on his deathbed that he would do whatever it took to keep the clan together.

It had been days since anyone had needed a fire bender, and as always, the supplies were running low. Everyone in his clan was now looking to him for answers, but Alexander still did not know what he was going to tell them. As if he did not have enough to worry about, it seemed as though the ground had gone mad because it was constantly shaking. He hoped the large city walls around Athena would hold. For the moment, the ground was not rattling, and he knew that if he did not find work for his people soon, he would have to lead them out of the safety of the city.

Alexander was starting to grow a bit impatient, and he would have left a long time ago if he had any other hope of finding work. He had been waiting well over an hour to meet with this elder. However, he was almost sure that this would not turn out any better than the last five interviews.

Several people seemed to talk for the elder, but none of them could tell him how long it would be before the man would have time to discuss business.

Finally, he was told to find the dirt master's daughter. The young woman had been coming and going for the last hour, but now he did not see her anywhere.

By the time Alexander found the girl, she appeared to be playing some kind game with half a dozen overweight juvenile dirt masters.

The girl was clearly a dirt master herself, but the six juvenile boys thought it was funny to pin her up with the small walls of dirt. She would move one wall, and three more would stop her from escaping.

Alexander did not understand what was going on but assumed it was a dirt master thing. He yelled loudly enough for the girl to hear him. "I understand that you have a task that you need to be done. Is there any way that you would have time to talk about it?"

The girl said nothing and just put up another dirt wall between herself and the other dirt masters.

The largest of the dirt masters turned toward Alexander and said, "Go away before you get hurt." The fat dirt master then pushed a wall of dirt up between them.

Alexander jumped over the small wall of dirt as the young girl walked by him through an opening in the dirt that she had made.

By this time, all six of the fat boys were standing a few cubits from Alexander and the other two fire benders.

Once again, the largest of the boys spoke, "I thought I told you to go away, but I guess that you did not understand."

As the young dirt master pulled the dirt from beneath his feet, Alexander and the other fire benders jumped out of the way.

As he landed on his feet, Alexander realized this was not some game. He quickly reached into his lantern and pulled out a flame he shared with his brothers.

This action was more than enough to change the dirt masters' minds. They turned and went through the holes in the dirt walls they had just made and left without another word.

Suddenly the girl reappeared and told Alexander, "Follow me. My father has a task for you and your clan."

It had been several days since his clan had started working for the council of elders, and although the pay was not great, it did keep them fed and out of trouble.

Alexander assumed that the council of elders was giving the orders, but so far, the only person he had talked to was the young dirt master named Maria. He expected to be doing all sorts of tasks, but there was only one thing a fire bender was good for, and everyone knew it. No matter how big or bad the other guilds thought they were, no one liked to play with fire.

It was not real work by any sense, but it did help feed his people even though there were too few of them to bring order to the entire city.

He had only been on duty for a few hours, and already he and his brother had broken up half a dozen fights. As he was instructed, he was once again looking for the young dirt master so that he could report everything his clan had done in the last twenty-four hours.

As usual, she seemed like she was trying to balance half a dozen other tasks, but as she had the last two days, she took the time to listen to what he had to say.

As she darted from one part of the stone room to another, he could not help but notice that for a dirt master, she was not the usual round shape.

Seconds later, he realized she had noticed him staring at her. He quickly stated, "We were able to disperse several groups, but I am afraid there is nothing to keep them from finding somewhere else to cause trouble."

She nodded her head and replied, "I know, but all we can do for the moment is keep it out of the public eye." She started to say something else when a messenger came into the room looking for her.

The messenger looked tired and was out of breath. After a few seconds, he was able to report, "A hunting party has discovered a large dragon that they believe is one of Haden's master dragons." The messenger took another deep breath and added, "Your father has called a council meeting to determine what is to be done. He has asked that you attend."

The young dirt master grabbed the few items she had brought with her and started out the door to follow the messenger. Before she got to the doorway, she turned. "Come on, fire bender. We have work to be done, and we cannot do it here."

By the time, Alexander and Maria arrived at the conference hall, the meeting had already started. To his surprise, the young dirt master grabbed his hand and pulled him toward the lower floor so that they could get closer to her father.

As they got near, she let go of his hand and started toward her father.

He believed that Maria let go of his hand so that the very large fat man she called her father would not notice him. He found a place where he could sit down but still see what was going on.

The old man who had led his dragon guild for the last year was being helped to the center of the floor so that he could address the council.

He had only seen the old man a few times since they had arrived in Athena. As he looked around, it was easy to see that most of the people in the hall were not dirt masters.

The old man waved his hand, and the hall fell silent as he began to speak. He started by saying, "Please hear me out before you judge. The dragon that has found its way to our doorstep is the just the tip of our problems."

All at once, the room filled with the hum of questions that at first were directed toward the old man. For what seemed like forever, the old man just stood as the group turned on each other. Finally, he waved his hand, and once again, the crowd became silent.

The old man continued. "I have not told you anything that you did not already know, but what we must do now is decide what to do with this information."

Maria's father stood up and replied, "I think that we should send a dozen horses toward the monster, and once it is fed, perhaps it will go away."

The hall again filled with an uproar of noise, and once again, the old man let the crowd yell at each other for a minute or two before he waved his hand to settle them.

He asked, "What if this monster likes being fed, or worse, what if the great armies of Haden come looking for their prize and find us instead?"

This time, everyone was almost speechless, for no one had thought about this possible consequence.

The old man shook his head. "I think that we should leave because although we are strong, I do not believe we would be a match for Haden's or any other major army."

Maria's father pushed his way to the center of the floor so that he was as much the center of attention as the old man. He announced, "We might be outnumbered, but I will not be a slave any longer. I say we fight or die."

This time, before the crowd had a chance to turn on each other, the old man waved his hand again, which once more settled the group.

After a moment, he added, "What if this dragon is used to attack this city, or worse, what if whoever comes for this dragon has Haden's other dragons? Will you be you be so quick to stay and fight then?"

He knew the dragon guilds would fight for their freedom, but he understood that a fight against one of these monsters was an exercise in futility, as did everyone in the room. He could see no one even wanted to entertain the thought of defending against a dragon this big, let alone multiple dragons this large. The old man looked at the faces of the crowd and did not need to speak what everyone was thinking, so he bowed his head. "We shall leave as soon as we can pack up."

No one wanted to leave, but no one could argue with the old man's logic either, even the large dirt master. Most of the group started moving slowly toward the back of the room.

Suddenly, Alexander stood up and shouted, "What if we capture this dragon? Would Haden's armies be so quick to come then?"

For several seconds, no one moved or said anything. Finally, the old man spoke, "Brave boy, we do not even know if this is one of the two light dragons."

He did not have a plan, but since the fire was the least of his worries, he ordered the flame from a nearby torch to dance around him and his thick skin.

Maria quickly ordered the ground beneath the young fire bender to rise so that everyone could see him making the fire dance around him. In a voice loud enough for all to hear, she exclaimed, "Together we can capture this monster and be free once and for all."

Everyone who knew anything about dragons was aware that magic would not work on the dragon. Luckily, the plan they had come up with did not depend on trying to use magic against the dragon.

The fire benders were resistant to fire, but even they would not be able to withstand the blast from a dragon. Therefore, while they were trying to distract the dragon, the dirt masters would build walls to hold the monster.

Besides fire benders and dirt masters, there were members from almost every discipline of magic to watch although most would not go near the dragon.

As reported, the dragon was lying in a field just south of the city walls as though it was hoping that someone would feed it.

Alexander believed that the old man was correct when he suggested that the only reason the monster would come this close to the city was that it had to be hungry.

They had several horses to feed the dragon, but first they had to get control of the beast so that once it was fed, it did not leave or worse, turn on them.

In total, some two-dozen people of various skills were trying to capture the dragon although most were either fire benders or dirt masters.

They had hoped to surround the monster before it even knew they were there, but it was obvious the dragon had seen them long before they got anywhere close to it.

As the group started to surround the monster, the ground suddenly started to shake to the point that it was hard to stand upright.

With the ground still shaking, Alexander quickly got back to his feet and then helped Maria up.

The dragon had not fallen, but it was stumbling and shifting its weight to try to stay on its feet. In the process, the giant creature could not balance itself long enough to take flight.

Alexander looked around and could see the other fire benders and dirt masters getting to their feet. He knew that this might be their only chance and shouted, "Get the ropes and chains—we do not have time to wait for the ground to stop shaking. We will only have one chance at this because when the ground stops, the dragon will take to the air." He started running toward the head of the dragon as fast as he could with Maria just a few steps behind him.

With its wide base, the dragon was staying on all fours, and although it could not take flight, it was clear that the monster was tracking the movement of everyone in the area.

Alexander and Maria were still about forty cubits from the dragon when suddenly, a large flame came toward them at an incredible speed.

He put his hands up just in time, but as he tried to hold the flame, he realized he could not hold it back for long.

Maria quickly lifted her hands to bring a wall of dirt up in front of them to deflect the flame. When the burst finally ended, the entire area was on fire. Alexander was burnt, but not too badly.

He looked at the dragon, but it seemed as though it could not tell if they were still there.

As the ground continued to shake, the wall of dirt in front of them started to break up.

Alexander picked up a flame. To his surprise, the dragon turned away as if it thought they were no longer there.

He started yelling, "Use fire to make it hard for the dragon to see you." It had taken almost a minute before the word spread to everyone trying to dodge the dragon's flame.

When the ground shaking began to slow down, the dragon started turning in circles as it tried to determine where everyone went. Within a couple of minutes, the group had managed to get at least two chains on the dragon. Within ten minutes, there were enough ropes and chains to keep the dragon from flying off.

Alexander told everyone, "Stop moving so that the dragon can see the horses," but there were so many flames that the dragon did not notice the horse being led into the area.

Maria and the other dirt masters had been burying the chains to add weight to them because there were not enough people to stop the dragon from leaving if it wanted. Alexander asked her to cover the flames so that the dragon could see the horses.

At first, she hesitated because she was afraid that the dragon would see them. However, once she started extinguishing the flames, the rest of the dirt masters did the same. As soon as the flames started to die down, the dragon realized there were three horses being lead to it.

The dragon, a female, settled down and waited until she could grab one of the horses. Within seconds, all three horses were dead, and the dragon was enjoying a meal.

# CHAPTER 14

# A WHISPER OF THE TRUTH

Technically, they were still at war, but most of the guards only watched as the three generals walked through the camp. Their plan was to see if they could negotiate peace with Lord Scorpion before everything was lost.

Two weeks had passed since the warmonger Haden was killed by the witch of Hela, and in that time, they had suffered huge losses.

Even without Haden or his dragons, the generals knew they were no match for Lord Scorpion's heavily armored seven legions. It had been a brutal struggle for power, and now most of their armies were more than happy to surrender to whoever was in charge of Haden's forces.

With rumors that every warmonger for a thousand leagues was on their way to this tiny kingdom to claim their piece of Haden's empire, it only made sense to form an alliance.

To seal the deal, Lord Scorpion was demanding that the generals report directly to his command center to give him an update on the status of their forces.

General Heron did not appreciate the guards' impassive stares. He was still a general, and he would serve Lord Scorpion for many years to come.

He thought, *At least someone is finally taking charge of Haden's army because we could all use some direction. We will see how these guards act when I take control of one of Lord Scorpion's legion.*

Heron understood they needed a strong hand to direct them, and now that Haden was dead, someone needed to take command. He had met many of Haden's children, and as far as he was concerned, Lord Scorpion would do as well as any of them. Besides, they had not done anything wrong. It was a bit embarrassing to have to walk through the camp like this, but the general was happy to pledge his allegiance to anyone who could unite Haden's forces.

He thought, *It was true that we had a few minor skirmishes with Lord Scorpion's forces a few days ago, but that was not my fault. Surely Lord Scorpion cannot blame me for that.*

As the three generals neared the middle of the camp, suddenly they were no longer the center of attention. They watched as the guards carried away the body of an old man who looked as though he had been beaten to death.

General Heron recognized the man as a druid priest that used to teach truth spells to the dragon guilds. He did not understand how the priest had stayed alive this long because, although he was a popular teacher, his power was not enough for him to defend himself.

He looked once again toward the dead man, but he could not see how the matter concerned him because he needed to prepare himself to meet his new commander.

General Heron directed the other two generals into Lord Scorpion's tent as they were directed. He could see that this son of Haden now considered himself the rightful heir to all that his father once commanded. As they would have done for Haden, the three generals bowed as Lord Scorpion entered the tent.

Lord Scorpion waved his hand to signal that they could rise and demanded, "If you wish to live, then I want to know what the hell you have done with my dragons."

General Virgo was not sure what the warmonger was expecting because they had barely been able to feed themselves over the last few weeks, let alone look for Haden's lost dragons. She hesitated to address

Lord Scorpion and was content for once that she was not the senior ranking person.

General Heron thought, *If I knew where these dragons were, we would not be having this conversation, or at least not from this perspective.* However, as the senior general, he stepped forward and waited for permission to speak.

Lord Scorpion repeated, "I don't have all day. I want to know where my dragons are and what efforts have been made to recover them."

General Heron cleared his throat and began explaining, "The dragons went mad when your father was killed, but as soon as I—"

Lord Scorpion cut him off midsentence. He demanded, "Were you there when my father was slaughtered? What exactly did you do to help him?"

Suddenly, General Heron began to tremble as he tried to think of something to tell his new master that would save his life. When nothing came to him, he began to plead for his life.

Lord Scorpion shook his head and pretended he did not hear the pleas. He turned toward the other two generals. "This is what happens when you get complacent and no longer respect your master." He turned as if to walk away from the pleading man, who was now on his knees. He took a deep breath, stroked his beard, and slowly started walking back toward General Heron. He whispered something in the general's ear and slowly walked away, all the while chanting something to himself.

For a few seconds, the general did not make a sound, and then he started whispering something that no one could make out. He tried to explain, "The dragons were uncontrollable moments after your father fell, and there was nothing anyone could do." With every word he spoke, it seemed harder for him to control what he was saying.

Lord Scorpion turned back around, but by this time, most people in the tent were focused on the eerie voice that did not seem to belong to General Heron.

Lord Scorpion smiled as he finished his chant and then walked over to the other two generals. He politely asked if they would like something to drink or eat because it must be difficult to find supplies these days.

The remaining generals looked at each other for a moment but were not sure what to say. When they looked at General Heron, it was clear they did not want to do anything that would cause them to end up in the same position.

General Heron was still talking but no longer pleading for his life. Instead, he was staring into nothing while babbling on about his mother playing peekaboo.

The other two generals quickly replied, "Yes, my lord. If it pleases you, we would be most honored to share your food and water."

Lord Scorpion commanded, "Bring me and my guests some food and water." He smiled, stroked his beard again, and added, "So that we can celebrate our new alliance and the start of the greatest empire to ever exist."

As General Heron continued to babble, General Vanessa Virgo sat down at the table that had been brought into the tent for their feast. She looked back at her mentor and lover to see whether he was going to be okay, but he was still staring at nothing and talking about his childhood.

An hour had passed when Lord Scorpion turned toward her and asked, "How many troops do you now control, and how long do you believe it will take to combine our forces?"

General Virgo replied without any hesitation, "Lord Scorpion, I can have your forces anywhere you want them in a matter a few weeks or sooner, if you need."

Lord Scorpion looked across the tent at the man still on his knees, who was now babbling about how his father was killed. He smiled. "I would like to see the forces combined as soon as possible."

She looked again at General Heron, nodded her head, and replied, "I am here to serve you, my lord."

Lord Scorpion started laughing and told her, "I have other plans for you, my dear, but I would like to see our forces combined."

She did not trust the warmonger because there was something about the way he looked at her that made her skin crawl. "Anything you wish, my lord."

She had never failed any mission, but she did not even want to imagine what Lord Scorpion planned for her. She looked over at her mentor on his knees and knew she could not fail this one.

For several hours, Lord Scorpion, his senior advisor, and his top generals sat eating food that was taken from the local countryside.

Although most people tried not to look at him, General Heron continued to talk about everything he could remember over his lifetime.

Lord Scorpion looked over at General Heron and then asked one of his advisors, "How old do you think our talkative friend is?"

The man looked at the general for a few moments and replied, "My lord, I am afraid the years have not been very good to the general." He looked at him again and took a few seconds to add something up in his head. He continued. "Although he looks to be seventy or eighty years old, my lord, I do not believe that he is older than fifty-five or maybe sixty."

Lord Scorpion looked over at the babbling man. "Hmm, I am not sure about that." He laughed. "I guess that we will see in a couple of weeks." He turned once again toward General Virgo and demanded, "I want the camps combined as soon as possible, and I want you back here in no more than twelve days."

She quickly replied, "I will see to it that the camps are combined." After a brief pause, she added, "Is there anything else that you require from me before I go to prepare the camps for movement?"

Lord Scorpion replied, "I need you to assemble a large raiding party of your best warriors. Keep in mind that if you fail me, it will be the last time you fail anyone."

It took well over three hours for General Virgo to make it back to her campsite. She knew it would take days to get all the patrols back to the camp and even longer to get everything broken down and packed. As soon as she was within sight of her camp, she began issuing orders to anyone and everyone that came anywhere near her.

~*~

It had been days since General Virgo had slept, but most of the tents were already broken down, and at least a half of them were partially packed. Although no one was standing around any longer, she ordered that anyone who did not have something to do to start packing the wagons and animals.

There were still a dozen things she needed to see get done before she moved on to the other camp, but there did not appear to be anything to keep her there much longer.

She had sent messengers to both of the other camps, but it had been a day since she had heard from either site.

General Virgo took a deep breath because it looked as if she was going to have her camp ready within the next day if she wanted to make sure the other camps had done as they were instructed.

Her horse had been saddled for the last hour, but she was hoping to see the wagons moving before she left.

According the last messenger she had spoken to, the other two camps were not quite as far along as her camp was, but she still had six days. She did not believe that was going to be a problem, but she would feel better when she saw the other camps for herself.

As she stood alone overlooking her camp, she watched as the last tent started coming down.

General Virgo suddenly realized she no longer had to shout orders at everyone and did not remember how long it had been since anyone had come near her.

She was taking another deep breath when she realized she had not even started assembling her raiding party.

She signaled for her horse to be brought to her. After she had mounted the horse, she instructed the young man holding the beast, "Tell my captains to assemble a large raiding party and to meet me at General Heron's camp."

~*~

When General Virgo relinquished command of her three legions, she had just enough time to make it back to see what Lord Scorpion had planned for her.

She arrived to find her mentor still on his knees in the same spot he was twelve days ago, and although he was still talking, his voice was now very hoarse.

Lord Scorpion welcomed her. "You are just in time to listen to the most important thing that your friend will ever have to say." He laughed and added, "Vanessa, I believe is your first name. If you would like, I can get you a transcript of what he said because your friend had a great deal to say about you."

She almost felt sorry for her mentor and lover except that she was glad it was not her there on her knees, telling everyone her most intimate thoughts. She looked at General Heron and replied, "Lord Scorpion, I do not believe that will be necessary." She could not take her eyes off the poor man as he relived the day when Haden was killed.

General Heron explained how Haden and his dragon suddenly landed in the middle of their camp. Then he explained how, out of nowhere, large objects started flying all over the camp. She listened to how he was nearly killed by the flying debris and was only able to survive by remaining in a low-lying area until the objects stopped flying. He then said something about a dragon guild and a witch who had done all this damage.

General Virgo had been thrown from her horse and barely remembered the witch, but she did recall that everyone seemed afraid of her.

Lord Scorpion started to chant again, and General Heron continued. "There were half a dozen healing witches there, and none of them could revive Haden."

He went on to tell how one of the dragons had been injured when they tried to capture it.

Lord Scorpion asked about the wielding witch, but all that Heron could remember was that she looked very young.

Before he could continue, the spellcaster demanded, "Tell me more about this dragon guild."

Heron explained, "The other three dragons soon returned without their riders but would only allow this one dragon guild near Haden. Finally, I ordered the guild to bury Haden beneath everything that the dragons would let them bring into the area. I also ordered the guild to take the witch that killed Haden back to the city of Hela."

He tried to shout out the orders to chain the dragons the same as he had done weeks ago but barely had enough breath to finish the story. Heron began speaking to someone no one else could see.

General Virgo remembered the dragons suddenly turning on them and General Heron trying to order everyone not to let the dragons get away. As he continued talking, she recalled that they did not have the resources to chain the dragons down.

He then yelled, "They will kill us all if we do not do something to drive the dragons away from this area!"

She could not remember the conversation her lover was now reliving, but she did recall that the dragons did not want to leave. As she tried to remember that day, she knew the dragons must have killed dozens—if not hundreds—of people before they fled the area in four different directions.

General Heron then said, "I know what we have done, but what choice did we have? These damn dragons would have killed us all if we did not do something to protect ourselves."

Lord Scorpion demanded that General Heron tell him where the dragons had gone.

He did not know and could barely speak. Even if he had any more to tell, General Heron had reached the end and fell dead to the ground.

Lord Scorpion turned toward General Virgo and commanded, "Your mission is to bring me the wench that killed my father alive, if possible." After a few seconds, he stomped his foot and demanded, "I want this wench alive. Do you understand me?"

Virgo quickly replied, "I have a raiding party ready to go, and I will make sure she is brought back alive." She was not sure if she should say anything else, but she soon found the courage to ask, "What about the dragons?"

Lord Scorpion looked at her for a few moments and then replied, "Yes, my dear, of course, you are right. I do need the dragons." He smiled and then added, "First things first, though. Bring me the wench because I have other plans for you."

# CHAPTER 15

# THE DECEPTION OF HELA

Angelina had finished the food the guardsmen had provided and was once again starting to calm down to the point that she was no longer glowing. She did not understand how the guardsmen knew so much about them or that she had killed Haden. However, she was glad they had been sent to find her.

According to Bryce, the captain in charge of the guardsmen, they had been trying to find her since the battle three weeks ago. Most of the north assumed that Haden's dragon guild either had killed her or had taken her with them.

As soon as they were found in the temple, Bryce had sent messengers to General Hortz in the north asking for more people, but she knew it might be a week or so before reinforcements arrived.

Angelina was not sure how many guardsmen the captain had brought with him, but as she watched the four men who surprised her try to bandage themselves, she guessed it was not many.

Suddenly, she noticed the young man who had come back for her sitting in the corner trying to fix the bow he had broken while trying to save her yet again. She was glad to see that he was not hurt, and even though everyone knew he was part of the dragon guild that had left her, no one seemed to care.

~*~

Likos did not believe that Angelina was safe, but for the moment, it was better than trying to make it north on their own when there were raiding parties everywhere.

Angelina had calmed down a lot in the week and was no longer lighting up the damp corridors of the stone temple. Although she was looking better, he was not sure she had been sleeping.

She did not like it, but the new guardsmen referred to her as the master wielding witch or just the witch of Hela.

Although few people had the courage to talk to her directly, there was always food and fresh water waiting for her wherever she went.

Likos had met many so-called masters of their trade over the years, but this young witch did not act like any master he had ever met. In his service to Haden and his dragon guild, he had learned that all masters of their trade loved to do two things—train others or direct them. As far as he could tell, this girl was not fond of either, but it had only been a week since she was left to die.

She had not made any demands for special treatment, nor had she asked for an apprentice. He knew it was only a matter of time before someone as powerful as this witch started making demands.

However, her behavior did nothing to stop people from treating her like a grand master. In the last two days alone, half a dozen people had showed up to receive training, but she had no interest in teaching or having an assistant.

Suddenly, he realized he was the only person this witch talked regularly other than Captain Bryce.

It had been an hour since anyone had bothered them, and as usual, Angelina was starting to relax and open up.

Likos was trying to restring his bow when she grabbed some of the fibers, he was using to make repairs. He smiled and asked, "What are you doing?"

As she was playing with the fibers, she replied, "I am bored and just want to talk."

While she was talking, he took the opportunity to grab the fibers out of her hands. He smiled. "So, what would you like to talk about?"

She returned the smile and said, "I don't know. Why don't you tell me how you got involved with Haden's dragon guild?"

He hesitated for a moment, but before he could say anything, someone knocked at the door.

As if someone had thrown a switch, Angelina changed from a normal twenty-year-old girl into a wielding master.

When Captain Bryce walked into the room, she smiled ruefully at Likos. "That will be all for now. I promised the captain of the guard that I would discuss city business."

Likos wanted to talk to the captain about leaving the city, but they were already engaged in conversation. He did not understand why they wanted to save Hela when there had to be safer places in the north. He knew that if Haden's armies came, they would destroy everything, but it seemed as if no one planned on leaving.

After a few minutes, Likos found himself walking away from the temple. He could see that Hela was in an absolute disarray of broken walls and doors. Most of the hundred guardsmen and scattered residents spent their time just trying to protect themselves from the weather.

He had heard the stories of how Haden's armies would flatten a city if it showed any resistance, but he had not expected this kind of damage especially since the warmonger was dead. He believed that if a raiding party showed up, they would not be able to defend the city for long. He knew that before Haden was killed, his dragons had hit the city for well over a week, and then three legions marched through to claim it. However, when Haden was killed, his legions abandoned the city, and Likos's guild scavenged the city for anything of value, driving away most of the residents.

The guardsmen had piled pieces of the wall and other large broken pieces of the city into the missing sections of the wall, which made the city somewhat defensible. He still did not want to stay here any longer because he knew it was only a matter of time before the warmongers came looking for the young witch. He just did not understand why neither Angelina nor the guardsmen seemed to be in any hurry to leave.

He decided to see if he could talk to one of the guardsmen about his concerns.

The sergeant who appeared to be in charge would only say, "We are following orders, and when it is time to pull back to the north, we will do so. Until then, we have other things to do."

He wanted Angelina to see if she could convince the guardsmen to abandon the city and move further north. However, all she would say was that this was her home, and she did not want to leave.

She had insisted that the northern region understood the situation and was planning to send additional forces but were waiting to see which way Lord Scorpion moved his legions.

He felt uneasy as he rolled this name around in his head because he had hoped he would never hear this warmonger's name again. He understood why the people of Utopia were waiting to see where Lord Scorpion would move next. He did not know Lord Scorpion personally but had heard the stories of how this man was without mercy and knew he would burn every city to the ground if he were given the chance.

In the last few days, Bryce had asked several times if he knew whether Angelina was sleeping.

Likos could see that her eyes were bloodshot, and she looked very tired. He suspected she was afraid to sleep because of her dreams. He tried but could not remember the last time he had seen her sleeping.

He watched her for a few seconds and asked, "Is there anything I can get for you?" After a few moments, he added, "When was the last time you slept?"

Angelina smiled slightly. "I wished it was that simple. I know you believe Haden is dead, but he is out there somewhere." She hesitated and then continued. "I know that he is coming for me."

He put his hand on her arm and asked, "What does this have to do with you not sleeping?"

She answered, "I have seen the way that people look at me when I am glowing. When I sleep, I dream about Haden, and when I am awake, I am glowing again, so I do not sleep."

She looked at him and smiled again. "If I can see him when I am sleeping, does that mean that he can see me?" After a few moments, she added, "I am scared because I am not the master that everyone thinks I am. I don't know that I could defend these people if I had to."

He looked at her for a few seconds. "So why don't we go somewhere safer?"

She shook her head. "I wished I could but this . . ." She did not finish.

After a moment, Likos commented, "The weather outside is nice. If you have time, we should walk around some."

She smiled. "Where would you have us walk to all alone?"

He turned slightly red because he only wanted to change the subject, not to flirt with her. To be honest, he did not want to think about Haden or Lord Scorpion and just wanted to find something else to do. He could not think of a way to change the subject again, so he said, "I want to do more to help fortify the gaps in the walls." He quickly added, "I don't believe it would take much for someone to figure out how to break through the makeshift barriers that the guardsmen have set up. I also do not believe that the guardsmen trust me enough to listen." He smiled at Angelina. "They would listen to you if you asked them to leave the city."

She shook her head and told him, "I would not worry about the gaps in the wall because we only plan to stay here until the reinforcements arrive from the north."

Likos thought to himself, *Even without Haden in the next month, there will be almost ten full legions in this area.* After a moment, he said, "I am not sure that there are enough people in this kingdom to stop them. I think that you would be better off to make your stand in the north, where you know the land and have the resources to defend yourselves."

She looked at him for a few moments and asked, "You do not expect us just to give these invaders the southern part of our kingdom, do you?"

He did not know how to reply, but after a few seconds, he muttered, "That is not what I meant." However, there was no real way to make the conversation better, so he decided he would find something else to do.

Likos had been pacing around for nearly an hour and needed to find something to do before he drove himself crazy. He thought to himself that if he could get out of the city, then he might be able to find some roots that would help Angelina sleep better.

It was never hard to find her, and as suspected, it only took about ten minutes this time.

He could tell she was stressed, so he asked her to come with him.

She hesitated for a few moments. "I would love to go with you and get out of the city, but that has not always worked out well for me."

He could only guess that she wanted to go with him, but for some reason, she felt safer in this old temple. He laughed. "I will make sure that you do not have to face another army on your own."

She looked at him for a minute. "How long do you expect to be outside the walls?"

Likos answered quickly, "Only a few hours. I need to find some roots that I can use to make some medicine for a friend." After a few seconds, he added, "Come on. It will do you good to get out for a while."

She did like the idea of getting out of the city, but at the same time, she did not want to leave the temple. For some reason she did not fully understand, she started shaking her head and replied, "I do not want to stay out very long because I have things I want to do."

He smiled. "It will not take long, and I will have you back here so that you can continue to protect this city."

It was not long before Likos and Angelina found themselves wandering in the wooded area about a thousand cubits from the edge of what was left of Hela.

He had found a plant that looked to be a variation of the root he needed. He was starting to dig up the plant when he heard several people approaching.

He looked up to see about a dozen people riding toward them in the distance.

They did not seem to be doing anything other than riding through the forest to get somewhere else.

Likos looked at Angelina, and although she was not panicking, it was clear she was not very comfortable with these people coming so close.

He quickly told her, "I do not believe that these people are any danger to us. I am sure they are only traveling through the forest so that it is harder for other people to see them. My dragon guild did it all the time, and if we are polite, these people might provide us with some news about what is going on in the rest of the kingdom."

Before she could say anything, he began waving down the riders. To her surprise, it did not take very long until one of the riders started toward them.

As the man approached, Likos held out his hands so that the rider could see that he did not have a weapon other than the bow across his shoulder. When the man stopped, Likos asked, "Would you like some of our water or maybe some fresh bread?"

The man replied, "I would not mind some water if you have any that you can spare."

He handed the man his small canteen and asked, "Where are you going, my friend, and do you have any news of how the war is going?"

The man almost laughed. "What war? Scorpion is raiding the cities to the east, and most of the armies of Utopia have pulled back to the north to make their stand."

Likos asked, "I was told that the north was amassing forces to push Scorpion and his armies out of Utopia. Do you know if they are moving south yet?"

The man shook his head. "Son, they are not coming, if that is what you are hoping." After a short pause, he added, "They have captured one of Haden's great dragons and have dug in to wait for Scorpion."

After the man had finished the rest of the water, he said, "Son, I need to get back with my people." He turned his horse and started to ride off. He turned once more and added, "If you and your woman have any sense, then you will get the hell out of here like the rest of us."

As soon as the man was far enough away that he could not hear them, Angelina said, "This is some kind of trick."

Likos shook his head. "I don't think so, and to be honest, I don't think they were ever coming for you. We should get back to the city to see if we can get the captain to leave this place before it is too late."

Angelina did not understand, but she was all for getting back to the safety of her city where she could see what Captain Bryce thought. She dropped the root they had dug up and followed as Likos started back toward Hela.

# CHAPTER 16

# THE COLLECTION OF INFORMATION

A few weeks ago, Airus was sure they were only a few days behind the army that had left them for dead. Now he did not want to admit it, but he was sure his companions were probably right. It had been a week since they had seen any sign of anyone from either Utopia or Haden's army.

The old woman had insisted that they try to make their way back to the city of Hela to see if they could get some much-needed supplies.

He did not like the idea but knew that if they could gather some bits of information about what had been happening, it might help them find the army.

They had been traveling through the backwoods of Utopia for weeks trying to catch Haden's army, but for some unknown reason, they had moved out of the area.

Airus had seen many trackers in his time, but he was still amazed at how the old woman seemed to know how to find her way back to Hela. He still did not trust her, and to make matters worse, he could not figure out why she stayed with them. He thought to himself, *If this old woman knows who we are, then why does she stay with us and what does she want?*

He still had her dagger, but he knew that was not the reason she did not leave because she had not even mentioned it in more than a week.

He looked at the old woman, and as usual, she was not more than a dozen cubits from the man who had united them. He could only guess that the old woman believed she would be rewarded if she helped them find Haden's army. Although he knew it was not true, he liked to think she was truly insane. He understood he might never figure it all out, but either way, she was one of the best guides he had ever met.

Airus could see a city in the far distance. Entering Hela this way was not the way he had planned. However, he was glad to be anywhere that might have some sort of civilization.

He was not sure whether the old woman was being serious, but every time he asked, she insisted, "I am just going to walk into the city like any normal person would do." Each time he thought about it, he would shake his head because it was just silliness. However, he was starting to believe she was crazy enough to do this. He could not imagine walking into a city that had been all but destroyed by an army he used to command.

Even from this distance, Airus could see that the main walls of Hela had been breached to expose the city. Although he did believe there could be many people left in the city, the old woman was convinced there would be plenty of people there to help them.

Suddenly, the old woman smacked Airus in the back of the head again.

When he turned around, she was rubbing her bony little forearms. He knew she was trying to tell him something, but he just did not understand what she wanted him to do.

Finally, the old woman shook her head and told him, "You need to cover your arms, dummy, because everyone in that city will know your symbols."

He hated it when she hit him. Although it did not hurt, it did aggravate him to no end. He did not know why, but she reminded him of his mother and his childhood. His mother would hit him like that to get him to listen. Nevertheless, he believed the only thing worse than being hit by this old woman was that she was always right.

As he looked at the man the old woman called Nedah, he was already covering his arms with mud so that no one could see the markings on his arms. Airus shook his head and reached down to get some mud to cover his arms.

~*~

As he sat overlooking the city, Airus was still hoping Nedah would come up a better idea than this. He thought, *Why not, we will just walk up to the city and ask, "Which way did my army go?"* He looked at the large man once again, but as far as he could tell, this man did not intend to stop them.

He looked at the large hole in the wall and began to wonder if there were smaller holes they could use to get into the city or get out of it if they needed to.

After several minutes, the old woman stated, "I think that we should go into the forest to see if we can find some roots or bark that could be used to make medicine."

Airus was not sure how making medicine was going to help, but he did not want the old woman to make him feel stupid again, so he said nothing. He smiled and thought, *Maybe this crazy old woman does have a plan other than just walking up into the city.*

As she walked by, she tapped her head with her bony fingers. "We can use the medicine to trade for supplies."

He looked at Nedah to see if he agreed, but he seemed a bit distracted as he covered himself up with a makeshift robe.

As Airus began to make his own makeshift robe from the blankets they had, he looked toward the old woman. He was not sure what she was planning, but he could see she was already starting to discuss this plan with herself. She went on about getting ginseng root and bark if she could find the right tree.

He shook his head and finished putting on his makeshift robe. He thought, *Anyone as old as this woman must know something about medicine even if she is crazy.*

The old woman never ceased to amaze him because they had not been in the forest for more than thirty minutes when she claimed to have found what they needed. The plant she wanted was a small, three-to-five-leaf green plant with red berries in the center. To his surprise, it was not the leaves she wanted but the roots of the plant, which forked and resembled the shape of a person.

It was another ten minutes before the old woman demanded he cut the bark from an odd-looking, off-green-colored tree. Airus could tell the tree was extremely old because its base had to be at least four cubits across. What he found strange was that the branches hung almost to the ground.

Before he started to cut the bark from the tree, he looked at Nedah and asked, "Do you understand why I need to cut the bark from a tree?" Again, the man appeared distracted as if he had something else on his mind.

Suddenly, the old woman smacked him in the back of the head again and replied, "Because you are the only person here with a steel blade, dummy."

He looked at the tree and then at the dagger and thought, *Does she want me to try to cut the tree down with a dagger?*

She quickly realized she needed to give him some direction. "Don't try to hack the bark off the tree but cut a deep groove in the bottom of the trunk and then pull the bark off in long strips." She looked at him for a few seconds and then walked away to continue looking for more of the root she had just dug up.

He shook his head from side to side and took the dagger from his belt to see if he could figure out what the old woman was telling him to do. As Airus held the dagger, he quickly realized it seemed to beckon him to use it, almost as though it was somehow enchanted. However, he knew that was impossible. As he walked closer to the large tree, he swung the dagger back and forth as he tried to understand the soothing effect the blade seemed to have on him.

The old woman turned and told him, "We need the green flexible skin of the tree that is just beneath the hard-brown outside." As she was walking away, she added, "When you are done, I want my dagger back."

Without thinking, Airus replied, "Of course."

He once again felt that there was something about the dagger that just beckoned him to use it as he sawed away at the tree bark.

Airus was so mesmerized by what he was doing that he did not realize his companions had wandered some four hundred cubits away to find more of the old woman's medicine.

An hour passed before Nedah and the old woman returned with several small bags of ginseng root.

Airus was still working on stripping the green skin beneath the bark. To his surprise, the old woman told him, "That should be enough to get what we need." After a moment, she added, "You can give my dagger back now if you do not mind."

Without so much as a moment of hesitation, he started to hand the old woman the dagger when something caught the old woman's attention. Suddenly, Airus realized he had no real reason to give the dagger back and placed it back into his belt.

The old woman and Airus both looked up as Nedah said, "About fifteen riders are coming toward us, but they do not seem to be in a hurry." He added, "I would guess that they are wanderers just trying to get away from the fighting."

Airus looked in the same direction as Nedah and the old woman were looking, but he had no reason to believe that anyone was coming their way.

To his surprise, after a couple of minutes, a small group emerged from the edge of the forest. The group consisted of mostly older people who seemed to be just passing through this section of this forest.

Airus waved one of the riders down to see if he could get some information on how the war was going and whether or not there were any signs of Haden's army in the area.

As the man slowly began to approach them, Airus put out his hands so that the man could see that he was not a threat to him or his group. He asked, "Can you help me and my family by sharing some information about the war?" When the man did not immediately answer, Airus asked, "Can I offer you some water or food for your trouble?"

The man smiled and replied, "I have enough food and water for the moment, but if you can spare some of the willow bark that you just cut, I would appreciate it."

He looked at Nedah and the old woman to see if they approved of the buying of information, but neither seemed to care. He honestly did not know the value of the bark and was not sure how much he needed to give. After a couple of seconds, he handed the man several long strips of the green bark.

The man thanked him for the generous gift and then complimented him on his technique. He was not sure whether the man was trying to be funny or whether he actually was thankful for the bark, so he just nodded his head.

The man smiled. "As I told your friends thirty minutes ago, the warmonger Scorpion is raiding most of the cities and towns in the south. Your forces are reestablishing their defenses in the north."

Airus asked, "How close are Lord Scorpion's forces to Hela?"

The man thought for a few seconds. "Most of Lord Scorpion's forces were heading west. It is the raiding parties that you need to worry about here because most of Lord Scorpion's men are looking for Haden's lost dragons."

He smiled and added, "I have heard your people managed to capture one of the large male dragons but have not yet been able to find someone who could ride the beast."

After a few seconds, the man said, "Friend, I have other things that I need to do and other places to be." As he rode away, he once again thanked Airus for the medicine and then disappeared into the forest to join the rest of his group.

As the man rode off, the old woman again asked Airus to give her the dagger back, but the moment had passed, and now he did not intend to give it up.

To change the subject and keep from answering the old woman, he asked, "Do we still need to go into Hela? We know where most of Haden's army is heading now."

The old woman looked at him for several seconds before answering. "We still need some supplies before we head north." In a low voice he could barely hear, he heard her add, "I have something in Hela that I would like to get back before I lose the chance."

Airus did not understand why the old woman wanted to go north except to avoid the raiding parties. She knew the lay of the land better than he did but heading north seemed so far out of their way. As he tried to figure out what the old woman was planning, he asked, "How long do you think it will take to catch Haden's army?"

The old woman quickly snapped at him and asked, "Why would we chase Haden's army when there is a dragon to the north?"

Again, Airus felt silly because it was a question, he wished he had not asked.

He had not thought about the dragons for a long time, but before he could reply to the old woman, Nedah interrupted. He announced, "North is a better direction than south or west, but we need to go to Hela first."

Airus did not understand why Nedah wanted to go into the heavily damaged city of Hela, but that did not matter. He wrapped up the bark and added, "I cannot think of a better place to go. I have heard marvelous things about this city."

## CHAPTER 17

# THE INFLUENCE OF THE TWO-FACED WITCH

Sabrina was not paying attention to the two-faced witch, but she needed to find something to do. For as long as she could remember, her father had been pushing his vast armies farther east, but she knew little about the world outside the palace. She understood that the Center Region held almost unlimited resources, but these kingdoms, such as Utopia, had lain just out of reach beyond the great rainforest.

She thought to herself, *Those cowards probably felt safe and sound until my father cut a path through the forest a thousand cubits across.* She laughed because it had only taken him over two months to cut his way through the rainforest. Now, nothing would stop her from being in Utopia by the end of the month.

She had never been allowed far from the palace because her father had always demanded that she spend her time studying the laws of existence. She never understood why he thought she could gain understanding of the world from such nonsense, but now the realm was hers to do with as she pleased.

The two-faced witch had been jabbering about something for the last hour, but all Sabrina could think about was what to do with her empire. She believed the only reason her father had kept her from doing anything as a child was because he did not want to share his power, but now he would never control anyone's life again.

Suddenly the two-faced witch said, "My dear, you will make a great queen when you gain control of all your father's forces."

Sabrina thought to herself, *I am so lucky to have not one but two of these witches as loyal advisors.*

~*~

It had been several hours since the witch had said anything, and Sabrina was starting to get a bit bored. As she sat the looking at the old woman, she could still remember when one of these women first told her of the prophecy to rid herself of her father.

Suddenly, she realized she did not know how to tell these two witches apart or what to call them. She believed that one or both of them had referred to the other as Jeannie, but that did nothing to identify the witch that was in the carriage with her.

As the ugly old witch mumbled to herself, Sabrina tried to remember if she had seen both witches together since they had left the palace. After a few moments, she convinced herself that she had talked to both at one point or another. Then again, maybe she had not.

Suddenly, some nonsense of her youth popped into her head as if she did not have enough to consume her thoughts. She could remember short chubby Master Pythagoras saying that according to the laws of existence, all answers are out there if you just know the right question to ask. She looked at the two-faced witch for a few seconds and asked, "Where is your sister today?"

The old hag stopped mumbling and replied, "My lady, I do not understand the question."

After a brief pause, Sabrina politely asked, "Is she not feeling well?"

The witch smiled, showing her nasty teeth, as she stared at the young girl. Finally, she replied, "My lady, Jeannie is always near, and you should not worry about my sister because she is more than capable of taking care of herself."

Sabrina quickly realized that the witch had not answered her question. However, she was not sure if she should demand that the old hag tell her where her sister was or whether she should try a softer approach.

Before she could make up her mind, the old witch tried to redirect the conversation. She asked, "My lady, do you not believe that you should push this legion harder before someone else tries to take what is rightfully yours?"

Sabrina immediately replied, "No one is going to take what is mine. Lord Haden made it clear that if anything was ever to happen to him, I was to have full control of his empire."

The two-faced witch smiled. "Now that Haden is gone, I am sure that no one will disagree with his choice of successors."

Sabrina knew the witch was just trying to see if she would get angry, so she tried not to show any emotions that could be used against her. She waved her hand as if to dismiss the witch's words and said, "The legions are moving as fast as they can."

The old hag shrugged her shoulders and replied, "If you say so, my lady."

After a few moments, curiosity got the better of her. Sabrina asked, "What would you have me to do?"

The old witch smiled again. "My lady, you have to show these people that you are in charge. Did not Master Pythagoras teach you that force is the start of all motion and all that people understand?"

Sabrina could not remember her teacher using force in this context, and she had a near-perfect memory. According to the laws of existence, every force had an equal and opposite force, but nothing the old witch said sounded familiar.

She had always believed there was more to the world than what her instructor talked about for hours and hours. She wished she knew where he had gone because he always insisted that everything she needed could be found in the laws of existence. However, she thought to herself, *Finally, I am starting to get some real education.*

~*~

Sabrina had tried for the last hour to get the words of the two-faced witch out of her head. She thought, *What if this witch is right? Maybe I do need to push these people a harder before someone tried to take my throne. After all, I am the queen, and if I want them to respect me as a leader, I must show them who is in charge.*

She knew that if her father wanted to be somewhere, he would not have hesitated to drive these people to their death.

She was just about to wake up the witch when the carriage suddenly stopped, and someone knocked on the door. The man announced, "My Queen, your royal guard wishes your permission to set up camp for a few hours while the scouting parties make sure that the area is safe to travel."

She had not noticed when the old witch had awoken, but she now had a big grin on her face as she nodded.

Without any warning, Sabrina shoved opened the door to the carriage and demanded to see the captain of the guard.

There were several dozen palace guards riding next to the carriage and a group of senior leaders riding just beyond her guards.

Ric Sochor, captain of the royal guard, commanded, "Cease all activity until the queen's needs are addressed."

Sabrina began yelling, "I have had enough of this treatment, and I will decide when we need to take a break! Do you think I am some fool who is too stupid to understand what is going on?"

The captain quickly bowed his head and replied, "My queen, I do not understand. No one is questioning your intelligence." He tried to choose his words wisely as he explained, "We need to give our scouts time to do their job, and I believe that you would like to get out of the carriage." He quickly dismounted his horse and knelt in front of the carriage to await her instructions.

She screamed, "I will decide when I want to get out of the carriage! I do not need anyone telling me what to do. I want you to keep the legions moving, or I will find someone who can lead the legions for me."

He did not have any control over the movement of the legions, but he looked up at her and quickly replied, "Yes, my Queen." He looked over at General Tempest and then added, "As you have commanded."

Sabrina looked back at the old witch to make sure she agreed and then demanded, "I want a horse now." She looked around until she found the finest horse she could. "Get off your horse. I want it." Just so that everyone knew she was serious, she added, "I am tired of being trapped inside this box and not being able to tell where I am going."

Although she did not realize it, Sabrina was taking the horse of one of her senior generals.

General Tempest grabbed what he could carry and dismounted his horse. He said, "As you wish, my Queen."

Sabrina jumped from the carriage and headed toward the general, who was holding the horse for her. He tried to tell her he could find her a better-suited horse, but she did not intend to let anyone tell her what she could ride.

She looked back once again at the witch, who seemed to giggle with delight. The witch nodded her head to let her know she approved of what she was doing.

As she moved close to the large horse, several men tried to steady the beast.

As she approached, it snorted and stomped its hooves against the ground. She had ridden some of the finest horses in the world but could not remember ever riding a warhorse.

She was not afraid of the horse, but as she got closer, she began to wish she had put more thought into her choice, but it was too late for that now. She did not want people to believe that she did not understand what she wanted.

This horse was one of the largest animals she had ever seen, and although she was sure she could ride it, there was not going to be anything pleasant about it. She thought, *When they figure out that I am not a child, I will have them bring me another horse. Maybe I will have them bring me a different horse every day just because I can.*

She hesitated for several seconds but finally dismissed the two soldiers that were there to help her mount the horse because she did not need anyone's help. She was going to show everyone that she was her father's daughter.

In a single movement, she jumped up, planted her right foot into the stirrup, and then swung her left leg across the back of the saddle. Immediately, she grabbed the reins with both hands. Instantly, she realized that the horse was so broad she could not put her feet in both stirrups.

~*~

After a few moments, Sabrina managed to gain control of the horse despite not being able to sit properly in the saddle. She could not reach both stirrups and could barely hold on, but at least the horse had not yet tried to throw her. Although she was not quite seated in the saddle, she began yelling and screaming at everyone as if she completely understood what they were supposed to be doing even though she really did not.

Within a few minutes, every general and advisor around her was trying to figure out what was going on or what she wanted. She demanded that every commander give her a status report. She demanded they tell her what they were doing to support her.

She wanted everyone to know that she was in charge and that they needed to respect her. She knew that her father's armies respected him, and she was going to demand the same.

Soon, the two-faced witch rode up beside her on a much smaller horse that appeared to have been prepared for the old hag. Sabrina did not know how the woman had managed to find such a nice horse in such a short time, but she was glad she was there. She wondered if she should make her trade horses but decided it would make her look weak.

The old witch spoke. "My lady, I must apologize that I have not been around for most of the day, but I had other things that I needed to do."

The witch was acting as if they had not talked all day. Sabrina looked at the ugly old hag for several moments, but she could not believe that this woman was not the person sitting with her just ten to fifteen minutes ago.

Although she was certain it was the same woman, she still asked, "Are you not the same woman who was just in the carriage with me?"

This two-faced witch smiled. "My lady, as I told you earlier, I have not talked to you all day." After a short pause, she continued. "My lady, you must have been talking to my sister, Jeannie."

She looked at the witch for almost a minute because she was sure that this old hag was lying. Suddenly, she knew what she needed to do and asked, "If your sister is named Jeannie, then what is your name?"

The old witch continued to smile as she replied, "My lady, you have known me for many years, and you know that my name is Jeannie."

Sabrina shook her head because she did not have time to play this game.

She began yelling at everyone except the witch again.

The witch followed her everywhere and made comments every chance she had.

Sabrina had been yelling orders for well over an hour when a young soldier from one of the scouting parties rode up to her. By this time, she could barely talk, so she waved her hand to signal him to speak.

He announced, "We believe that we have found one of your father's dragons, but we need far more people if we are going to chain it."

Sabrina now knew who her senior officers were, so she looked at them to see if anyone was willing to help her. Most of them did not want to look at her because they had had enough of her temper. However, General Tempest nodded his head. He offered, "We need to hurry because this may be the only chance that we have to chain this dragon."

Sabrina started ordering everyone to get what was needed to chain this dragon.

General Tempest ordered the captain of the guard to bring at least a hundred soldiers.

Sabrina then added, "Include anyone who knows anything about dragons."

The truth of the matter was that few people, other than Haden's most trusted, knew anything about dragons.

## CHAPTER 18

# LOST IN THE LIGHT

When Anna first flew into the great glow, she had no way of determining which way she needed to go to get back to the dark because she could not see. By the time she could see again, she was confused as to which way the darkness lay.

At the time, she did not understand that the darkness, unlike the light, did not stand out and would not be so easy to find once she left it.

Although she only planned on flying into the glow so that she could see the forest, she had now been in the light for what she could only guess was days. She understood that when she first entered the light, she would have trouble seeing, but she did not expect to be so disorientated that she would not be able to find her way back home.

Anna thought to herself, *It was so easy to find the light because all I had to do was fly toward the glow.* As she thought back, she realized it was not so easy to find the dark because the light hid everything.

She had always been told not to go into the light without an experienced rider, but that did not change the fact that she was now lost. She looked at the distant horizon and took a deep breath because she knew she needed to remain calm or she would die out here in the light.

Finally, she remembered that the Kingdom of Acoma had gardens just beyond the great glow.

Once she could see, she began looking for these gardens hidden away in the mountains. She believed if she could find the gardens, then she would be able to wait for someone to find her. The problem was that she had never seen the gardens and did not know which mountains to start for them. She had spent most of the first day looking for these gardens, but when she could not find them, she once again tried to find the darkness. Every horizon looked dark until she spent hours getting there, only to find that it was still light.

She wanted to keep looking for the darkness, but she knew that if she could find the gardens, she would be able to find to eat. Once again, she looked at the distant horizon, but nothing looked dark anymore.

Anna knew that these gardens were in a deep valley so that outsiders would not be able to get there without a dragon. She decided to sweep the mountain ranges once to see if she could find the gardens of her people, but she was starting to believe that she was never going to find her way home.

Anna had always been independent and did not have any problems finding food for herself, but it was a different situation for her dragon. Her father's riders had always taken care of providing food for the dragons. Although she knew what dragons ate, she did not know how to find it in sufficient amounts. There were some fruits and vegetables the dragon would eat. However, because she had to stay away from other people, they were in short supply.

She knew that what her dragon wanted was meat, but the best she had managed to snare were a few small rodents and a scrawny rabbit. That amount of meat was barely enough even to be considered as a treat, let alone a meal, for something so large. She had tried to catch a deer a few days ago, but she could not get close enough to kill it. She felt that she was spending as much time gathering fruit and hunting rodents as she was trying to get home.

Anna had been flying over this mountain range for hours and finally spotted an opening in the meadow near some foothills. She pulled slightly on the harness to adjust her flight path because she would have to guide the dragon into the opening.

Her father had explained to her as a young child that a dragon's vision, as with most reptiles, was very different from that of a human.

She could see that there were far too many trees and very few rocky surfaces for her dragon to navigate to the rocky clearing on its own.

It really would not have mattered where she wanted to land because Paytah trusted her without question. With a few tugs on his harness, he was easily directed to the tall grass near the rocky opening.

As soon as the dragon's feet touched the ground, Anna dismounted and began looking for something to feed her dragon. Within a matter of minutes, she was using her dagger to cut down some wild berry bushes when a deer suddenly jumped from the bush and ran past her.

By the time she returned, the dragon had managed to catch the deer as it was trying to cross the meadow where he was lying. She felt sorry for the deer as it fought for its life, but she understood that the deer was a far better meal than the wild berry bushes.

She sat down and started picking the berries off the thorny bush as she watched Paytah begin eating the deer.

It had been a long time since she had felt at peace. Anna did not know how long she had been lost in the light, but at least her dragon was fed. She knew he would be good for at least a couple of days, if not longer.

She was tired, but she understood that they would probably need to leave soon. She was glad just to sit and pick berries from this bush.

She looked around, but all she could see beyond the meadow was a dense forest. She thought, *I think we will be safe for a while, and Paytah will know long before anyone gets close enough to be of any danger.*

She could not remember how long it had been since she had slept, but she felt safe, so she lay down. It only took a few moments until she noticed what appeared to be the moon behind the broken clouds. As she looked up, she started wondering if this was the same moon that could be seen on a clear night in the Dark Lands. If this was the same moon, then, by its position in the sky, she had been in the light for twenty-five to twenty-eight days.

She soon convinced herself that the moon was in the same position as it was on the night, she had gotten lost. She lay on the grass, gazing at the beauty of the moon, just glad to have a moment to rest. Suddenly, she realized that the moon was the solution to her problems because she could follow it back to the Dark Lands.

She quickly sat up and looked at her dragon because she wanted to tell him it was going to be okay, but by this time, he had finished the deer and made himself comfortable. She realized it would probably take as long to get back to the Dark Lands as it took to get to wherever she was now. She took a deep breath, exhaled, and lay back down so that she could rest for a while before they started back home.

Anna was barely awake and had not yet decided to get up. It was peaceful and she could not remember the last time she had slept this well, but she had things to do. After a few moments, she sat up to see if Paytah had woken up yet, but as she had expected, he was still sleeping. Before she could stand up, the dragon sensed she was starting to move around and quickly awoke to greet her.

Although her dragon had eaten several hours ago and would not need food for two or three days, she was not so lucky and was starving. She stood up and started brushing off her leathers so that she could find something to eat. She made sure that her dagger was secure and started walking toward the woods to see if she could find more berries. Long before she reached the small shrubs, she found some hanging fruit but decided she would like to have more of the berries.

All at once, she heard a sound that was unmistakable. As she looked at her dragon, there was no doubt he had also heard the squeal of another dragon. For several seconds, she stood motionless, unsure as to what to do next as she waited to hear the dragon again.

Before the second squeal was finished, she was running at full speed toward her dragon, who was already kneeling and preparing to be mounted. In a single motion, she planted her right foot and swung into the correct position for the dragon to take flight.

Paytah had done this maneuver a thousand times. As he leaped into the air, he spread his wings to catch as much air as possible. With three or four strokes of his large wings, the dragon was a dozen cubits above the tree line and would continue to climb until he was told to do something else. Anna knew that there was only way she would find the other dragon, and that was to go as high as she could and hope the other rider would see her.

~*~

It was Paytah that first spotted the dragon in the opening in the forest, and even from this height, Anna knew this was the largest dragon she had ever seen.

Anna also saw, far below, a large army too occupied with whatever they were doing to notice her and her dragon. They were too close to the dragon not to know it was there, but as far as she could tell, there was no one near the dragon yet.

Other than the physical aspects of the dragon, she had no way of knowing anything about it and was not about to put her dragon in harm's way. With a firm pull of the reins, she guided her dragon to the edge of the rocky area where the large dragon was resting.

She did not have any desire to frighten the beautiful creature, which had to be at least sixty cubits from its head to the tip of its tail. Even with its massive wings, she did not understand how something so big could ever fly.

She could see from the harness on the dragon that it had been tamed at one time. However, she had no way of knowing how long it had been since the dragon had human contact.

As she slowly advanced toward the dragon, she began to wonder why it was not curious about her or her dragon. Normally, dragons did not like people they were not used to, but this one did not seem frightened of her. She stopped, aware that this meant one of two things.

The first reason a dragon without a rider would not be interested in another rider was that it had been too long since it had had contact with humans. The only other reason she could think of was that this was a light dragon that could breathe fire. As she slowly started moving again toward the dragon, she was certain that it was a male. She took a deep breath, relieved because at least she would not have to worry about finding the dragon's eggs.

Once she was within about thirty cubits, she could see that the dragon had several branches stuck in one of his wing's center joints, and he probably could not fly. The closer she got, the more she believed he was a light dragon. She also knew that if the dragon had not had human contact for a while, then he would have learned not to fly so close to the trees by now.

Anna knew more than most people about light dragons because from time to time, they would be rescued from the outsiders, and she had always helped when her father asked her. She even believed that someday, Paytah would breathe fire. She took another deep breath because she knew that a dragon this large could probably breathe fire for a hundred cubits or more.

From the way the dragon shifted its weight, she was certain he was not comfortable with her being so close. She also knew she needed to remove the tree branches out of his wing. If she were not patient, the dragon would scorch half of the forest before she could help the poor creature.

As she got closer to the dragon, she could see that he seemed to get more nervous. Finally, she decided to sit down to let the dragon relax. As she expected, the dragon calmed down, and it did not take long before he started to move closer to her.

After a few minutes, Anna had the dragon nudging her, which, of course, meant that he was hungry. She did not have any idea what or how she was going to feed something this massive. She pulled out her dagger very slowly so that the dragon could see it and understand that it was not a threat.

At first the dragon was curious, but after a few seconds, he lost interest in the small blade and nudged her arm again. Anna wanted to remove the branches from his wing, and without thinking, she gave him the command to spread his wings for inspection.

To her surprise, the dragon spread his wings and allowed her to cut the branches to free his wing.

She was certain that someone had trained the dragon at one time.

By this time, Anna could see that her dragon was starting to get restless. She gave the large dragon a command to stay. When he settled down, she started walking back to where Paytah had been patiently waiting for her to return.

Even though she had gained the large dragon's trust, she was still not comfortable enough to bring Paytah any closer. She was not sure if it was because she did not want the dragon to feel threatened or if she just did not want her dragon exposed to a light dragon.

She knew dragons were territorial when left to fend for themselves. Although this dragon appeared to be trained, the truth of the matter was that Paytah could be an ass sometimes. She knew that the last thing she needed was for him to start something with a dragon four or five times his size.

As she was cutting some berry bushes to get some food for the large dragon, Paytah suddenly started looking at something that was coming through the woods. She quickly ran to him and ordered him to kneel, and although there was clearly someone coming, the dragon did as he was told. It only took a few seconds for them to be airborne.

The men who came through the woods were so concerned with the large dragon that they did not even notice her and Paytah.

Just as quickly as they entered, they turned and left. Anna assumed it would not be long before they would return with many more men.

As soon as the men were out of sight, she landed once again to see if she could help the dragon.

She ran back to him, which seemed to calm him down. She did not know whether the dragon understood, but she stroked his head and told him she did not have any way to feed him. After a few seconds, she added, "Soon people will come to capture you, but they will have food." She apologized because she had to leave but promised she would return as soon as she could.

As Anna mounted Paytah, she looked back at the dragon and felt that somehow, he understood.

# CHAPTER 19

# THE SACRIFICE FOR THE DRAGON

It had been several hours since a scouting party found a large male dragon, and still, Sabrina was not sure how to capture the beast without hurting it.

They were still a few days from Utopia and were completely unprepared to deal with a dragon here in the middle of the forest. She doubted they even had enough chains to restrain the monster if they could figure out how to get close enough to capture it. She knew that regardless of whether or not they were ready, there was no way she could pass up such an opportunity.

To make matters worse, no one knew if it was a light dragon that could breathe fire or a dark dragon whose loyalty to Haden would be hard to break.

Sabrina had hoped that someone else would have already found and chained all her father's dragons by now.

Captain Sochor managed to gather at least 250 people to help chain the dragon if they came up with a plan. She had ordered the group to surround the dragon to keep it from escaping. However, now she just thought it was silly because dragons could fly. No one seemed to notice; everyone was so frightened of the dragon that they did not have time to criticize her decisions. Even if she ordered it, no one was brave enough to go any closer than a couple hundred cubits to the monster.

Everyone knew that if they had any chance of taming the dragon, then at some point, they needed to chain the monster so that they could feed it and tend to its damaged wing.

Anyone who had ever served Haden knew what his dragons were capable of doing, and so did Sabrina. She understood it was only a matter of time before they had to do something, but no one wanted to get any closer to the monster than they had to at the moment.

Sabrina had long gotten over her temper tantrum. She was now being followed by most of her senior staff, but none of them would come forward to help her. She wished she knew more about the rank structure so that she could identify whom to ask for help. She also wished she had not rushed out of the carriage and made such hasty decisions. Although she believed she needed to show that she was in charge, she was clearly in over her head and had made many poor choices.

She could barely move because she had rubbed the inside of her thighs raw, and her back hurt from riding such a large horse. She probably needed to dismount so that she could figure out the best way to approach the dragon. The truth of the matter, though, was that she was not sure if she could stand. She tried to shift so that she would be more comfortable. However, the horse was just too large.

Despite her condition, at least one of the two-faced witches had finally appeared next to her.

It did not take long before the old hag commented, "This should be fun, my dear."

Sabrina looked at the two-faced witch and wondered whether this was the same woman she had just talked to a few hours ago. She had to admit she had not paid enough attention to the horse to know the difference and definitely could not tell the witches apart. As she rode next to the witch, she asked, "Do you or your sister have any words of wisdom that would help us to chain this dragon?"

The hag smiled as her eyes lit up with the delight of a schoolchild. She replied "Yes, my dear, don't let it kill you because death by fire is most certainly not the best way for you to die."

She was not sure how to take the witch's comments, so all she could do was look dumbfounded at the excited old woman. After a few seconds, the old witch turned her horse and rode up to one of the generals. Sabrina listened as the old woman told the general, "This is probably a dark dragon, and if you want to chain it, there are certain things that you need to do." She looked back to see if Sabrina was listening and added, "All you need to do is approach the dragon with a few horses because the creature is probably hungry."

Sabrina knew that dark dragons were not as dangerous as light ones, so she hoped the witch was correct. As she listened to the old hag try to persuade the general to send some men in with horses for the dragon to eat, she thought it was at least worth a try.

When General Tempest looked at her to see if she agreed, she nodded her head to let him know she did not have any problem with the witch's plan.

After about thirty minutes, two horses were selected to be fed to the dragon. Sabrina watched as this general ordered several men to bring the horses forward for the general to inspect. Six other men followed with the chains they were hoping to use to restrain the dragon.

She now knew that the captain of the guard was only in charge of her personal guard, yet he followed the men with the horses.

Captain Sochor covered each of the horse's heads with a blanket so that they could not tell where they were going.

As Sabrina watched the men and horses edge closer to the massive dragon, she suddenly remembered the twisted words of the two-faced witch and realized that the words were not directed at her. She began yelling, "Stop! I believe that this is a light dragon!" but she was too late. By the time the men heard her voice, the dragon had begun to scorch the land around them.

The horses and the men leading them did not have a chance to take cover. They were instantly caught in the burst of flames. The men dropped the chains and scrambled to get out of the dragon's way.

Sabrina watched in dismay as the dragon killed both horses and the two men leading them. The hungry beast grabbed one of the horses and turned away to consume its meal. The rest of the men took the opportunity to scramble out of range of the monster.

Sabrina had never seen anyone killed before and could not take her eyes off the smoldering bodies of the dead men.

As the remaining badly burnt men began to return to the safety of the group, they looked at her as if she had caused the dragon to turn on them. Although she wanted to help them, she was not sure she knew how.

The old hag had found a place behind the main group where she would be safe and could watch the whole spectacle. Sabrina found it hard to think over the giggling of the old woman. She did not see the point of the two-faced witch's game and almost felt sorry for the men who had been burned by the dragon.

Finally, she thought to herself, *At least their sacrifice was not in vain because now it is clear that we must plan for dealing with a light dragon.*

Sabrina knew the only way to capture the dragon was to blindfold it until the monster started to trust them.

As she turned around, she could see that the healers were still treating the wounded. She wondered how she was going to convince these people that they needed to try to blindfold this monster.

It was several minutes before the group regained their composure. By this time, the dragon was starting to tear the second horse apart.

Sabrina rejoined her senior staff, but she was not sure that any of them cared to hear what she had to say. It was now clear to her that the man whose horse she had taken was in charge. She could see that General Tempest was planning to capture the monster by sheer force and had already ordered a hundred men and women to prepare to charge it.

Not that she cared about these people, but Sabrina knew that a hundred people were no match for a dragon, especially one of this size. At best, the only value their deaths would bring was that the dragon might tire enough so that the remaining warriors would be able to chain it.

She decided she would ride up to the general to make sure she understood his plan.

General Tempest asked, "My lady, do you have any other advice for my warriors as we try to capture this dragon for you?"

She looked back at the man who she only knew as her captain of the guard, and a healing witch was still working on him. She informed the general, "If you charge this dragon, your men will die a miserable death, and I still will not have a dragon."

He looked at her for a few seconds. "What would you have us do, my lady?"

She looked at him and wanted to apologize for taking the horse she was riding, but she believed he would think she was weak. She replied, "I want fifteen of your best light-footed warriors so that I can attempt to blindfold this monster before it kills all of you."

She did not wait for him to reply before she dismounted the large horse and started stripping off her clothes. She knew she needed to put on some armor before she tried to blindfold the beast.

She did not know why, but she decided to wear the cheaper and lighter leather armor instead of the metal armor her generals demanded.

She shook her head because it was hard to believe that although most of these people had been around her father for years, none of them seemed to know anything about dragons.

By the time she was dressed, there were fifteen of the worst-looking warriors she had ever seen waiting for her. Although she knew no one in his or her right mind would volunteer to blindfold this monster, she had hoped for a little more.

She could see why the dragon had chosen this area. There were few trees to block the light and plenty of large rocks for him to lie on to stay warm. Unfortunately, the openness made it difficult to approach him unnoticed.

Sabrina ordered the fifteen soldiers to spread out and approach the dragon from different directions as slowly as they could. She told them, "If the dragon starts moving, remain still until he has lost track of you."

As she looked at the fifteen frightened warriors, she realized they were still carrying their longswords and shields as she was. No one would be happy about leaving their swords and shields behind. However, she knew there was nothing that would get a dragon's attention as fast as something shiny would.

Sabrina took off her weapons. She then laid them on the ground and ordered the others to do the same. Without taking the time to listen to them complain, she also ordered everyone to bring with them as many blankets as they could find.

They quickly demanded to know how they were supposed to fight a dragon without their swords or shields.

She replied, "We are not fighting this dragon because we would not have a chance in hell. We are trying to capture a light dragon by blindfolding it."

She grabbed several blankets to cover herself and started slowly walking toward the dragon, and the others quickly did the same.

Sabrina had worn the skin off the inside of her thighs and was so stiff from having to lean forward that she was not sure how she was going to make it all the way to the dragon. To make matters worse, the leather armor she was wearing made it hard to move and burned her raw flesh. Most of all, she was not sure how she was going to be able to capture the dragon if the others did not join her.

Despite her fear, one by one, they decided—or were forced—to join her. Either way, there were sixteen people, armed only with blankets, sneaking toward one of the scariest monsters on the planet. She was not sure the others would understand what they needed to do, but to her amazement, everyone was now about twenty to twenty-five cubits from the dragon.

Luckily for them, the dragon was still busy tearing apart one of the horse carcasses.

She had read a lot about dragons but could not believe this plan was working so well. Suddenly, she noticed the metal plating on the person just to her left, and if she had noticed it, then the dragon would have long ago seen it.

Abruptly, the dragon turned and lurched forward.

Sabrina froze in her tracks to let the dragon pass by to investigate the shiny object. When the dragon moved, everyone in front of the dragon panicked, dropped their blankets, and ran.

Without hesitation, the dragon scorched everything that moved.

Sabrina quickly realized she only had one chance at this point, and that was to jump on the head of the dragon as it moved past her. She jumped up and dropped her blanket over the dragon's eyes.

Within a few seconds, several other people joined her in her efforts to blindfold the dragon. It was not long before they had covered the dragon's head with the blankets, which in turn made the dragon believe that it was sleeping. The dragon immediately stopped spraying fire all over the place.

The dragon lay motionless beneath the blankets. Sabrina looked around, and although half of the people who were helping her were burnt or dead, she felt victorious because she had managed to capture a dragon.

Although she was in a great deal of pain, she stood up and turned around to find one of the ugly two-faced witches standing behind her with a nasty grin on her face.

Sabrina smiled because she believed the witch would be proud of what she had just accomplished. She thought to herself, *I am a hero to these people who will now follow me anywhere.* When she smiled again at the two-faced witch, the old hag smiled back and showed her nasty teeth.

Suddenly, Sabrina felt something hit the back of her head, and she lost consciousness, falling face first into the dirt.

# CHAPTER 20

# THE LOST COMPANION

It had been several hours since they had talked to the traveler, but Airus was still not sure that just walking into the city of Hela was a good idea.

The old woman had suggested that Nedah stay outside the city walls until they were sure it was safe for him to enter.

Airus, on the other hand, did not like the idea of splitting up, but his friend no longer showed any interest in going into the city. He did not understand why, but he assumed that his friend was staying where he was because the old woman had suggested it. Although he could not put his finger on what was wrong, he seemed distant.

To Airus, this seemed like the perfect chance for the old woman to separate them so that she could betray them both.

Nedah had found a place for them to set up camp about a thousand cubits in front of a large section of the city wall that had been destroyed. From this point, they could see half of the city, but it would be hard for people inside the city to see them. Nedah did not seem concerned with what his companions were doing and sat down on a rock so that he could look into the city.

Airus watched as the old woman finished grinding up the roots and bark. He could see that it would not be long before she was ready to enter the city. When he looked back, the man sitting on the rock still seemed distracted, and it was clear that he did not intend to join them.

As he sat turning the dagger in his hand, a thousand thoughts went through his head, and he did not like the idea of the old woman going into the city alone or leaving Nedah by himself. He did not realize the old woman had moved until suddenly she was standing behind him, knocking on his skull again with her little bony fist.

He took a deep breath and placed the dagger back into his belt. He got up to see if the old woman was ready to go. To his surprise, she had something in her hand that she wanted him to eat.

He sniffed it and asked, "What is this?"

She quickly replied, "It is medicine from the bark." After a moment, she added, "It will help you feel better."

Airus looked back at Nedah to see if he knew what this was and if he should eat it.

Nedah nodded his head and turned once again so that he could stare mindlessly into the city of Hela.

As he finished the last bit of the odd-tasting paste, the old woman smiled. She told him, "Good. I was afraid that I had the wrong tree, but I guess it is okay because you are not dead yet." She smiled again and added, "I must have gotten it right this time."

He tried to spit, but his efforts were in vain because there was nothing left to spit out. He hated this old woman's games, but for the moment, it was clear that she was ready to enter the city.

Instead of waiting for the city guards to come to them, the old woman quickly walked toward the guards and met them halfway.

Airus could not hear what she was saying to the guards, but it was something about her son and that they wanted to trade medicine before headed north.

The guards looked at him for a few moments and then spoke to the old woman before waving them through the large hole in the wall.

His heart pounded as he followed her by the twenty people guarding the hole in the city wall. To his surprise, the small group of men barely looked up as they passed.

The old woman did exactly as she said she would and walked into the center of the city. Within a few minutes, she began peddling her homemade medicine to anyone who would look her way. There was not much money to be made, but people were quick to trade what they did have for the medicine or offer information, which the old woman gladly accepted.

As far as he could tell, these people seemed to trust the old woman, and not once did she try to draw attention to him or his friend. He could also see why it was so easy for her to sell this medicine. He only had a small amount of the paste, but his ribs were already starting to feel a lot better.

It only took about an hour for the old woman to run out of medicine.

Airus was very happy with their take even though most of the information was the same as what the traveler had told them.

As he was going through their inventory, the old woman suddenly started knocking on his skull with her bony little fist. He looked up and quickly asked, "What do you want this time?"

She grinned and replied, "There is something that I need to find, but I cannot take you." After a few moments, she added, "I just want to make sure you are not going to do anything stupid if I leave you here."

He looked at her in disbelief because he did not intend to just let her turn his friend into the local authorities. He jumped up in the hope of catching her before she escaped, but before he was able to gather up the items they got for the medicine, she had disappeared around the corner of a building.

He looked around, but as far as he could tell, she had left him in one of the most desolate areas of the city. He now wished he had paid more attention to how he got here because he did not know how to get back to Nedah.

He looked around until he found a safe place to hide their supplies. He then walked into the open so that he could figure out where he was and if he could see the old woman.

It did not take very long before he was able to locate the stone temple in the center of the city, but he still could not see the hole in the wall through which they had entered. He decided to walk toward the stone temple to see if he could find the spot where he came into the city. He thought to himself, *If nothing else, I might be able to warn my friend that the old woman is about to betray us as I expected.*

~*~

It only took about five minutes for Airus to find the large opening in the city wall. He looked to see where Nedah was, but he could not see his friend. He began to wonder if he could make it through the opening without the old woman.

He did not understand how these backwoods people ever thought they could defend this opening. The glare alone from the western sun made it nearly impossible to see anything. He lifted his arms so that he could cover his eyes with his hands, and although he could see a little better, he exposed the branded marks on his forearms. Although he had covered the marks with mud before entering the city, he did not realize he had sweated enough to expose them.

He heard someone yelling, and when he looked up, he could see three people coming toward him. The hole in the wall was too far away for him to make it out of the city, and he did not want to lead these men to his friend.

He decided he would lead them away from the opening before making his stand.

Although the medicine the old woman had given him helped a lot, he knew he would not be able to run for long. He thought to himself, *I probably will not be able to put up much of a fight, but at least they don't know about Nedah.*

He was only able to make it a few dozen cubits before the men caught and surrounded him, but for the moment, there were only three of them.

As the first man charged at him, Airus fell to the ground and allowed the man to fly over his head and directly into one of the other men chasing him. He then grabbed the third man's leg as he was getting up and pulled him off his feet.

He returned to his feet, semi happy with his performance, but he was struck with a blunt object before he could make his escape.

He had not planned to make his stand just yet, but it was quickly becoming apparent that he would not have any choice in the matter.

The blow to his head had knocked him off his feet, but he was still not ready to give up so soon. Airus swept a fourth man's feet out from beneath him and then slammed him into the ground. He put his hand down to steady his balance as he tried once again to get up and escape.

Seconds later, he was struck again, but this blow hit his lower rib cage, causing him to fall back to the ground.

By this time, the other three men were on their feet and had rejoined the fight. They continued to kick and stomp him until it was clear that he did not have any fight left.

Airus did not know how long he had been out, but he was now awake. His hands were tied behind his back, and his body hurt like hell, but he thought, *At least I am alive.*

He was surprised to see a familiar face among his captives, but he could not remember the young man's name from the dragon guild. As they started to pick him up, he could only hope the boy did not recognize him.

Likos smiled. "General, I am glad that you are back with us. It seems as though you are not as dead as people thought, but you are a bit out of place here."

Airus look at the boy for a few seconds. "I could say the same about you. Where are the leaders of your guild?"

Before Likos could answer, a young woman walked up to Airus and asked, "Where did you get this dagger?"

Angelina grabbed him. "Do you know who this dagger belongs to?" Suddenly, she realized this man was among those she had attacked. She cried, "What did you do to the old woman?" Unexpectedly, she started having flashbacks from the battle.

Angelina quickly pulled her hand back, took a deep breath, and stared at Airus. She asked, "Where is Haden? Is he with you?" After a few seconds, she was glowing and screaming, "Is he alive? Tell me!"

Without hesitation, Airus replied, "Haden is gone, and you have no reason to fear him any longer."

She put the dagger to his throat and demanded that he tell her the truth.

He had no fear of death, so he told her, "The warmonger Haden is gone."

Likos gently took Angelina's hand and told her, "You need to calm down because we all know that Haden is dead." After a few moments, he added, "I saw his body with my own eyes, and we buried him beneath a pile of rocks and dead horses for the whole world to see."

She screamed, "Then why is this man here?"

Likos replied, "I do not know the answer, but I will take a dozen men, and we will search inside and outside the city to confirm that no one is with him. My guess is that he was left for dead and somehow managed to make it to Hela in hopes of finding his army."

Angelina took a deep breath to try to calm down. "I would feel better if you did but do not stay long." She then remembered the dagger she was holding and added, "If you find a little old woman, she is a friend."

Likos nodded and left the room to see if he could find a dozen men to help him search the city for anyone who might have helped General Airus make it to Hela.

Although Angelina was still glowing, she had managed to calm down enough to continue asking the general questions, but she dared not touch him again. She asked again, "Where did you get this dagger?"

He replied, "You are correct, it does belong to an old woman, but I do not know where she is right now."

She leaned forward with the dagger as if she was going to stab him. "Where is she?"

Suddenly, a small figure appeared in the doorway and replied, "My dear, I am here." After a moment, she added, "If you are through playing with that, I would like to get it back now," and pointed to the dagger.

Angelina could not believe that the old woman was alive and standing a few cubits from her. She dropped the dagger and ran to hug the old woman.

After a few seconds, the old woman begged, "Please let me go. I am very old, and I am afraid that you are going to squeeze me in half."

Once Angelina let her go, she walked over, picked up the dagger, and started walking toward Airus.

To his surprise, she cut the ropes that bound his hands and then thumped him on top of his head. After a second, she replied, "Didn't I tell you not to do anything stupid?" The old woman then turned toward Angelina and added, "Didn't I tell you not to do anything stupid also?"

Angelina smiled. "So, tell me what I need to do now because I am scared, and I do not know what to do."

# CHAPTER 21

# THE FIRST CONTACT

Likos had promised Angelina to see if he could find General Airus's companions, but the truth was he was restless, and he needed to get out of the city. Even if he did not believe he would find anyone, at least he could see just how badly the city walls were damaged.

Captain Bryce Hunter and eleven other guardsmen had agreed to help him do a perimeter check around the city walls.

He knew that without Angelina, he would not have been able to get anyone to check the perimeter. These guardsmen and the residents of Hela worshipped her though, and they would do anything she asked. He believed that even if he had asked for twice as many riders, he would have been able to get them.

He had also asked that some of the remaining guardsmen look through the city to see if General Airus had any accomplices on the inside. He was not sure if the search would be effective because there were not enough guardsmen left, and although the city was in ruins, there were many places to hide.

As the thirteen riders prepared to leave the city, Likos thought, *I need to look around this city myself when I get back. There could be half of Haden's army inside the city, and these people would still think they were safe.*

~*~

As the thirteen men rode through the enormous hole in the wall, Likos looked around, but as far as he could tell, nothing had changed since he had entered the city.

He asked Captain Bryce Hunter, "Can you split up your men and ride around the city walls in opposite directions?"

Captain Hunter nodded his head and then divided his men into two groups as requested.

As the groups started moving, Likos added, "Can you also have them take note of where the city could be penetrated by smaller groups?"

Captain Hunter hesitated for a moment and then replied, "This will be much easier once the reinforcements arrive from the north." He smiled and added, "When they get here, we can start repairing the wall."

When the captain finished, Likos added, "Angelina just wants to make sure that the city does not take any further losses before the reinforcements arrived. If it is okay with you, I am going to check out the area in front this hole in the wall." He took a deep breath. "If you do not think it is needed, you are welcome to discuss the matter with her."

Captain Hunter looked at him for a few moments and then ordered the groups to inspect the city wall as well.

As the groups began to move in different directions, the captain picked one man from each group. He then ordered, "Stay with Likos and assist him with anything that he needs."

Although Likos had heard the captain's instruction, he knew they were there more to watch him and make sure he stayed out of trouble.

As he watched the two groups of five men each ride off in different directions, he just hoped that they inspected the city's walls as they said they would. He was hoping that if they realized just how vulnerable the city was, then maybe he could talk them into leaving.

Likos knew it would be twenty to thirty minutes before either group returned. Therefore, he decided to ride out about five hundred cubits just to see how bad the wall was and whether there was any chance of defending the city.

He and the two guardsmen had only gone about two hundred cubits when he realized that someone had set up a small camp directly in front of the large hole.

Likos could not believe the guardsmen were so blind that someone could set up camp right in front of the hole. He shook his head because he knew no one had detected the camp, and if they had, no one had said anything.

As they rode closer to the camp, he thought that perhaps the guardsmen had set the camp up as an early warning. He smiled. "Finally, they must have figured out that they could not see out of the hole in the wall."

As Likos rode up, he noticed a single person who did not appear to have any weapons. The man stood with his back to them as his torch lit up the area for fifty cubits. He began to wonder why they would send someone out here without a weapon. Although he did not recognize the large man, it was easy to see that the large man was a warrior.

Likos asked, but the guardsmen did not seem to know the stranger either. After a few moments, he signaled the guardsmen to dismount their horses before they approached this man.

The man did not seem to notice as they rode up or was deliberately not facing them. The three men drew their weapons and slowly started toward him.

About fifteen cubits away, Likos stopped and asked, "Sir, can you turn around so that we can see who you are?"

The stranger did not turn around but only replied, "There is a large raiding party heading toward this city."

Once again, Likos asked, "Sir, can you please turn around so that we can see who you are?"

Still the man did not make any effort to acknowledge him and only replied, "They will be here in about fifteen to twenty minutes. You must get your people out of the city."

Likos looked in the same direction as the man but could not see anything, and his eyesight was better than most. This time, he then demanded, "Turn around so that I can see who you are!"

Finally, the man turned around, and Likos could see that his eyes were glowing like bright embers. He gasped because he had absolutely no doubt about the identity of the man.

Unwittingly, he dropped his weapons to the ground, and he muttered, "Son of a bitch." As he tried to walk away, he stumbled and fell to the ground next to his weapon.

Not knowing who this man was or what else to do, the other two men charged toward him with their swords in hand.

In a single motion, the man grabbed one guard's hand as the blade swung past his head and used the butt of the sword to smack the other guard in the face.

Within a fraction of a second, both men had been disarmed and beaten, and they were lying on the ground.

If by his size alone he was not threatening enough, the man now held a sword in each hand.

In a much louder voice, Haden once again told the three men, "A large raiding party is heading this way." He took a deep breath and added, "This raiding party will kill every person they find in what remains of your city."

Although the other two men were barely moving, Likos was already trying to find his bow so he could get the hell out there. He quickly grabbed both men and tried to drag them away from this monster.

He had managed to drag the guardsmen four or five cubits when Haden yelled, "Get up and warn the people in the city!"

Likos slung his bow across his shoulder and crawled back until he felt that it was safe to get up. Bowing, he replied, "Yes, my lord," before helping the other two men to their feet.

The first man to his feet asked, "Who does this guy think he is?"

Likos did not take the time to answer the man's question but instead demanded that they get back on their horses. He was sick to his stomach and had never been so afraid in his whole life, but he could only think of one thing. He knew without a doubt that he needed to get Angelina as far from this place as he could.

Within moments, the three men had mounted their horses and were riding back toward the hole in the wall.

One of the men asked, "Do you know who that was?"

Likos tried to clear his head by taking deep breaths because he was not sure if he should say the man's name aloud. After several seconds, he muttered, "Haden," but he was not sure whether anyone heard him.

The guard was speechless for almost a minute and then replied, "Are you sure? I thought he was dead." Before Likos could answer, the other guard asked, "What do you think we should do?"

Likos thought for a second and then replied, "Run like a bat out of hell if we have time, and if we do not, then we will have to fight."

Both guardsmen tried to keep up, but neither of them believed this was Haden. Finally, one of the guardsmen replied, "I think he has lost his mind or is playing a game to get us to leave before reinforcements arrive."

It only took a few minutes for the men to make it back to the large hole in the wall. When Likos looked back, he could not see any trace of Haden or his camp.

He understood why Haden's army had broken through the wall where they did because now, they were blind to everything more than a few hundred cubits away.

Soon after returning to the inside of the city, the two guards started relaying Haden's message to the twenty or so guardsmen who were assigned to guarding the opening in the wall. Likos did not even take the time to tie up his horse as he dismounted the animal. All he could think about was that he needed to find Angelina so that they could get out of this place.

To Likos's surprise, Angelina, along with a little old woman, General Airus, and several of her personal guards were already coming toward the opening in the wall.

He wanted to tell her she was right about Haden, but the last thing he needed was for her to get any more upset than she already was.

He took a couple of deep breaths to calm himself and to figure out what he was going to tell Angelina. As the young witch approached, he was finally starting to regain his composure, but he knew he still needed to get her out of here. He grabbed her and then replied, "We need to leave because there is a raiding party on the way to the city."

Neither of the guardsmen wanted to say Haden was standing outside the hole in the wall. Finally, one of the guardsmen replied, "There is a man about thousand cubits in front of the wall who says there is a raiding party heading this way."

As the group began to discuss what to do, the other two sets of mounted guards returned through the opening in the wall.

Captain Hunter demanded, "I want to know why everyone is suddenly in such an uproar."

Likos explained, "There is a man camped about a thousand cubits in front of the hole in the wall who claims that there is a large raiding party heading this way. I believe we need to leave as soon as Angelina is ready."

The old woman put her hand up so she could try to look through the hole to see whether there were any signs of a raiding party and if she could see Nedah.

Captain Hunter looked at Airus and asked, "Do you know who this man is? Is there a raiding party heading for the city?"

Airus quickly replied, "If he says there is a raiding party coming this way, I would believe him. You need to leave this place as fast as you can."

The captain looked at him for a moment. "Why should we listen to you?"

Airus turned away as if he was not listening and then told Angelina, "If you want to live, then you had better do as he says and leave this damn city."

The old woman interrupted. "There are a lot of them, at least five hundred by my count, if not more. Maybe even a thousand. It is hard to tell."

Captain Hunter did not know why he should listen to the old woman. However, when he looked to where she was pointing, it was true that the sky was darker.

He looked at Angelina to see if she had orders for him but also to see if she was going to do anything to help them.

Angelina stated, "We have the advantage here within the city walls, and we will stand our ground until reinforcements arrive from the north."

The captain nodded his head and started yelling out orders to the crowd that was forming around them.

The old woman interrupted again. "Don't be stupid. They will pour through the large gaping holes in the wall and kill everyone in this city."

By this time, the young witch was glowing so brightly that she was lighting up everything around her. She asked the old woman, "What would you have us do if you do not think we can defend the city?"

The old woman quickly asked, "Is there any other way out of the city other than the large hole that we are looking through?"

Captain Hunter replied, "The main entrance on the north side was barricaded so that we only had to worry about one entry point."

One of the other guards added, "There are several smaller holes in the wall on the east side of the city."

The old woman began issuing orders to half of the group. Although most were doing as she told them, others were uncertain and were waiting for Captain Hunter's orders.

Captain Hunter looked at Angelina again to see what she wanted to do. Angelina nodded her head and told the captain, "Do as the old woman says."

The captain immediately started repeating what the old woman was telling everyone to do. It was not long until she found something to stand on and was shouting orders at everyone who passed, followed by the captain ordering them to do the same.

Likos wanted nothing more than for Angelina to leave with the rest of the people evacuating the city. However, she was determined to do whatever she could to help as many people as possible to escape.

Suddenly, the old woman came up to Angelina and told her, "We must go, but first I need to make sure that someone else is safe."

The old woman was not asking for permission. Therefore, she did not stay long enough for Angelina to object.

Angelina watched as the old woman started walking toward the large hole in the city wall. She thought, *I cannot let her get away again*, and she started following her. She did not understand why, but the closer she got to the hole, the more she felt as if she was losing control.

# CHAPTER 22

# STUCK BETWEEN THE LIGHTS

General Virgo had been able to see the ruins of this city for the last ten minutes. However, she was not quite ready to take the city because she knew she would only have one chance to figure this out. She did not expect Hela's defenses to be more than a hundred guardsmen.

As she looked at what appeared to be a helpless city, she had a nagging feeling that something was not right, but she just could not figure out what it was. The locals had built two large bonfires to make it harder to see into the city. She had to admit this was a very clever trick.

She gave the order for the rest of the raiding party to stop so that she could try to figure out what the city defenders had planned.

Sergeant Jarvis rode up next to her and asked, "Ma'am, are we setting up camp to wait out the residents of the city?"

She replied, "I don't think that we need to set camp. I just need a little time to make sure that we are not running into a trap."

The sergeant nodded his head, turned his horse, and started yelling, "We have been given orders to hold fast until the situation can be evaluated. If you have a problem with this, now is the time to say so."

A few people dismounted their horse, but no one came forward to complain. General Virgo was not sure how long she had, but she did not need long because she this was going to happen.

As she watched sergeant ride back deeper into the group, she could tell they were eager to get this raid started.

General Virgo turned attention once again toward the city. She thought, *I understand the purpose of the bonfire inside of the city walls because now we cannot see into the city. However, I cannot figure out what the purpose of the second bonfire.*

~*~

An hour ago, General Virgo had sent a dozen of her best warriors to investigate the second flame and another dozen to check out the area around the city. As of yet, not one of them had returned, and she knew that her sergeant could not calm this group forever.

She thought, *Could these savages have come up with a way to defend the city?* She knew she had to remain calm so that her men would not see how anxious she was. She turned once again to look at the bonfires as she debated on whether or not to send more men.

She could see that her raiding party was getting a bit restless, but she had no clue as to what was happening. General Virgo did not want to waste any more of her raiding party and knew it was only a matter of time before she would take the city and claim her prize. For the moment, however, she just wished she had more information about the city's defenses.

She looked up as the scouting parties finally returned with several prisoners tied across their horses.

As she looked over the prisoners, she could tell that most of them were in bad shape. Finally, she was able to find someone who was still able to speak.

General Virgo grabbed the first man she came to and demanded, "Tell me why none of my people come back your city and what the purpose of the bonfire outside your walls is."

The man pleaded, "Please, I don't know anything about a flame outside our city walls."

She grabbed the man and once again demanded, "Tell me, what kind of deception is this, and where are my people?"

He stammered, "I don't know what you are talking about when you say a fire on the outside of the city."

She turned the man's head toward the city so he could see the two bright lights.

The man knew the light inside the city was the witch of Hela—she was glowing when he left—but he did not have any idea what was causing the second light. He thought about it but could not come up with anything, so he turned and started begging the general to let him live.

She grabbed the man by his hair so that she could direct his attention to the glow of a large fire in the distance. She asked, "So you would like me to believe that you don't know what is going on here?" She once again demanded, "Tell me what kind of deception this is before I kill you myself."

The man continued begging for his life, but soon it became apparent that this woman was going to kill him no matter what he said. He straightened and uttered, "Long may the wielding witch of Hela live."

Virgo again grabbed the man by his hair, yanked off the horse, and then tossed him to the ground. She waved her hand for someone to take him out of her sight.

Sergeant Jarvis rode up behind her and asked, "Ma'am, what are your orders?"

She had stalled about as long as she dared, and she knew it was time. She jumped back on her horse and replied, "Prepare what is left of my command for this raid."

The sergeant turned his horse and started yelling at the other sergeants.

She looked at the bright flame that stood between her and the city of Hela. If this wielding witch were the reason that no one was coming back, then she would not be so easy to capture alive. She thought to herself, *I cannot go back without this wench, and even she cannot stop a thousand people.*

The general quickly mounted her horse so that she could get ready to charge the city and confront the witch. She then ordered Sergeant Jarvis to take half of the raiding party to charge the light outside the wall while she took the other half to see what the witch was doing inside the city.

Sergeant Jarvis nodded his head and then turned once again to give orders to the sergeants of arms.

General Virgo then ordered the other half of her forces to follow her toward the hole in the wall. She was determined to stop the witch and whatever tricks she had waiting for them.

~*~

As General Virgo's forces started through the city wall, rocks and debris began raining down on them.

There were so many bits and pieces of material flying around that General Virgo could not tell where the debris was coming from or how many of her people made it through the wall.

She directed her horse from one safe spot to another. However, she could barely see fifteen cubits in front of her. She wondered, "Are the rest of my forces having this much trouble?" She knew that if the witch was causing the damage inside the city, then there was nothing to investigate outside the city wall.

As far as General Virgo could tell, the rocks and debris were not directed at any one person. If she could figure out where the witch was, she might be able to sneak up on her. However, despite her best efforts, she was knocked from her horse.

As she leaped from spot to spot, the smoke and dust seemed to get worse until the only things she could see were the two bright lights. Even as she fought for her life, she did not understand how the witch could be in two places at once. With every passing minute, she grew more confused and soon was not sure which light was the witch and which one was a decoy.

Suddenly, a dozen rocks whizzed past her head and slammed into six of her warriors. She realized that these rocks must be coming from the witch and started working her way once again toward the source.

Movement through the flying debris was very slow because she never knew when another bombardment of rocks would come flying toward her. To make matters worse, she was lucky if she could see any further than ten to fifteen cubits in front of her.

Even with all the dust and debris, two things were still easy to see. These lights were the only way she had to gauge where she was going. By this time, General Virgo had lost sight and control of the raiding party although from time to time, she would stumble over someone trying to get back on their feet. Despite the damage, what bothered her the most was that no matter how close to the light in front of her she was able to get, the light behind her continued to get closer. She thought, *If I did not know better, I would think that these lights are moving toward each other.*

General Virgo was bruised and beaten to a point where she could barely move, but she was still slowly making her way toward the witch. For some reason she did not understand, the second light had stopped just before the hole in the wall some time ago. She had no way of knowing how long it had been since she was knocked off her horse, but at least she had almost made it to the source of one of the lights.

She tried to smile as she could now see the silhouette of the witch as she continued to make her way toward the light.

She could not stop thinking about the second light. She turned once more to look for it. For some reason she did not understand, she was very afraid of the second light. As she looked around, she could see that most of her raiding party had been stopped before they entered the city.

She still could not figure out how the witch could be in two places at once. She only hoped that the witch was distracted by everything she was doing that she would not be seen as she approached.

She had long ago lost her sword, and there was very little she could find to use as a weapon because the witch had cleared almost everything out of the area. By now, she could clearly see the witch in the center of the bright glow. She could also see that there was only one man armed with a bow defending her. She just wished she could find something to use as a weapon.

Once she was within a few dozen cubits, Virgo realized that the man with the bow no longer had any arrows. She took a deep breath, and with all the strength she had left, she charged at the witch and the man with the bow.

She had hoped to get to the witch before the man had a chance to react. She had not expected the man to shift sides so quickly. Within seconds, she was standing just a few cubits away from the man with the bow.

He clearly saw her coming and was ready to swing the bow as soon as she was close enough.

General Virgo stopped a cubit short of the bow's range, exhaled, and waited for the man to make his move.

Once Likos swung the bow as she had expected, she swept his feet from beneath him and took the bow from his hands as he fell to the ground.

Virgo knew she would only have one chance to get to the witch before he got back to his feet. Once the witch was distracted, the odds would again be a thousand to one, and victory would be hers.

Virgo charged toward the witch who, as she expected, was preoccupied with summoning rocks and debris.

Meanwhile, Angelina had only once felt such power, and now, with every word she spoke and every hand gesture she made, another dozen objects came to life to do her bidding.

With a single swing of the bow, General Virgo knocked the young witch to the ground.

A thousand objects immediately fell to the ground because, without the witch, they had lost their will to continue the fight. She smiled as she fell to her knees because she knew that victory was hers, and now there was nothing to stop her army from flooding through the wall.

It felt like time stopped, and she could barely remember to breathe as she waited for her army. Her celebration was short-lived because as she waited, no one came through the wall, and there was no one left inside the wall to attack the witch.

General Virgo looked back once more to see whether the second light was still on the outside of the wall. She took a deep breath and thought, *Maybe there are two witches.* As she looked for the second light, she could not see it and started wondering if it ever existed or had only been her imagination. She wanted to get up and run before she was discovered, but she did not know where to go even if she had possessed the strength to get up.

She looked back at the hole in the wall, once more hoping that someone would come to her aid. To her disappointment, very few of her soldiers had made it through. The only thing she could see for two hundred cubits was trash and debris.

General Virgo could see that the young man whose bow she had taken was now getting to his feet. Even in her weakened condition, she knew that Likos lacked experience and that he was not her primary concern. She was exhausted, and more than that, her will to fight back had been broken. She had one hope left; she needed to see if the man slowly coming up behind the young man was truly the person, she thought he was.

She barely managed to smile because if she could buy just a few seconds until Airus made it to her, then maybe her old friend would save her.

As Likos grabbed General Virgo, she tried to sweep his feet out from beneath him again, but this time, he was ready for her, and he quickly moved out of her way.

She reached out in the hope that Airus would rush to her aid. Instead, the oldest woman she had ever seen was standing in front of her.

Without saying a word, the old woman cracked her in the center of her skull with a rock she held in her bony little hand.

# CHAPTER 23

# THE MEETING OF LOST SOULS

Without her army, the place seemed quiet now, and it gave her a chance to think. Sabrina had been awake for a little while, but she still had not found the strength to get up and find something to eat. As she lay on the cold ground, she had no way of knowing how long she had been unconscious or how far away her army had gone without her.

The two-faced witches had left a knot on the back of her head that was almost as big as her fist. Both her thighs were rubbed raw from riding the horse she had taken, and every bone in her body hurt from the encounter with the dragon. Although she was alive for the moment, she was not sure she even cared because she had lost everything and was never going to get it back.

She thought, *I am sure if I just lay here, sooner or later, something will come along to put me out of my misery.*

Unfortunately for her, as the hours continued to pass, it became clear that no one was coming to take her life. Although she did not believe that anyone would care if she starved to death, she knew that eventually, she was going to have to get up. She was starting to realize that she was hungry now, and it would take a while for her to starve to death.

She looked around and finally decided she would see if she could sit up, which did nothing to help her feel any better. As Sabrina sat looking over the rocky opening in the forest, she began to wonder why she had ever thought she could trust the two-faced witches. She thought back to many years ago, when she had first met what she thought was a single witch and how, even then, they had been setting her up. The one thing that bothered her more than anything else was that she had helped destroy the only person in the world who would have protected her from them.

Thinking about the witches just made her angry, so she started wondering if she could stand. Other than finding something to eat, all she wanted to do was get even with the witches. With every passing moment, she found another reason to hate the two-faced witches and to want to live.

Suddenly, for reasons that she did not yet understand, more of Professor Pythagoras's nonsense began to enter her head. She could hear him saying, "Any object, living or not, that does not experience the force of another is free to continue the path of least resistance." She realized that if she ever hoped to get revenge on the witches, then she had to get up. She needed to find something to eat before she died in her own self-pity.

Sabrina looked around. "This is a rainforest. Surely, I can find something to eat. If I can just get off my ass, it will not take me long."

As she tried to stand, she quickly realized there was something wrong with her left leg because she could not put any weight on it. She did not remember doing anything to her leg but then thought, *Maybe it happened when I was trying to capture the dragon*. After a few moments, she was able to gain her balance, but she still could not stand on her left leg. The leg was far too sore for her to walk on, let alone try to catch up to her army any time soon.

After realizing that she was not going to be able to walk, Sabrina decided that she had tried enough and fell back to the ground.

As she examined her leg, Sabrina would have cried if she could remember how. It was apparent that someone had deliberately cut a gash in her lower left calf. As she ran her hand down the back of her leg, there was a clean slice on the back of her leather pants just between her knee and ankle. The two-faced witches had gone so far as to treat the wound with something because other than being sore, when she stood, there was no pain or blood.

For almost ten minutes, Sabrina looked at the treated wound and tried to convince herself that the witches had tried to help her. She then tried to convince herself that the treatment would keep her leg from being infected. She had many other wounds that hurt far more than her leg, and she did not understand why the witches had treated just this one wound. She wanted to believe that she had misjudged the two-faced witches, but at this point, she did not know what to believe. She suddenly realized that the two-faced witches had cut her leg and then treated it only to prolong her misery.

Since she could barely stand, and it was clear that she could not walk far, she began to wonder how she was even supposed to gather food for herself. As she thought about what the witches had done to her, she became enraged once again, but there was nothing she could do. As if she did not have enough problems, the two-faced witches had ensured that her death would be long and miserable.

Although she thought she had forgotten how to cry, the tears began to roll down the side of her face. She lost her will to get up and fight, so she lay back down to die slowly. She had not cried since she was five years old when one of the witches had stopped her. One of the two-faced witches had told her, "Only babies cry, not queens."

As her anger grew, it felt good to cry, not that she could have stopped if she wanted. Although she knew she needed to get up and find something to eat, she had all but lost her will to live. The only reason she could think of to continue was that she wanted to make the witches pay for everything they had ever done to her. However, in her current state, she could not see how that would ever happen.

Sabrina felt warm and comfortable beneath the blanket as she began to wake and did not want to move. Suddenly, she realized that this was the same blanket she had used to sneak up on the dragon, but she could not remember whether or not she had the blanket when she fell asleep. She thought that perhaps the two-faced witches had returned to help her. She could not see much from the angle at which she was lying, but she thought she could hear some movement behind her.

She lay motionless so that she would not give away the fact that she was awake. For several minutes, she tried to figure out how she was going to turn over so that she wouldn't lose her element of surprise. She then heard an unfamiliar voice coming from behind her.

The female voice said, "I hope that you are feeling a little better now." After a moment, the voice added, "I was not sure you were ever going to wake up."

Sabrina was not sure how this person knew she was awake because she was sure she had not made a sound. She replied, "I am doing okay. Who are you, and what do you want from me?"

The person acted as if she did not hear her and added, "I watched your efforts to catch the dragon a few days ago. It was clever to use the blankets to hide from the dragon but flat out stupid to take so many people that close to a dragon that did not know you."

Sabrina expected to turn around and see one of her warriors or someone who she at least knew. She assumed the witches sent someone to make sure she died. Instead, she found a young girl she did not recognize dressed in leather armor. After a moment, she smiled and asked, "So what makes you an expert on dragons?"

The girl replied, "I am no master, but I sure as hell know more about dragons than you do."

Sabrina looked at the girl, who was several years younger than she was, and asked, "Child, have you ever seen a dragon?"

The girl laughed and replied, "The only reason I let your people anywhere near him was that he could not fly yet and I did not know how I was going to feed him."

Sabrina smiled again. "How old are you?"

The girl shook her head and said, "Obviously, this dragon does not belong to you, but at least you knew enough not to get yourself killed this time." After a pause, she asked, "Are you hungry, and do you know who that dragon belongs to or why he was so far from where he belonged?"

Sabrina did not know where to start because it seemed as if the girl wanted to know everything all at once, and she did not know how to separate her questions. She decided to start by introducing herself to see if her name had any meaning to the girl. "My name is Sabrina, and you are right—the dragon was not mine. He did belong to my father, who was a great dragon master."

The young girl quickly replied, "My name is Anna. If your father trained this dragon, where he is now, and why were you trying to capture it?" After a moment, she added, "The dragon was well trained, so why then did you not use the commands to get closer to him instead of trying to sneak up on him?"

Sabrina tried to stretch her back and thought, *Now someone ask why I didn't use the commands.*

She shook her head because again, she did not know how to answer so many questions all at once. She tried to break them down. First, she responded, "Yes, my father trained this dragon and his other three, but he is gone now because of me."

Anna stopped for a moment because she had not imagined there could be more than one of these master dragons. Also, there was something familiar about this story that she had heard before that made her want to hear more.

Sabrina continued. "Yes, my father, Lord Haden, has had these dragons for a very long time."

Anna knew the Dark Land would not have any defenses against four master dragons. She knew that an attack by the dragons was the biggest fear her people had, but because Haden had never shown any interest in the Dark Lands, they had felt safe. With Haden dead and his dragons scattered, she knew her people were in great danger. She could not believe what she had gotten herself into and fell to her knees. She cried, "What have I done? I had a chance to bring one of Nedah's dragons back home."

When she got up, she thought to herself, *At least I can rid the world of one of Haden's offspring.*

Anna drew her dagger and tried to convince herself she was doing the right thing. As she approached Sabrina, she said, "Your father damned us all when he killed the dragon master Nedah. Nedah was the only person who could return the magic to the ground." After a moment, she added, "Now, when enough magic has been taken, the world will no longer be able to hold itself together."

Anna was holding the dagger so that Sabrina could see it, but she had never killed anyone. As she hesitated, she told herself, "I don't know if I can do this, but the world demands justice." Gathering her courage, she started charging toward the woman lying on the ground, but to her surprise, Sabrina did not try to stop her.

Anna stood above her with the dagger in her hand, ready to kill her, but she just could not find the courage to do it.

Sabrina started screaming. "What are you waiting for? I am not going to beg for my life if that is what you want!"

From the moment that Anna stopped, Sabrina was certain the girl was not going to follow through with her threats. Without thinking about it, she kicked the girl's legs from beneath her.

As Anna stumbled, she dropped the dagger. The steel blade fell toward the ground and stabbed Sabrina in her side, causing her to scream out.

Sabrina grabbed the dagger and started to pull it out when Anna thumped her on the head and told her "Don't be stupid, you will bleed to death before I can close the wound."

Just the small amount that Sabrina had moved the blade had caused blood to gush out of the wound. With the loss of blood and a weakness from hunger, she did not have the strength to stop Anna from doing anything she wanted to do.

Suddenly, she realized she really did not want to die. However, there was nothing she could do to stop it. As her vision began to fade, she watched the young girl try to remove the dagger and stop her bleeding.

~*~

As she slowly regained consciousness, Sabrina did not know how long she had been out, but at least she was still alive. She ran her hand down her side to where the dagger had pierced her, and although it was sore, the dagger had been removed, and she had been bandaged up. She also noticed that someone had removed her leather armor so that the wounds on her legs could be treated. Even the knot on the back of her head seemed to feel better. When she realized she was not alone, she asked, "Why save me? I will only turn on you the first chance that I get."

Anna smiled and replied, "I am not sure that is true because you are not the person that you thought you were. As Gaho-Meda would say, we are only what the world will let us be."

Sabrina sat up so that she could see the girl who had decided not to kill her. To her surprise, there was a dragon perched on the rocks behind Anna. She realized instantly that the girl was a dragon rider from the Dark Lands, and that was how she knew so much about Haden's dragons.

Sabrina thought for a few moments and then told Anna, "If you will let me do what I need to do, I will help you get the dragon safely back to the Dark Lands."

## CHAPTER 24

# THE SECOND MEETING

Finally, the ground had stopped shaking, and the dust was starting to settle. Likos was bruised and battered, but he felt guilty that he had not been able to protect Angelina. He knew they needed to leave but could also see that this witch needed medical attention. He had talked to the old woman already about Angelina's face. He understood there were other people who were in greater need, but he had to find a way to get Angelina out of this place. While he was waiting for the old woman, he found some water to cool the marks on the young girl's face.

Even though the side of her face was already starting to swell and change color, Angelina insisted it was not that bad, and she was trying to sit up.

When the old woman arrived, Likos watched everything she was doing as tried to figure out how he was going to get this girl out of here.

The old woman waved her bony little hand for him to get out of the way as she started treating the side of Angelina's face. Finally, she told him, "I will look at this. Why don't you go see if the captain of the guard needs some help?"

He was not sure that Angelina was ready to travel, but General Airus had been gone for several minutes now, and like all good generals, he would soon report to his master.

Likos had been pacing back and forth for several minutes as he watched the old woman talk to Angelina. He knew she needed help, but all he could think about was how he was going to get her out of this place before Haden showed up. Finally, he asked, "Is she going to be okay, and how long before she can travel?" Before the old woman could say anything, he muttered, "We cannot stay because she is not safe here."

The old woman looked around and replied, "You are correct, son. We cannot stay here, but we have some time." After a few seconds, she added, "Why don't you relax for a few minutes while I clean this wound, or go see if you can be useful until we are ready to go?"

He believed the old woman was right, but he just wanted to scream, "Haden is coming!" However, the last thing Likos wanted to do was to let Angelina know that the warmonger was so close and that she was right all along. Nonetheless, he believed that they needed to get moving before Haden figured out that she was here.

He reached down to help Angelina up, but the old woman smacked his hand with a stick that happened to be lying next to the young girl.

She looked up at him. "I told you to go make yourself useful. It will not take long, and then we can leave."

Likos quickly pulled his hand back and cursed under his breath. He stood looking at Angelina and the old woman, who now waved the stick at him.

The old woman laid the stick down and turned her attention back to Angelina. As he started to come toward her again, she exclaimed, "Boy, I am not going to tell you again. Go find something else to do!" She added, "We appear to be safe for a few minutes, and as soon as we can, we will leave."

He stopped for a moment and then once again started toward the young witch because they just could not stay any longer.

He was still several cubits away from Angelina when the old woman picked up the stick again and waved it at him.

He stopped just short of being hit because he knew Angelina trusted this woman, and the last thing he needed now was for her to start glowing. Likos could see Bryce Hunter in the distance and, looking down at Angelina, replied, "You are right. I think I see the captain of the guard. I will go see if there is anything that I can do to help him."

Airus could see the few remaining guardsmen were beaten and battered but were starting to pick themselves out of the mess. He was not sure if they had done much to defend the city, but they were clearly caught in the crossfire. He had no doubt the witch was responsible for the flying debris, but almost all the wounded and dead were outside the city walls. He was not sure what that meant, but he was on his way to find Haden. There were pieces of rocks and wood lying all over the city, but most of what was left of the raiding party appeared to be just outside the wall.

By all accounts, the raiding party should have been more than the few dozen guardsmen could handle. He believed that everyone inside and outside the city should have been killed, but instead, a thousand well-trained warriors had been beaten down and defeated.

Because most of the warriors were lying on the ground outside the city wall, Airus suspected that Haden was responsible for saving everyone in the city. Everyone else believed that it was this witch of Hela who was responsible for saving everyone. However, he thought to himself, *She probably was responsible for the flying debris inside the city, but the child was not responsible for the death and destruction outside the wall.*

As Airus walked around the bodies, it was easy to see that they had been sliced or stabbed. He still could not see how one person could have done this much damage even if this one person was Haden.

Haden, or Nedah, did not appear to have any injuries. He was sitting on the ground, although he had found some water to drink.

It had been about twenty minutes since Airus had left the city, and he had just received word that the young witch was up and moving around. It would not be long before Haden was also up on his feet, which meant they would be leaving soon.

Although there were bodies lying all over the place, he knew that some of the raiding party must have escaped, and it would not be long before they returned with more people.

Airus had enough of trying to figure everything out, and he decided it was time to find the old woman. If he could convince her that they needed to leave, then it would not be hard to convince the witch or Haden. As he turned around, to his surprise, the old woman had walked up behind him. He had nearly walked over her before he realized it, but she did not try to move out of his way.

The old woman finally stepped to one side and let the general go past her.

As he stumbled to avoid hurting her, he began to lose his balance and fell to one knee.

Now that he was on one knee, he was much closer to being eye to eye with the little old woman, who was now standing less than a cubit from his face.

She reached up with her bony little fist and once again began knocking on his skull. She told him, "You need to be more careful. You are going to hurt yourself, and then what use are you?" After a few moments, she added, "I think we need a new plan because I am not sure this army of yours can help us."

He nodded his head to let her know he agreed.

She smiled at him and said, "I think that we need to find somewhere else to be before a larger part of your army shows up to see what happened."

As he was getting to his feet, she told him, "Go see how long Angelina and her friend are going to be because we need to leave within the hour."

Airus did not believe the witch trusted him, so he was still not comfortable talking to her. However, he needed to get their supplies, if he could find them, and there was nothing he could do for Haden at the moment. He knew the old woman was not going to leave without the witch and whomever she still had with her. He pulled himself up and once again nodded his head so that the old woman would leave him alone.

~*~

By the time Airus returned to the city, Angelina was up and trying to help the few guardsmen who were still left in the city gathering a few supplies.

Likos and the captain of the guard arrived and began trying to get the young witch to leave, with or without the supplies.

She did not understand why Likos was being so pushy all of a sudden, but she continued to insist, "I am not leaving without—" Angelina could not believe she did not know the old woman's name, so she just added, ". . . without the old woman."

Likos tried to explain. "We do not have time to wait for her," but the truth of the matter was that he wanted to get as far away from her as they could. He had long ago figured out that the old woman and Haden were traveling together, but he did not want Angelina to start panicking.

He grabbed her hand to try to lead her away, but she just did not understand what he was trying to do. The more he tried to get her to leave, the more upset she became, until finally she started screaming.

Likos was not sure if she realized why he was trying to get her out of the city or if she was just starting to get angry with him. Either way, she was starting to glow again, and there was nothing he could do about it.

To make matter worse, a small crowd was starting to form around them.

Although Angelina was clearly getting upset, Bryce and the other guardsmen began to help Likos drag her out of the city before it was too late. They surrounded her and were planning to cover her with blankets so they could carry her out of the city.

Before they could get enough blankets to cover her, the old woman grabbed Bryce by his ear and yanked him back until he went down on one knee.

He quickly demanded that everyone stop what they were doing.

Now that she had everyone's attention, the old woman asked, "What the hell is going on here? Don't you think that this girl is stressed enough?"

Angelina realized that the old woman was right and took a deep breath to see if she could regain some her composure. She took a few more breaths but could feel the energy surging through her.

The old woman let go of the captain and then walked up to Angelina and grabbed her hand. Angelina was starting to calm herself down a bit. However, her moment of calmness was not meant to last because Haden stepped into her sightline.

She trembled as she stared at the warmonger whom she was told she had killed. As her nightmare became reality, she began to glow uncontrollably, and the ground once again began to shake.

Likos and the guardsmen saw Haden coming and moved between Angelina and the warmonger.

Soon hundreds of objects took flight, and the air was filled with so much dust that it was difficult to see anything other than herself and Haden. To make matters worse, the ground was shaking so violently that it was hard for everyone else to stay on their feet.

The old woman stared at the young witch as Likos and the guardsmen continued to try to stand between Angelina and Haden. They were yelling at the warmonger, who just stood there as if he did not see them.

The old woman grabbed the young witch's hand even tighter. "Girl, you have to stop this before you kill us all," she said, but Angelina was far too focused to hear her. When she realized she could not get Angelina's attention, she smacked the young witch.

Angelina quickly looked at the old woman. "I cannot stop. He is going to kill me if I do not try to do something to defend myself."

The old woman softly replied, "Child, this man is not going to hurt you because he does not even know who you are, and he does not have a grudge against you."

Angelina, with tears in her eyes, cried. "I tried to kill him. He is the warmonger Haden."

The old woman smiled. "He is not the man he used to be, but he is still my son although he does not know it."

Suddenly the ground stopped shaking, and everything fell to the ground. Angelina dropped to her knees, grabbed the old woman, and begged her not to let Haden kill her.

~*~

It had been almost an hour since the old woman had stopped Angelina and Nedah from destroying what was left of this city.

Airus had never felt the ground shake as it did an hour ago, but he believed that it had something to do with the witch and the man he once knew as Haden.

Likos managed to find another half a dozen guardsman who were still alive, but their injuries would only slow them down for a while.

He also did not understand where the old woman had found two old mules, but he thought to himself, *At least they are better than nothing*.

Likos and his guardsmen had loaded a makeshift wagon with some supplies which meant they would be leaving the city fairly soon.

Although everyone was starting to gather, Airus knew there was still one thing he needed to do before everyone left.

Just as he had expected, she was still lying on the ground where he had left her hours ago, but he had no doubt that she was awake even if she lay motionlessly. He reached down and started loosening the ropes that bound General Virgo's hands.

When he had removed her bonds, she continued to lay motionless on the ground.

He told her, "I wish that there were more I could do for you. You know you do not belong here, and when we are out of sight, you need to run as far from here as you can."

He had only made it a few cubits away when he heard General Virgo ask, "What are you doing? Come with me."

He did not turn around as he replied, "This is where I belong, and even if it were not, he needs me."

She did not say anything for several moments, but then she asked, "Is this where Haden belongs?"

Although she could not see, he lost all color in his face. He answered, "I know what you think you saw, but Haden is dead," and he walked away. Even though Haden had not entered the city, he was sure she had seen the confrontation.

He turned toward her and said, "My friend, I fear for you, and if I could, I would help get you out of this place."

# CHAPTER 25

# TWO HALVES OF A WHOLE

It had been a week since they had seen anyone from Lord Scorpion's army, but they knew that did not mean they were not being followed. The two-faced witches believed they needed to get the dragon as far away from Utopia as fast as they could before the one who walked in Haden's place came looking for it.

They understood that if the factions of Haden's army were fighting each other, then they would not have time to search for the dragon. They also believed that with so many people pouring into this small kingdom to grab their piece of Haden's empire, no one would notice them leaving.

The dragon was well trained and, once he was chained, was easy to lead. Even if his wing had mended, they would not let the dragon fly without a rider because they had to make sure that the beast would come back to them.

Jeannie could hear her sister's voice in her head, and it was the same as it had been for weeks now. The voice repeated, "Find someone to ride this dragon because if we can control him, we will be queens of more land than we can see in a month."

She snubbed her nose and thought loud enough for her sister to hear, "Who do you think you are? Of course, we need a rider, but first we have to find the right person."

Her sister replied, "You know that the wielding stones demand that we go east to find the rider."

Jeannie again snubbed her nose and asked, "What do we do about this army that keeps deserting?"

Although her sister could not see her, she shook her head and replied, "The fewer people around, the better. We don't need them anyway."

She smiled her nasty grin. "If you understood the value of this dragon, then you understand that we don't have enough people to protect the beast."

Once again, she shook her head. "Just do what you need to do, and I will take care of the dragon."

The witches were so afraid to let anyone be alone with the dragon that one witch always stayed with the dragon while the other made sure the group kept moving.

They believed the dragon could fly, but the beast had already killed half a dozen people who had attempted to get close to him. It was not that they cared how many people the dragon killed, but with each person killed, another hundred people deserted. They knew it was not helping the dragon to be chained all the time, but until the beast accepted a rider, they were afraid that the creature would fly away if given the chance.

In the weeks since they had found the dragon, the beast had eaten a dozen horses and killed a dozen people, and still the witches did not know if he could even fly. Neither of them was brave enough to get any closer to the dragon than they had to, and they did not trust anyone else to ride the dragon. All that they could do was continue traveling east until they could figure out what they were going to do with their prize.

Neither Jeannie nor her sister knew who was in the small camp that was a mere league in front of them, but they had come too far to let a few hundred people stop them now. Even from this distance, the two-faced witches could tell that the group of people was from the east.

She looked at her sister. "It was only matter of time before these Easters started showing up like vultures to claim whatever small piece of Haden's empire that they can get." She waved her hand and replied, "My sister, this small dragon guild is not worth our time. We can just go around them."

The other witch gnashed her teeth. "There will be others and maybe even larger armies."

She looked at the small dragon guild camp in the distance. She then replied, "Yes, I agree, but we are no better off if we turn back now because Lord Scorpion has started to unite the factions of Haden's army."

The other witch suggested, "Why then do we not turn south?"

She smiled. "As always, sister, you know there are opportunities in the south, but you know as well as I do that the stones do not lie." Once more, she looked toward the small camp and added, "What say you to this dragon guild that lies sleeping so helpless in front of us?"

Jeannie smiled, showing the gaps in her teeth. "Yes, my dear, we must feed the dragon."

Even before the words came from the old hag's mouth, her sister knew she meant to unleash this dragon on the camp so that those who followed might not be willing to come so close.

Even without the help of the dragon, this small guild would not have been much of a match for the small army that the two-faced witches now controlled. It took less than an hour for the witches' army to surround the guild and push them into a defensive position in the center of their camp.

The two-faced witches had given clear instructions that they wanted as many people alive as possible.

Several dozen people of the guild had changed into large animals to protect the group so that the rest had time to set up their defenses. It was common for a dragon guild to set up a center defensive posture such as this, and the witches knew it. This posture had been developed so that they could use each other's powers to defend the group.

Most of the guild appeared to be shapeshifters, who charged the attacking army so that the rest of the guild would have time to set up their defensive position. Due to the damage they would receive, an army this small would not normally attack a dragon guild this large.

The witches had never planned to attack the guild directly. Instead, the point was to get the dragon guild to set up a defensive posture so that they could test the dragon.

Xio Ying had ordered that everyone get set up in their defensive positions, but he did not understand why the army was not attacking until he saw the large dragon being led in their direction. Most of his guild had seen dragons before, but none of them had ever seen anything to compare to the creature coming toward them.

With every second that ticked away, he could see the dragon being led closer to them. The ground rumbled with every step the creature took. However, for the moment, Xio needed to try to determine how to save his guild because, once again, his master was nowhere to be found.

He could see that the dragon was being led by two groups who clearly did not know what they were doing. Xio knew that if this dragon had not been so well trained, he would have tossed them long ago. He wished his master was here, but as always, it was up to him to make decisions for the guild.

Xio took a deep breath because it had been many years since he had been so close to such a dragon, and he could not ever remember seeing a dragon this large.

He watched as the dragon kept coming forward, and the rest of his guild took a defensive position with whatever they could find as a weapon.

He looked around and then suddenly demanded that everyone put away his or her weapons.

Most of his guild did not even look back in fear of drawing his attention, but it was going to take more than a few words from a mad man to get them to disarm. Once again, he demanded, "Put your weapons away!" This time, he added, "Dragons like things that are shiny." However, some hesitated until he yelled, "If you do not wish to be killed, put your damn weapons away!"

His screaming was more than enough for most people, who quickly started trying to remove or cover up any metal that could be seen.

By this time, the two groups that were leading the dragons were starting to walk around the guild and blend into the surrounding army.

Suddenly, Yang Hon appeared out of nowhere and ordered everyone to attack the people on the lead ropes because it would confuse the dragon.

Again, the dragon guild hesitated until the old man yelled, "If you want to live, then attack the people leading the dragon!"

The shapeshifters were the first to leap into the well-armored army, but it was not long before the entire guild was attacking the surrounding army.

It only took an instant before the two-faced witches figured out what the dragon guild was trying to do. However, no matter how much they ordered their army to stop, it was too late.

For the first few moments, most people did not realize what was going on until the dragon started attacking the inner circle of the two-faced witches' army. Suddenly, the army was being dragged as the dragon continued to attack everything on his right side.

Within seconds, hundreds of people were scrambling to get out of the way of the giant beast that was now trampling them.

The two-faced witches were screaming, "Do not harm the dragon, or I will tear out your heart with my bare hands!" However, few people cared as the dragon snapped at anyone who showed their shiny weapons.

For several minutes, the dragon's attention was pulled from one shiny object to another until the creature had killed or injured dozens—if not hundreds—of people. Finally, the dragon started to get tangled in the chains being used to lead it.

Even though most people were long out of the area by this time, several people were injured or killed as the beast tried to untangle itself before eventually falling to the ground.

Although once again he had no idea when his master had showed up, Xio suddenly heard Yang yelling at him, "Do not let anyone hurt this dragon because we need him!" As he looked toward the dragon, there were already four or five people gathering around the beast with their weapons drawn.

By this time, the dragon had wrapped the chain around his front legs and could no longer walk freely. The more the dragon tried to untangle himself, the more entangled he became, until the poor creature could no longer turn to watch the area around him.

Xio understood that this was a light dragon, and even if he could not freely move to defend himself, he could still breathe fire. Xio had to be very careful as he approached the dragon to see if he could help it.

He could see that he was not the only person who saw the vulnerability of this creature who had just killed or injured hundreds of people in a matter of minutes. By the time he was close to the dragon, there were already half a dozen warriors ready to strike it down. He knew as soon as they were able to muster enough courage to get close enough to strike the beautiful creature that they would try to kill it. He was not sure they would succeed, but he was certain they could do a lot of damage before the dragon killed them.

Xio tried to position himself between the dragon and the fools who now believed that they needed to exact justice.

As he went past the dragon, he ran his hand as high as he could along the dragon's side so that it knew he was there. As he came around the head of the dragon, he continued to run his hand alongside the creature's massive head, and then he lightly tapped the creature's nose.

The dragon exhaled a large gust of very hot air and then lay down as comfortably as possible.

He did not need his master Yang to tell him that there was going to be a lot of people who wanted this dragon dead.

Now that the dragon knew he was there, Xio was free to draw his long blade to defend the dragon. Most of his guild had fled, as they should have done.

Yang suddenly appeared out of nowhere, but thankfully, the dragon did not appear to notice he was even there and continued to lie on the ground as he had been directed.

Finally, one of the warriors built up the courage to come close enough to strike the dragon. Before he could make his move, however, Yang grabbed him from behind.

Xio hated it when Yang played these games, but somehow, Yang was now holding the long blade Xio was holding just moments ago.

Xio did not have any desire to kill the man, but he could do nothing to stop Yang from stabbing him with the long blade. He could only watch as Yang stabbed two more warriors. Even though he was far older than either one of them, Yang quickly killed them.

The other three warriors had no intentions of waiting for this crazy old man to attack them, so they ran toward him.

Xio knew that Yang had only been able to beat the first three men because he had managed to take them by surprise, but he was not able to do anything to help his master. The three warriors remaining would not be surprised by Yang even if they did not seem to notice where he was. Xio also knew that if he ordered the dragon to attack, it would not be able to tell where Yang was. He thought to himself, *If they want a fight, I'm going to make sure that the dragon has a fighting chance.*

Before he could signal the dragon to get ready to attack, however, the two-faced witches appeared behind the two trailing warriors and stabbed them in the back.

Before the third man could surrender, Yang had appeared once again, carrying the long blade he used to behead the remaining warrior.

Xio watched in horror, but even before the man's body fell to the ground, the blade was once again in his hand.

As the two witches got closer, he raised the long blade. "We will not let you harm this dragon."

The two-faced witches looked at each other, smiled, and replied, "Friend, I think we need to talk."

# CHAPTER 26

# THE GIANT AND THE SPELLCASTER

It had been well over a month since he had taken his forces from his father's training camp. The reports Lord Taron had received just a few hours ago was all the confirmation he needed. He expected it, but now he knew his brother was not going to answer his request for information.

In the last month, the giant had time to regain his composure, but he still had more questions than answers. It had been a long, grueling trip for most of his young army, and he was starting to realize that he had probably pushed them harder than he should have.

Most of his troops had held up well especially during the first few weeks, but now most of them could barely walk or ride. It was obvious that even if he did stop soon, most of his troops would not be of any use in a battle. To make matters worse, they had not packed well, and now their supplies were running very low.

Taron had listened to his generals complain about as much as he could, but he understood he probably needed to set up camp soon. He toyed with the idea of putting the sergeants of arms in charge because they had not made a single comment about needing to stop. He laughed as he thought to himself, *I believe that if I decided to march all the way to Hela right now, they would not question my orders.*

As he looked around, he knew the generals were right. He could see that his army could not go on much longer. Finally, he stopped his horse and ordered, "Prepare to make camp. We are stopping until we can resupply and figure out our location."

Everyone who could hear his voice stopped moving forward so that they could find a place to sit down and rest.

He watched as word quickly spread through the ranks as the four legions began to slow down and stop. Soon people by the hundreds seemed to fall to the ground.

Lord Taron had barely gotten off his horse when the ground began to shake vigorously again just as it had been doing for weeks. He thought, *If the ground always shakes this much, then why in the world does anyone care for this place?* Although the horses could maintain their balance much better than most humans could, they were more likely to be seriously injured if they fell to the ground. Even though he believed the ground would only shake for a little while, Taron stood with both hands on his horse to steady the beast.

As the shaking continued, he thought, *Surely this cannot be normal. I have never known the ground to shake for the entire month.* He began to wonder how far away the shaking could be felt because they had covered a lot of area over the last month.

After ten minutes, when it seemed as if the ground was never going to stop shaking, the vibrations lessened enough that everyone could get back to their feet.

Although they had lost several dozen horses in the last month, it finally seemed that the troops were learning how to keep the horses steady. He smiled because from where he was standing, he could see that not a single horse had fallen.

It had been five days since Lord Taron had stopped his four legions, and the message was starting to spread through the ranks that they were near the Utopia border.

According to the reports he was receiving, Taron believed they were less than half a day's travel from the border of the Kingdom of Utopia. As of yet, none of the scouting parties had seen any sign of the Utopian forces or his brother's legions.

He knew that his brother was extremely devious and that he was probably being watched.

The supplies were starting to arrive, and most of his sergeants were trying to determine how many people they had lost along the way or were tending to their duties.

Although he was tired of waiting, Taron was not going to move any farther until he had a plan. He needed to know what his brother was doing before moving into the kingdom that had taken his father.

His father had taught him that logistics and being able to understand your enemy's reason for their actions were the first steps in defeating any army. As he stood looking into the Kingdom of Utopia, Taron knew that all his brother wanted was power and that he would try to trick him into making a mistake. He thought, *I bet he expects me to get tired of waiting and then charge in at the first chance I get.* After a few moments, he started to shake his head because he knew he was right.

Without a second thought, he grabbed the first person who was not experienced enough to know to stay away from him. He lifted the man off the ground and demanded, "Tell my master of arms to prepare the ranks to start moving at once." He then dropped the man back to the ground where he had found him.

The man quickly got to his feet and scrambled to obey the giant's command. Before he could get very far, however, the giant demanded, "I want to see my generals in my quarters within the hour. Do you understand?"

The man quickly snapped to attention and replied, "Yes, Lord Taron, as you have commanded." Before the giant could say anything else, the man was off to find the sergeants of arms and as many generals as he could on such short notice.

~*~

It had been three days since they had crossed into the Kingdom of Utopia, yet there had been no sign of an army waiting for them.

Sergeant William Minton, the master of arms, had been on many campaigns over the years and knew that this meant one of two things. The first option was that his master, Lord Taron, was wrong about his brother expecting them, which he doubted. The second option was that Lord Scorpion did not want to be seen and was waiting for the right moment to make his move.

Minton understood that it was not his job to make decisions about which way to go or to tell the generals how to lead. His job was to do as he was told, which meant that he needed to make sure the ranks were ready for anything. Lord Taron had told him personally to make sure that the troops were ready to fight.

His master had also told him, "If you run into my brother's forces, do not engage unless you have to defend yourself."

He shook his head. He would have liked to have been able to gather a few extra supplies before they started moving. He then thought, *At least Utopia is a center kingdom, and hopefully, we can find what we need along the way.* He understood it did not matter what any of the generals wanted because he was going to make sure the ranks were ready to fight. Minton pulled the straps of his armor tight and then demanded that everyone make sure their armor was secure. Whatever was waiting for them, he had his orders, and he was going to make sure the formations were ready.

Ever since he was selected as master of arms two years ago, Minton realized there was more to Taron the Destroyer than just his rage and anger, although most people could not see it. He was not sure if this image was the way his master wanted it or if it was just because of his size. There were only a few people in the world whom he trusted, and the giant was among them.

Five days had passed since Minton had been given his orders. He laughed at the generals because they whined and complained about having to wear armor, but he knew not one of them was going to tell him they did not have to do so.

He had his orders and did not care if no one else understood why they had to wear armor and the ranks had to move in this formation. No one had to tell him how to do his job, but he also understood that it would have been much easier if the giant was actually on the lead horse instead of a stick figure. He did not have to know what the giant was planning because he understood what the giant wanted.

Lord Taron had told very few people what he was planning, which left most of them guessing. The most common rumor was that the giant was afraid of magic. Minton could not imagine that this was the case because in the two years he had known the giant, he had never seen him run from anything, including magic. There was also a rumor that Lord Scorpion had struck the giant down with some spell and that they were being led to join his army. Although he did not know what was going on, he did know that his master was not afraid of anyone, especially his brother.

Lord Scorpion had demanded a full report of every move his brother made from the first time he received a message that his brother was coming to Utopia. Now that his brother had been in this area for a while, he had his best scouts tracking his every movement.

Just as he expected, the oversized buffoon had charged in without taking the time to resupply or rest his troops. He knew it was only a matter of time before his brother would have to set up camp again, and from the direction the army was advancing, he believed he could guess the location.

The spellcaster knew this day would come long before his father was killed, but he had not expected his younger brother to be stupid enough to march against him. If he were lucky, it would only be a day or two before he controlled his brother's forces. Lord Scorpion laughed because although his brother did not know it, the big dumb oaf was on his way back to where he belonged.

He thought, *The buffoon will do well controlling the mines and providing recruits for the greatest warmonger this planet has ever seen.*

~*~

A messenger had just arrived and was asking to speak to him about the movement of the giant and his troops. The spellcaster smiled because he knew that his plan was coming together, and he signaled for someone to show the messenger into the center court.

As he waited, he leaned to the side so that he could speak to one of his generals. He whispered, "I want every available warrior ready to go within an hour. It is time that we taught these fools a lesson," and then took another drink.

As soon as his master finished speaking and just before the messenger entered the courtyard, the general and most of the senior staff left to prepare the legions to move.

~*~

The messenger slowly walked in and bowed down about ten cubits from Lord Scorpion. The messenger did as he was taught and continued to bow without looking up until he was given permission to speak.

Several minutes passed before the spellcaster finally acknowledged him with a wave of his hand. He asked, "Tell me, messenger, does my brother lead from the front or the back of his little army?"

Without thinking, the messenger looked up and replied, "My lord, your brother rides at the front of his army but never gets off his horse."

The spellcaster had been waiting for this messenger to make a mistake and had planned his entertainment around the chance that the messenger had not been well trained.

As soon as he realized he had made a mistake, the messenger quickly bowed his head and waited to see if his master had any other questions.

The spellcaster slowly began speaking in a strange language that few in the courtyard knew.

At first, the messenger wondered whether the spellcaster was done with him, so he did not move. He was willing to wait if he needed to because he was instructed not to show Lord Scorpion any disrespect, or he would not be forgiven.

Suddenly, the messenger began to feel a sharp pain in his upper back and lower neck area. After a moment, he realized he could no longer move his head.

Lord Scorpion knew his brother's rage would get the better of him someday, but he never expected his brother's stupidity to provide him with such an army. He thought, *With my brother's fifty thousand new recruits, my army will number well over a hundred and twenty thousand, and then no one will be able to stop me.*

He smiled as he watched a new messenger arrive. The man stopped to ask the captain of the guard for permission to enter the center court. He knew that another messenger so soon could only mean that his brother had made camp and that he did not need to waste his time with listening to this fool.

The new messenger stopped and bowed as he was supposed to, but the spellcaster did not even take the time to acknowledge the man.

As Lord Scorpion prepared to mount his horse so that he could oversee the battle, he suddenly noticed a dozen men charging toward him. One of them was unmistakably Lord Taron.

He thought that if he could get to his horse before his brother could get to him, then he might be able to get away. By the time he mounted, however, the giant had eliminated most of his guards and was standing a few cubits in front of him. He dug his boot spikes into the horse's side, which made the horse rear up on his back legs.

The moment the horse's front legs touched the ground, the giant swung his huge right hand and hit the horse on the left side of its head.

The blow was so hard that it broke the horse's neck instantly, causing the beast to collapse to the ground and pin Lord Scorpion underneath its weight.

The spellcaster was at the mercy of the giant with nothing he could do except hope that his brother did not kill him.

Lord Taron grabbed his brother by the head. "I think that we need to discuss what action has been taken to avenge our father." He tightened his grip on his brother's head and added, "If you make any effort to cast a spell on me, I will kill you where you stand. Do you understand?"

Lord Scorpion was able to signal he understood the threat. As his brother lifted the horse that had pinned him, he thought, *You have the upper hand for now, brother, but my day will come.*

## CHAPTER 27

# THE WITCH AND THE WARMONGER

Although it had been days since they had started moving away from her home, Angelina was still dragging her feet in the hopes that they would turn around and go back to Hela.

Everyone was thankful Angelina had been able to protect them from the raiding party, but they were also glad that the old woman had convinced her that it was not safe to stay in Hela.

Angelina tried not to think about the last few days, but she still did not understand what happened during the battle with the raiders. If she thought that people feared her before, that was nothing compared to the way they acted around her now.

They would not even talk around her, and if she tried to talk to them, she had to keep them from trying to bow down to her.

She wanted to help the old woman look after the twenty or so injured guardsmen, but she did not know what her friend was doing.

Ever since they left the remains of Hela, she had watched the warmonger Haden and his general walking parallel to the rest of the group. She was not sure whether he was setting them up or whether it was as the old woman said, and he just did not feel comfortable around other people.

When she was not treating the wounded, the old woman spent most of her time with Nedah, as she called him.

The old woman had tried to convince Angelina that the man was no danger to her or anyone else in the group, but she would feel better if he was not so close.

She knew that Likos, more than all the others, did not like having Nedah so close and was rarely more than a dozen cubits from her. She knew so little about the young man who claimed to be her protector and had no idea where she would be if he had not been there for her.

Although she had not seen him sleep since they left Hela, Likos had finally found a quiet place to lie down for a while. She knew she needed to get some rest while she could, but she also knew the nightmares would return if she made any effort to sleep. She wanted to get up and take a walk to see if she could clear her head, but she knew that if she started moving around, she would wake Likos.

Angelina knew she was dreaming and tried to wake herself up, but it was just a matter of time before Haden's monster landed as it always did.

The warmonger stood alone at the edge of the forest. She could hear him although he never said a word to anyone other than his general and the old woman.

As her dream unfolded, fear once again consumed her, and she froze, unable to make herself run as she wanted to do.

As she watched in horror, Lord Haden summoned a dragon, and she knew she was not going to live.

Unexpectedly, Lord Haden began to speak again. "Angelina, you need not fear this dragon, for it cannot harm you." She believed she was still dreaming, she but could not figure out why no one else could hear him.

As Lord Haden continued to speak, she became more confused, and she was not certain whether she was still dreaming or whether this was really happening. To make matters worse, she could not remember if Haden had ever spoken to her before in her dreams. She tried to focus on the warmonger, but she soon realized there was something on the other side of him.

As she leaned to see what was on the other side of the warmonger, she lost track of what he was saying until she heard someone say, "Dragon." She gasped as the image of the dragon came into focus. She took another shaky breath as she started to realize that the monster did not appear to be as large as she remembered.

By this time, she truly did not know whether she was dreaming or not when the sky suddenly went dark. As she looked up, she realized the monster had grown many times its size and was just a hundred cubits above her head.

She tried to scream for help, but before she could make a sound, she awoke to find the old woman holding her hand.

In a soft voice, the old woman asked, "My child, are you okay? Is this why you don't sleep?"

The young witch shook her head and replied, "We need to go somewhere else. Likos has enough to worry about without having to deal with my dumb dreams."

The little old woman smiled. "He will not wake up for another hour at least, if I know anything about medicine."

Angelina stared at the young man sleeping and was glad to see he was finally getting some rest.

As she started to get up, the old woman told her, "Child, you still need to get some rest. Nedah will want to start moving again in a few hours."

Angelina looked down, but she had had enough of the nightmares for now. She looked at the old woman and replied, "I will be fine, but first I need to clear my head."

The old woman asked, "Do you want to talk about the dreams, or is there anything else I can do for you, my child?"

The young witch shook her head and replied, "No. I just need some time before we start moving again."

The old woman looked at the young woman for a few moments and then continued to see if there was anything she could do for the wounded.

~*~

Angelina did not want to leave the safety of the group, so she sat on a rock where she could look back at the camp. She began wondering how she had ever gotten herself into this mess. Many times, her teachers had told her that if she did not learn to use her power, she would find herself lost and without hope. Now she was lost, and to make matters worse, she knew what the warmonger had planned for her. She could not help but wonder how they had known that this was going to happen. She wondered if she would ever learn to use her power.

As she sat on the stone, she asked, "Can I make one rock do as I command, or will I bring every rock in this forest down on me?" No matter how much she wanted to try, she just could not find the courage to say the words. Finally, she decided she would leave the rocks for another day. She then turned her attention to her dreams to see if she could make any sense of them.

As she sat there trying to figure out what she was going to do about her nightmares, she heard a voice behind her. When she turned, she quickly recognized the large figure of the warmonger Haden.

Once again, she could not remember whether she was sleeping or if this time, he had come to take her power. She fell to the ground, gasping for what she believed was her last breath of air.

Suddenly, she remembered the rocks and gave the command. "Come to me, I need your help." Almost immediately, every rock and piece of wood within a hundred cubits began racing toward the young witch.

Haden stepped forward and towered over Angelina as she waited for the rocks and loose pieces of wood to start raining down on both of them.

When nothing happened, she knew she had failed. She closed her eyes to wait for her inevitable death at the hands of this warmonger. After a few seconds, she realized she was not dead, and as far as she could tell, her power was not being drained. She slowly opened her eyes to see why Haden had not killed her and to see if the rocks had come to save her.

At first, all she could see was Haden standing over her. Within seconds, she realized there were hundreds of rocks stopped midair.

Even more amazing was that the warmonger stood with his right hand extended to help her to her feet.

She could only stare in astonishment as the rocks seemed to be stopped in time and the man, she feared more than anything stood motionless with his hand extended. Her shock intensified when Haden said, "I am not going to hurt you."

Likos could not figure out how Angelina was able to leave the camp without waking him up, but he could only guess that Haden had cast some kind of spell on him to make him sleep. He had already spoken to the captain of the guard, and he had agreed to leave two guards with her at all times.

He was glad the young witch was unharmed, but he was not going to let Haden get anywhere near her again. Now he was looking for the old woman to find out what she was going to do about the warmonger. He was determined to figure out why and how had Haden been allowed to get so close to Angelina in the first place.

After a few minutes, Likos found the old woman, who was trying to bandage up a young guardsman.

He wished the old woman would take Haden and leave the group even if she did know a little about medicine. He knew if Haden left, everything would be much easier. Even after her encounter with the warmonger though, Angelina would not leave without the old woman. Likos wanted to convince the old woman to leave, but she seemed content to stay.

He did not understand what power this little old woman had over people or why they did not stand up to her.

She had those who could walk out gathering wood and those who could not walk helping to take care of the ones who had not yet awoken. Although there was a captain of the guard, a general, and possibly the most powerful warmonger of all time in their group, the old woman was clearly in charge.

She did not turn around as he walked up behind her. She was bent over one of the guardsmen who had somehow stabbed himself with his blade. Before Likos could say anything, she said, "Come here, boy, I need your help. This fool will not sit still so that I can remove his blade."

He was certain she could not possibly know he was behind her, so he looked around to see if there was anyone else that the old woman might be talking to.

Without turning, she continued. "Don't just stand there, Likos, I need your help." After a few seconds, she added, "I think that is what Angelina called you. I need your help if I am going to treat this fool."

Likos could see that the guardsman had stabbed himself in the leg, and although there were two other people trying to hold him down, the old woman was still having trouble removing the blade.

She was busy going through the bits and pieces of what she called her medical kit and never looked up as she told him to sit on the guardsman's leg.

He stood there for a few moments because he could not see how sitting on an injured leg was going to help.

The old woman again said, "Sit down, boy. He is not going to bite you from that end." After he sat on the guardsman's leg, she handed him a couple of clean rags and instructed, "Hold this. When I pull the blade out, you will need to apply pressure above the wound."

Before he could ask if she thought that was a good idea, the old woman pulled the blade out of the man's leg. Almost immediately, the blood started gushing from the wound.

Likos was surprised by the amount of blood and watched in fascination until the old woman smacked him on the top of the head. She scolded, "I told you to apply pressure when I removed the blade." He quickly leaned forward and grabbed the upper part of the man's leg, which slowed the flow of blood from the open wound.

As the old woman worked to clean the wound, she told him, "Put your weight into it and do not let him move his leg."

Without a moment of hesitation, Likos did as he was told this time, and to his surprise, the flow of blood nearly stopped except for a small trickle.

The old woman suddenly produced a red-hot knife, which she used to seal the man's wound.

After a few minutes, the old woman finished working on the man's leg and told everyone, "I think that this fool will live. You can let him go now." As she was cleaning up, she turned and asked Likos, "Why were you looking for me?"

He had wanted to ask if she would take the warmonger she cared so much about and leave. Now he was not so sure about what he wanted, so he replied, "It can wait until another time."

As he started walking away, he thought, *I must find something to do because I just can't think right now.* He remembered that he had promised to help gather supplies if the guardsmen would keep an eye on Angelina. He found his bow and headed into the forest to see if he could find a deer or some other type of meat for Angelina and the guardsmen.

Likos had been tracking a small herd of deer for over an hour, and he still had not been able to get close enough to get a clear shot. Somehow, every time he got close enough to take a shot, something would scare them away. He was certain he was not doing anything to scare them, but according to the smaller wildlife, he was not alone in the forest. After the second time the deer were spooked, he decided to find a place where he could get a better view of the area. It was not long before he found a spot where he could see a hundred cubits in almost every direction.

In a few minutes, he saw the large familiar figure of Haden. Why was the warmonger so far away from the camp, and why did he seemed to be constantly looking toward the sky? As he raised his bow, Likos thought to himself, *With one well-placed arrow, I could solve all my problems in a matter of seconds.*

Before he could release the arrow, he noticed a small animal run past him. He turned his bow just in time to shoot a man who was about to stab him. He tried to grab another arrow, but another man broke the bow with the swing of a sword. Likos kicked the man in his right knee so that he could escape. He had only managed to pull away a few cubits when, out of nowhere, Haden stepped in front of him.

With a single kick, Haden buckled the man's knees and quickly took his weapon. It only took a few moments for the warmonger to defeat two more men.

Soon, all attention focused on Haden, who was standing in the middle of a group of armed men with another person in his grip.

Likos grabbed a sword and began to engage the closest person he could find, but it quickly became apparent that the man was better skilled with a blade than he was. He was able to defend himself for several minutes until his opponent knocked the sword from his hand.

The man was about to kill Likos when he suddenly fell to the ground, stabbed by the warmonger.

The young man quickly got back to his feet, but the fight was over, and the scouting party had been defeated.

Haden took a deep breath, as though he had just finished a light workout, and said, "We need to return to the camp. We cannot stay here any longer."

Likos did not understand why this man would kill his people just to save him, but as he looked around, he had to agree they could not stay.

## CHAPTER 28

# RISE OF THE DRAGON MASTER

It had been thirty-six hours since the old man who talked to himself had taken control of their dragon and army. All that either of the two-faced witches had thought about for the last few weeks was that they needed to find some place safe for their dragon. They were not sure this crazy old man had enough forces to protect and care for the creature, but the wielding stones continued to indicate that he could. To make matters worse, the old witches were having visions of the one that walked in Haden's place. This man was who they feared above all else, yet they needed his blood for their stones to help them.

Most of their forces had deserted when they found the dragon, and now that the beast had killed another hundred or so, they were down to just over ten thousand people.

Ying Xio had taken control of all operations in the short time that the two-faced witches had known him. He clearly knew more about dragons than they did, and people listened to him, which was more than they could say when they were in charge. If the old women wanted him to do something, they only had to say that Yang wanted it done, and he would see that the task was completed.

~*~

The witches needed answers and had been looking for Xio to determine his plans. They finally found him with the dragon, but they were not willing to go near the beast. They decided to wait for him just beyond the reach of the dragon.

As Xio finally began to walk toward her, the old witch quickly pulled her thoughts together. Her sister had left her with instruction to make this man happy. She started walking toward him with the food she had taken from the captain of the guard. Crazy or not, he was their best hope of using the dragon to build their empire. All they had to do was keep him happy while they let him believe he was in control.

As Xio came closer, the old witch asked, "My dear, are you hungry? I have made some food for you." She handed him the food as she added, "I hope that you like it."

He could not remember the last time someone had brought him food, so he took it without hesitation and asked, "Where is your sister?"

She did not want to explain her sister's actions, but she smiled so that she would not have to tell him this. She replied, "My sister is with Master Yang. He is very demanding, as you know."

As they started walking toward the tent, she asked, "How soon before we can start east again?"

He smiled. "What is your hurry? We have a dragon, and we can do anything we want."

She hesitated for a moment. "My dear, I am afraid that we don't have enough people to defend this dragon." When her words did not seem to affect him, she added, "With all the deserters out there, it is only a matter of time before Lord Scorpion starts looking for the dragon."

He stopped and looked at the old witch. "We cannot go east because the warmongers are heading toward us. Truthfully, Lord Ojak is probably only a few days from here."

She did not know who Lord Ojak was, so she just stared at the old man, waiting for him to continue.

Xio explained, "He is a powerful warmonger who has an army fifty thousand strong and two dozen hatchlings. Lord Ojak would like nothing more than to get his hands on this dragon so that he could use it to train those hatchlings."

The witch hesitated before she replied. "We have to go east because the one who walks in Haden's place is gaining power, and he is coming for all of us."

He did not have any idea what the witch was talking about, but he certainly was not going back east. He repeated, "Lord Ojak would like nothing more than to get his hands on this dragon so that he could use it to train his two dozen hatchlings." After a few moments, he added, "I am not sure that it would be safe for us to go in any direction because every warmonger out there wants a piece of Haden's empire."

She did not need the wielding stones to know he was correct, and with so many unknowns, it was hard for her and her sister to foresee the future. Even with all of this, she could not stop thinking about the one who walked in Haden's place.

Suddenly, Xio thoughtfully repeated the same thing he had said several times already. "Lord Ojak would like nothing more than to get his hands on this dragon." As he spoke, he realized the weakness in Lord Ojak's army. He looked at the old witch. "I think that I have an idea that will give us an army." He smiled and added, "If I am right, it will allow us to get more dragons, but first I need to find Yang."

The witch looked at him for a few moments, but she did not trust anyone other than her sister. She believed the man who talked to an imaginary master was truly crazy, but he controlled their dragon and army.

When Xio looked up, Yang and the other two-faced witch was coming toward them. Even from this distance, he could see that Yang was smiling. His master's appearance could only mean one thing—he had already read his mind and knew what he planned to do with the dragon.

It had been more years than he cared to remember since he had been on the back of a dragon, and even then, he had never ridden one so large or well trained. As he sat on the back of the massive creature, he could not help but wonder, if Haden had three other dragons as large as this one, then what kept him from ruling the world?

It had been so many years since he had trained with the great dragon master Nedah that Xio was not even sure he would remember where to sit.

His worries were short-lived because as soon as the creature started to move forward, memories of his youth came rushing back to him. He leaned forward, bent his knees, and planted his feet so that he could shift his weight.

There was something about the beautiful creature that reminded him of the dragon he once rode for Nedah. As the creature began to gain momentum, the old man could not help himself and yelled, "Higher, Eostre!" He pulled the reins to guide the dragon higher.

As he rose above the landscape, he looked back to see if his master was still watching. He thought, *At least Yang cannot play his stupid games if I am on the back of a dragon.* It was a freedom he had long forgotten, and if he had any place else to go, he would have left the death stalker and his dragon guild far behind.

Now two hundred cubits off the ground, he looked back and saw the forces the two witches were preparing for the other phase of the operation.

Xio had found exactly what he was looking for, but he had to wait until the witches moved their army into position.

Lord Ojak was not making any effort to hide his forces, and it did not take long for the witches to find the warmonger's camp.

As he circled high above, Xio could see that the young hatchlings sensed that the great dragon was near. He could not believe Lord Ojak's people knew so little about dragons that no one in the camp thought to look up.

He expected that the large tent near the dragon yard was that of Lord Ojak's, because he knew the warmonger would not be far from his hatchlings. Xio knew it would be easy to land anywhere he wanted.

As the witches moved their forces into place, he assumed Yang was directing them to defendable positions.

As he watched, both sides adjusted their troops for the pending battle, unaware of the great dragon. He wanted to take the dragon and his rediscovered freedom to anywhere else, but he knew the witches and his forces would be crushed if he did not do as he originally planned.

He circled the area a few times just to see if anyone noticed him flying above. After a few minutes though, it was clear that no one was watching the skies. He turned the dragon toward the center of the dragon yard.

Most of the camp was moving west as was to be expected, which left few people in the dragon yards. Most of the young hatchlings were already starting to come toward his dragon long before he was anywhere near the ground.

He landed the dragon in the middle of the yard and waited for the rest of the hatchlings to notice him. As soon as he was sure they all had seen him, he returned to the air, followed by the two dozen hatchlings.

Thirty seconds later, the dragon master and the two dozen hatchlings landed again, but Xio now had control of all the dragons, and if he attacked, then the two dozen hatchlings would also attack.

Even if Lord Ojak had ordered his forces to attack, most of them knew what the small dragons could do, and no one wanted to confront the large dragon.

The dragon master quickly demanded, "Lay down your weapons, or I will start killing people by the hundreds, and there is nothing you can do to stop me."

The guild leader was known for his brutality, and no one wanted to provoke him. Despite Lord Ojak demanding that they stand fast, everyone within the sound of Xio's voice dropped their weapons and bowed down before the dragon master.

Seconds later, the warmonger was shoved into the open. He responded, "I am here, and I am at your mercy." He then fell to one knee and waited to see what the dragon master demanded of him.

The old man dismounted and started walking toward the warmonger so that everyone could see that he was now in charge of everything that had once belonged to this man.

Lord Ojak knew that if he wanted to live, then he had to submit to the leader of the dragon guild. He was familiar with the protocol of surrender and waited on one knee, ready to pledge his loyalty to his new master until he could once again turn the tables.

As Xio stepped forward to relieve the warmonger of his command, Yang once again appeared out of nowhere. As the warmonger began to rise, Yang grabbed him and drove his dagger deep into the side of the helpless man even though they already controlled his dragons and a huge army.

Lord Ojak did not take his eyes off Xio until the dagger was removed, when he fell helpless to the ground and died.

Xio did not understand how Yang, who knew nothing about dragons, could stand in the middle of so many, and yet they did not seem to notice he was there. The old man thought to himself, *Dragons are not supposed to be affected by magic, but Yang's power must be so great that he can fool even them.*

Lord Ojak, as did most warmongers of the time, ruled with an iron fist. When he was defeated, few people questioned their new master's authority. Xio still did not understand why his master saw the need to murder the warmonger in front of everyone, but he thought to himself, *Maybe it was a message for me.* It had been at least fifty years since he had come under the control of Yang, but he had never known him to be so violent or unpredictable.

Xio hated the fact that the bastard could manipulate and control his very thoughts. He could not help but wonder if it was the tainted magic his master stole from his victims that made him that way.

He had not seen his master since he had taken control of the army, but he assumed he was with the witches.

He had never overseen so many and did not understand what it took to keep an army so large functioning, let alone determine what to do next. He had no interest in leading the army, but someone had to because Yang would not.

Xio had spent the better part of the last two hours listening to his generals. Although some of the things they said made sense, he did not care about most of the information as he would have preferred to be with the witches.

~*~

Xio now knew more about the hierarchy and structure of the army than he ever wanted. Although he was sure his new generals did not like it, he appointed only those he knew to positions of power and influence.

Soon he asked about the care of the dragons. It took several minutes before a skinny man in poor health was brought before his counsel.

The man was dressed in leather although it looked as though it had been many cycles since he had taken them off.

Xio asked, "Dragon keep, what is your name, and where did you learn about dragons?"

The old man lowered his head as he had been taught to do. He then replied, "My mother used to call me Ciqala, and she was once a dragon rider for the warmonger Haden." After a few moments and almost as a second thought, he added, "I am afraid that I do not know a lot about dragons. My knowledge of these creatures is just enough to keep them from killing me and to call them back when their work is complete."

The dragon master was amazed at how little these people knew about these powerful creatures. They did not have riders and had one trainer, if that is what you want to call him, and they had lost hundreds of warriors just trying to keep them fed. He stood up and told the man, "Come here. I wish to discuss training the young hatchlings so that they may carry riders."

The man lowered his head and replied, "Lord, I cannot come any closer," and after a few moments, he displayed the tether that kept him from coming any closer. He then added, "Lord Ojak believed that I would run if I ever had the chance."

~*~

It had been an hour since Xio had dismissed his senior counsel and the dragon keep. He was glad to see that the two witches had finished their inspection because there was much, he wanted to discuss with them.

He welcomed the witches back and asked, "How did your inspection go, and are they ready to fight for us?"

Both witches spoke as one person and replied, "Yes, my lord. They are a fine army and will serve us well."

He then asked, "What should we do with this army now? Have either of you seen Master Yang since we took the dragons?"

The two witches looked at each other, and then the witch on his left side replied, "Lord Xio, we do not need Yang."

The other witch snared her nose and added, "You, my lord, are the dragon master."

He pushed them away. "Yang hears everything, and he will kill you just to make me suffer if it pleases him." He looked around, but there was no sign that his master was near.

Both witches then asked, "What do you think that your master will want to do with this army and all the beautiful dragons that we now control?"

The old man leaned his head back as though he was thinking. "I believe that my master would like Haden's other master dragons."

Both witches squealed and demanded, "What about the one who walks in Haden's place?"

One of the witches started to speak when her sister interrupted, "Don't mention the bastard's name."

The first witch stepped back, paused, and then continued. "The one who walks in Haden's place will also being looking for those dragons, my lord."

He then began to think to himself that his master would not run from anyone, and when he looked up, Yang was standing just ten cubits away.

He could hear his master demanding, "Ask the witches about the one who walks in Haden's place and why they are so afraid of him."

He did not understand why he needed to ask the witches when they could hear as well as he could, but he knew better than to question his master. He turned to ask the witches, but they were gone. He thought to himself, *I will ask them later, but I need to prepare the forces for this person who wants my master's dragons.*

# CHAPTER 29

# THE DRAGON PURSUIT

Although it had only been a week since she had been stabbed, it had been days since the wound had bled enough to worry her. Sabrina still did not understand why this girl from the Dark Lands had not killed her when she had the chance or why she helped treat her wounds.

She knew Anna could have killed her at any time but believed she must want something from her. However, she could not figure out what it was.

Once again, she was pretending to be sleeping so that she could see what Anna was doing or planning.

As she always did, Anna left the dragon to himself about fifty cubits from the campsite.

Sabrina did not know whether this was to keep her from getting too close to the dragon or whether it was to keep the dragon from getting too close to her. Either way, even from this distance, she could tell that the monster had caught some kind of large animal. She watched as the girl dismounted and then ran her hand down the side of the beast until she stood directly in front of it.

Anna used her dagger to cut off a piece of the animal the dragon was tearing apart. As the dragon lay down to finish his meal, she turned and started walking toward the campsite with the piece of meat in one hand and her dagger in the other hand.

Sabrina did not know why she cared if the girl knew whether she was awake or not, but for some reason, she closed her eyes as if she had been sleeping for hours.

Anna walked past Sabrina and then started treating the piece of meat with some spice she kept in a small bag. After a few moments, she announced, "It is time that you start getting up and moving around because I will need to leave soon."

Sabrina did believe she was ready to get up because she had not tried to move much, let alone stand up. As she sat up, she replied, "You know that I am not going to eat that because your monster had it in its mouth, right?"

The young dragon rider did not understand if the warmonger's daughter was just trying to be funny or if she did not eat meat. She looked back at her for a few seconds and then continued preparing the meat.

By the time the meat started to cook, Sabrina had made it to her feet and was standing on her own.

Anna was still roasting the meat, and as far Sabrina could tell, she was not going to come help her.

Although she was slow and very sore, the more she moved around, the easier it became.

Soon she was standing near the fire, watching Anna. She asked, "Are you really going to eat that?" When Anna did not answer, she asked, "Aren't you afraid of disease?"

Anna looked up and replied, "Paytah would not eat it if there were something wrong with it."

Sabrina did not understand how this girl could pull the meat from a dragon's mouth and expect her to eat it.

~*~

It was unusual for Anna to not be talking about something, but it had been hours since Sabrina had heard her say anything.

Suddenly, the young girl stood up in front of her. She was talking so fast about so many things that Sabrina did not know where to start untangling what Anna was saying. The only thing she understood was that Anna had something she needed to do. After a few moments, Sabrina interjected, "I am getting better every day. Can I go with you?"

Anna shook her head. "I need to take the dragon home. It cannot stay here." After taking a deep breath, she added, "It is my fault that he is still here, and this is not where he belongs."

Although she did not understand why Anna cared so much about whether or not the dragon stayed, Sabrina was finally starting to figure out why she was so upset. It occurred to her that she might not know that there were three other dragons. After listening to the young girl for several minutes, she finally interrupted, "Anna, there are four dragons in total like the one you saw."

Anna could not believe that Nedah's four master dragons could be returned to the Dark Lands. She demanded, "Tell me how to find these dragons, or I will kill you where you stand."

Sabrina wanted to tell her how to find her father's dragons, but she did not even know where she was, let alone have any way of knowing where to find them. Although she believed she was well enough to defend herself, she had no reason to hurt Anna, so she tried to get her to calm down. When she could not, she shook her head and replied, "I don't know where these dragons are, but I will help you find them."

Anna stepped back because for some reason, she believed Sabrina when she said she did not know where to find the dragons. After a few moments, she replied, "I don't know if you are healthy enough to help."

Sabrina did not say anything for almost a minute but then added, "I don't have anywhere else to go."

It had been hours since Anna had agreed to take her to find her father's dragons, but it was just starting to sink in what that entailed.

Her father had taught her at an early age how to overcome her fear, but Sabrina was not sure she was willing to deal with a dragon again so soon. The last time she was this close to a dragon, she had one of the worst beatings of her life and was then betrayed. The old witches had left her to die, but she could only hope it would be different this time.

Anna had told her how to approach the dragon. She explained, "When you get close to Paytah, you need to make sure that he knows that you are there."

Sabrina could remember she had also said something about how dragons do not like to be surprised but could not remember her exact words.

During most of the conversation, she was more concerned with what the dragon was doing, and she only partially listened to Anna. By the time, she realized what the young girl was telling her, they were halfway to the dragon. She stopped moving forward and asked, "Are you sure? I would think it would be better if he did not know that I was near."

Anna smiled and replied, "You cannot sneak up on dragons because they see all living thing, but they struggle to see variations. We believe that they only see changes in temperature, if that makes any sense, and this makes it hard for them to see differences in people." She smiled again and added, "This is why you cannot sneak up on a dragon."

Sabrina looked at the young girl for a few seconds before she asked, "So I need to get his attention without surprising him so that he does not try to kill me? Sounds easy enough."

The young dragon rider smiled again. "Paytah already knows we are here. Dragons have great eyesight; it is just different from ours. All you need to do is talk to him like a friend."

Sabrina tried to remember if she had ever had a friend other than the two-faced witch, or witches, but could not think of anyone. She already knew she was committed to approaching the dragon, and her fears no longer mattered. However, she still did not know what she was supposed to say or what Anna was planning on doing when they got to Paytah.

They were within about twenty cubits when Anna turned around and said, "See how he keeps his legs in front of him?"

Sabrina looked up but did not understand why this was important.

Anna continued. "It is because he anticipates that we will use his legs to help get up on his back."

Sabrina almost stopped because surely, Anna did not expect her to ride this monster so soon. She had always had a fear of heights although it had never stopped her when she wanted to go to the top of the palace towers to spy on people.

Anna then told her, "Just before you make contact, speak to him and then run your hand along the side of his head before you attempt to mount him."

As she got closer, Anna put out her hand and ran it along the dragon's head as she said, "Good boy, Paytah. I need you to be nice to Sabrina." Then she swiftly moved past the dragon's head and, in a single motion, stepped on his massive foreleg, swung herself up, and seated herself low on the back of the creature. After a few moments, she waved her hand and told Sabrina, "Come on, he will not wait forever."

Before she had time to talk herself out of this, Sabrina took a deep breath and put out her arm the same way as she had seen Anna do before starting toward Paytah. The scales on the side of the monster's head felt as if they were made of highly polished glass. As she went past him, she managed to say, "Hello."

When she reached the base of the dragon's foreleg, she suddenly realized she might not be strong enough to make it onto the dragon's back as Anna had done just moments before. At this point though, it did not matter if she was strong enough because she was already committed to trying, so she stepped forward and started looking for something to grab. To her surprise, Anna extended her hand and was waiting for her when she made the leap.

Anna grabbed her and, with all her strength, pulled her across the lower part of the neck of the dragon, just in front of where she was sitting.

Anna told her, "Lean forward, bend your knees, and find a place to plant your feet."

As she did as she was told, Anna lay against her back and grabbed the harness just in front of her.

Sabrina was not used to being this close to anyone, but when the dragon took to the air, nothing else mattered except finding a way to hang on.

Within a few seconds, the dragon was a dozen cubits above the tree line and was getting higher with every passing second.

Sabrina suddenly remembered she needed to breathe if she did not want to pass out. Once she was breathing normally again, she realized that although the dragon was wider than the horse she had ridden not long ago, she was more comfortable.

~*~

It had been four days since they had left their camp to look for the dragons, and still Sabrina held on so tight that she would lose the color in her hands. Although she did not want to say anything, she did not believe the two-faced witches would stay in the area with so many of her father's warriors nearby.

They had circled the small city below, and as far as Sabrina could tell, it had been nearly destroyed. However, she was sure Anna would want to look to look through the rubble.

Sabrina was not sure what Anna hope to find in this mess, but she was just glad to move her hands again and stretch her legs.

As Anna picked through some of the debris, she became convinced that a dragon had been here. However, Sabrina was starting to believe that young girl did not know what she was doing because she did not see any signs of a dragon.

It was true that something had destroyed the entire city, and maybe it was one of her father's dragons, but she did not understand how that information was going to help them. She did not like being so close to any city because, after all, she was the daughter of the person responsible for all the damage. Sabrina wondered why they did not just search from the air because something as big as a dragon could not just hide behind a rock.

The walls around the city had been breached, and most of the city had been burnt to the ground. Although Anna was sure a dragon had been there, she insisted the damage was not caused by a dragon.

Once again, Sabrina did not understand why Anna believed a dragon had been here if she did not believe the dragon had caused all the damage. What else could have destroyed the city? The strangest part she did not understand was on the outside of the wall, where something had killed hundreds of people from her father's army, yet there were no other bodies.

Anna explained that the deaths were not caused by a dragon because dragons do not kill like this, but she could not explain why there were no other bodies.

When they came to one spot just on the outside of the wall, Anna seemed a bit confused as she looked through the rubble. She explained, "Most of the fighting took place here although the debris came from inside the city." After a few moments, she added, "A very powerful master of magic—no, two powerful masters of magic did this."

When Sabrina looked at the same ground, she did not see any of the normal bending of the ground or burning of the vegetation that would indicate the use of magic. All she saw were large cracks in the dirt and piles of debris.

Anna then pointed to an area just fifteen cubits from where they were standing. "A great dragon stood here, and she was looking for something." She ran her hand across the air as though she was counting something. She shook her head as she continued. "The dragon was looking for the man who stood here and caused the ground to crack." Suddenly, as though some great truth was revealed to her, she turned to Sabrina. "Yes, that is it. We have to go—now."

Anna called her dragon. Within seconds, Paytah swooped down from the sky. As soon as the dragon came closer to the ground, Anna was running toward the creature. By the time Sabrina was able to get to the dragon, Anna was already mounted and was extending out her hand to help.

As they took to the air once again, Sabrina was sure the creature was somehow trying harder as though it knew something she did not.

~*~

For the last four hours, they had jumped from one site to another, and each time, Anna was sure they had just missed the dragon. Sabrina did not understand how she could determine this because she could not see any evidence that a dragon had been anywhere near these locations.

As Anna looked round, Sabrina took the opportunity to get something to drink. She knew that once this girl found what she was looking for, they would be off in search of the next spot.

As she finished her water and waited for Anna to finish sifting through the dirt and grass, she realized she was standing next to the dragon. She could not remember whether she had been this close to Paytah without Anna, so she put her hand on his side. She was sure the creature could not feel her hand through the thick scales, but at the same time, he seemed as though it liked her touch.

After a few minutes, Anna came running back toward the dragon once again.

She started yelling, "I am sorry, but we have to go. We cannot be far from this dragon, but I don't think it is the same dragon that tossed you around." She jumped on top of the dragon and signaled for Sabrina to hurry up.

By now, Sabrina knew the routine and ran as fast as she could with her bad leg and jumped on the dragon next to Anna.

Moments later, the dragon took to the air, and they were off to the next place so that Anna could sift through the dirt again in search of this dragon.

# CHAPTER 30

# THE DAY OF NIGHTMARES

Although he would surely have been captured or killed if Haden had not shown up when he did, Likos still did not like him being so close to Angelina. To make matters worse, the warmonger would not listen to anyone. He decided he was going to go in whatever direction he wanted.

Just an hour ago, he had talked with the warmonger's general, and they agreed to continue north, but now, for some reason, Haden was determined he was going to head south again.

He had tried to talk to Angelina, but he did not even know why he bothered. Regardless of what everyone else thought, he knew the old woman was in charge, and she did whatever Haden wanted. The only reason he cared was that Angelina did whatever the old woman wanted, and everyone else did whatever Angelina wanted.

As they continued to travel back the way they had just come a few hours ago, Likos could not help but notice that Haden seemed driven to get back to the edge of the forest. As the warmonger's pace increased, most of the group fell back some hundred cubits. Likos was determined that he was going to stay with Haden so that if he tried anything, everyone else would have time to get away.

When they got to the edge of the forest, Likos looked back and saw that the rest of the group had stopped for some reason, but from this distance, he could not tell why. When he turned back around, Haden was standing about forty cubits on the other side of the tree line, looking up.

Likos also looked up, but he could not see anything. As he began to walk out of the forest, the sky suddenly went dark. He looked up again and saw the most terrifying thing he had ever seen. He fell to the ground and was barely able to reach for an arrow. He knew he had to do something to save Angelina and the rest of the group.

After a few seconds, he somehow regained his composure and, instead of fumbling with his bow, managed to get to his feet. He knew he needed to make it back to the edge of the woods so that he could warn the others. He could see that Angelina was glowing so brightly that he could barely see the old woman next to her. He started yelling for them to run, but before he could start moving toward them, Haden grabbed him from behind.

The warmonger calmly told him, "Stop, boy. The dragon will think you are food, and if you try to run, you will not make it to the edge of the forest."

By now, the dragon was hovering just twenty or so cubits above them. Haden let him go, but Likos did not intend to be fed to the dragon, so he started trying to run. He had not gotten more than a few steps when Haden grabbed him again and knocked him unconscious.

Once again, Angelina could not tell if she was dreaming as the warmonger stood alone at the edge of the forest. Although he never said a word, it appeared as if he was calling to something. Likos and the old woman were also there, which added to her confusion.

Likos had got into a confrontation with the warmonger, and although the old woman never said anything, she held her bony little hand out and pointed toward the sky.

Angelina wanted to run to Likos, but fear had once again consumed her.

As she watched the scene unfold, Haden again grabbed the boy and, with a single blow from his large hands, knocked him to the ground.

Unexpectedly, Haden spoke, "Angelina, look at me. You need not fear the dragon, for it cannot harm you." She looked around, but no one else seemed to notice that the warmonger was speaking.

Angelina was not sure whether she was dreaming or whether it was real this time.

They had been in the air for about thirty minutes when Sabrina realized she had to hold on tighter just to maintain her position. For a few moments, she was sure she could see something in front of them, but she quickly lost it in the clouds. Despite her difficulty seeing, she continued to search the horizon for anything that might be a dragon.

Anna seemed firmly planted behind her, and as far as she could tell, the girl never moved.

Suddenly, something occurred to her. "What if we do find this dragon, then what?" A hundred different thoughts went through her head as she again caught sight of something just beyond the distant horizon.

Sabrina could not believe the small silhouette in the far distance could be anything other than a large bird. Most of her thoughts were focused on the distant object that either just landed or went below the horizon. Suddenly, she realized she was holding on so tight that she could barely feel her hands. As she tried to loosen her grip just a little, she started to shift, but before she could slide, Anna pushed her closer to the dragon.

Sabrina could see the dragon below them, but still she did not have any idea what they were going to do with the massive creature. She did not understand why Anna did not land and was beginning to wonder if she had thought the situation through. They were making their fourth circle when she noticed something other than the dragon.

Sabrina could see a man standing between the dragon and the edge of the forest. Although there was something familiar about him, she could not quite figure out what it was from this distance.

Anna circled the large dragon several more times and then finally landed her dragon on the opposite side of the man.

Sabrina knew it was going to take a little while for her to get off the dragon, but Anna quickly jumped off and drew the only weapon she had. She started slowly walking toward the man because she did not want to frighten the dragon. She announced, "I don't know what you think you are doing, but if you value your life, you will slowly walk away from this creature."

She suddenly realized there was a second man lying on the ground.

As the second man got to his knees, the larger man started walking toward the dragon.

She had not anticipated this action and walked a dozen steps closer to the large creature she had come to save. She made sure the large man could see her. Then she repeated, "I don't know what you think you are doing, but if you value your life, you will walk away from this dragon."

Sabrina had finally gotten off the dragon. She ran her hand along the dragon's head as she had seen Anna do many times.

Paytah roared and then lay down as he was directed.

As the large man continued to walk toward the dragon, Sabrina suddenly got a good look at him and finally realized who he was. If she could have run toward him, she would have. As she hobbled toward him, the large dragon next to him roared so loudly that it echoed throughout the area.

Anna quickly grabbed her. "Girl, have you not learned anything? Go back to Paytah before you kill us all." She turned and once again started walking toward the dragon.

Sabrina did not know how to warn her friend about the man standing next to the dragon, but she also had no intentions of letting her find out on her own. She quickly yelled, loud enough for everyone to hear, "Stop, or you will die."

Anna turned to see what was wrong with Sabrina, and as she looked back, it was clear that even her dragon seemed uneasy. When she turned back to see where the large man was, he was already running his hand along the side of the dragon's head. Instantly, the dragon lay as it was directed.

As Anna watched the dragon lay down, she could not believe she had been so wrong about the man. She thought to herself, *So he knows a little about dragons, but that does not mean that I am just going to give up.* She slowly continued to walk toward the dragon with her dagger in her hand. She then announced, "I am not leaving this dragon here. It belongs back in the Dark Lands."

Although she knew it was dangerous, Sabrina followed the young dragon rider and once again tried to tell her she needed to stop.

Although neither dragon seemed comfortable with Sabrina's movement or speech, Anna's dragon seemed as if it wanted to get up.

Anna quickly turned around replied, "I don't have time for this, and you need to go back to Paytah." She pointed to her dragon and added, "Keep him calm like I taught you. Do you understand?"

Sabrina looked back at the dragon, and it did appear as though he was going to get up at any moment. She looked at her father, and although she could not tell from his blank expression what his intentions were, she was sure the massive dragon was staring at her. She did not know how to convince Anna to stop and knew all too well that her father was a cold-blooded killer who would not have any problem killing the young girl if she continued toward him.

As Anna once again started moving toward the dragon and her father, Sabrina did not know what else to do, so she screamed as loudly as she could, "Stop, he is my father!"

Paytah sprang up and started walking toward the two girls to see if he could figure out what his master was doing and if he could help.

To everyone's surprise, Haden clapped his hands and then ran his left hand along the ground. After a few seconds, Anna's dragon lay back down.

Although Anna was still trying to figure out why Sabrina was screaming between two dragons, what bothered her more was how this man was able to order her dragon to lay down. As she began to put Sabrina's words together, she realized the man was Haden, the killer of Nedah, and she was suddenly filled with rage. She tried to hold onto her courage as she continued to walk toward the man who had destroyed the world.

When she found herself face to face with this killer, she heard a voice she thought she might never hear again. She looked up and could not believe her eyes. Just twenty-five cubits away stood her teacher and friend, Gaho-Meda.

The old woman held out her bony little hands and said, "My child, do you want to die like this? There must be a better way that we can resolve this situation. Please put down the dagger, and we will talk about this over a hot meal."

Of course, Anna dropped the dagger and started walking toward the old woman. However, she quickly realized that although this old woman looked and sounded like her old friend, it was not her.

Before Anna could change her mind, the old woman grabbed and hugged her. The old woman picked up her dagger and started leading Anna back to the edge of the forest.

Anna took the dagger back. "You are not Gaho-Meda, are you?"

The old woman hesitated for a moment and replied, "No, child. My name is Pangaea."

Anna could not help but ask, "Why would you let this warmonger so close to this dragon?" Suddenly, she remembered her dragon and turned to see what had become of Paytah.

The old woman grabbed her arm and asked, "Do they not still teach of Nedah the Master of Dragons in the Dark Lands?"

Anna did not understand how this man could be both Haden and Nedah, but there was little doubt the man with her dragon was a dragon master.

Likos did not like the whole situation before Haden had two dragons, and he sure did not like it now that these monsters had shown up. He sat on a rock watching Haden, who had not left the dragons since they dropped out of the sky. He was not sure what he was supposed to do now or how he would be able to protect Angelina.

The old woman had said that Angelina would be fine and all she needed was some rest, but he still wished there were something more he could do.

As the old woman had directed, most of the camp was helping to find food for the dragons. He did not know where the two young women who rode on the smaller dragon had gone to, but he assumed they were with the old woman.

Suddenly, Likos could hear voices coming from Haden and his dragons. As he walked closer to the dragons, it was clear that the other two voices were coming from the dragons. Although he had always been able to hear animals in a way few others could, he had never heard animals talk as these dragons did. It was not just broken words but stories such as he had never heard before.

He soon realized that Haden knew he was there because every so often, he would look up at him. Likos did not care because he wanted to hear what these beautiful creatures had to say.

## CHAPTER 31

# IN THE WAY OF DREAMS

Angelina did not know a lot about dragons and had only once seen these monsters when she encountered Haden for the first time.

She had fallen behind the rest of the group, but she did not care if the monsters were fed.

She wanted to talk to the old woman, but as soon as they started out, she took Haden's general and disappeared. She did not believe the old woman was in any danger but thought, *It would be nice if she were around to talk to or to tell me what to do.* She had barely ever been out of Hela and had no idea what a dragon ate other than meat, which, of course, she had no way of getting.

As she lingered behind, she tried to remember the day Haden summoned the dragons and still could not figure out what the two young girls had to do with the warmonger or the dragons. She remembered being frightened, but even now, she was not sure how much was real or how much had been a dream.

Angelina was not thinking clearly because once again, it had been days since she had slept. Although she was no longer having the same nightmares, she was still having bad dreams.

She looked around and did not see the old woman anywhere. Her guards were only a dozen cubits away, but she knew they would not talk to her anyway. Finally, she decided to find a place where she could rest and wait for the others to return. She thought, *Maybe dragons eat sticks because everyone else seems to have one.* She laughed and then began to fall into a light sleep.

Angelina looked around but could not remember how she got to this place or who most of these people were. There were so many people for as far as she could see that she believed that once again she was must be dreaming, but she had no way to know for sure.

Suddenly, she realized she was bleeding from somewhere in her midsection. There was so much pain that she could not stand it any longer and fell to her knees. When she looked up, Haden was also on one knee.

Finally, she heard Haden scream, "Enough!" When she opened her eyes, all she could see was the warmonger looking back at her.

She closed her eyes again to see if she could clear her thoughts or wake from this dream. She could feel the ground shaking beneath her, and when she opened her eyes again, Haden was standing with his arms extended. There were dead bodies everywhere and more people falling for as far as she could see.

Likos was not sure if it was the right thing to do, but he shook Angelina again because he had to do something before, she killed them all.

Finally, the rocks and sticks began to fall as the young witch started to awaken.

She gasped for air, but it only took a second for her to realize that breathing was much easier than she had expected. She sat up and slowly began to exhale while she tried to regain her composure.

Likos grabbed her hand and asked, "Are you okay?"

She nodded her head, but she knew she could not let Haden kill millions of people in her name. She also knew she had always misunderstood her dream but could still see people dying by the thousands. Now, more than ever, she wished that she could talk to the old woman, but she was still with Haden's general.

Finally, she decided there was no reason to worry about this new dream because even Haden would not kill so many people.

She extended her hand to Likos and decided she would talk to the old woman the first chance she had. There was no way she would let Haden cause so much death.

They had only been back in the camp for about an hour, but the old woman still had not returned. Angelina could not imagine that Airus would do anything to harm the old woman even if she kept knocking on his head. She could not imagine the warmonger would let his general do anything to the old woman, but she still wished she knew where she was.

As she sat in the camp tearing apart the weeds the old woman had asked her to collect, she watched Haden as she had found herself doing so many times in the last few days. If she did not know better, she would have thought that Haden and the younger of the two girls were fighting.

The girl would continue to get on the dragon, and without mercy, he would throw her to the ground. He would then scold the girl, and seconds later, she would mount the dragon again, only to be thrown off it.

She thought for a moment and whispered, "Anna. Yes, that is her name. I don't understand what she is doing with the warmonger." She watched as time after time, the young girl would climb on the smaller dragon, and after a few seconds, Haden would throw her from the creature as if she was a sack of potatoes.

Angelina was not sure where Likos was although he was probably cleaning the small animals he had managed to catch earlier.

The other girl walked up and asked, "Can I sit down? I have some questions that I need to ask, and you seem to be in charge."

She nodded her head and then looked to see whether Haden was still there. She was not sure whether she trusted Haden, Nedah, or whatever his name was. With the new dream though, she no longer feared for her life but for the millions he would kill in her name.

Sabrina sat down and asked, "How do you know my father, and do you know what happened to him?"

She tried not to act surprised, but the young girl's words pierced through her head like a shape knife. After a few moments, Angelina shook her head and replied, "I do not really know anything about him." She turned and asked, "Did you say that Haden is your father?"

Sabrina bowed her head. "Yes. When I heard that he was dead, I never shed one tear. When I found him alive and realized that he did not know me, I never felt so much pain in all my life."

Angelina looked at her for a few seconds and then asked, "Is he the monster that so many people fear?" She looked once again to see what the warmonger was doing. "It is not your fault that he is a warmonger who does not care about anything except himself and, apparently, dragons."

Sabrina replied, "It was not like that at all. It is true that he was a warmonger who has destroyed more kingdoms than I care to try to remember." She took a deep breath and continued. "He is my father, and now that I look back on it, he never did anything that was not in my best interest. He always made sure that I had the best teachers and that my every whim was met. At the time, I did not understand, and now he does not even know who I am."

Angelina had never thought of Haden as being a father or anything other than a warmonger. She started wondering what else she did not know about him. She asked, "Do you know anything about someone named Nedah?"

Sabrina thought for a moment and replied, "He was a legendary warrior from the Dark Lands that was supposed to save the world, but I am not sure he was even real."

Angelina laughed. "According to the old woman, your father Haden and her son Nedah are the same person."

Sabrina looked at her father and Anna before replying, "I'm not sure that is possible. Nedah was defeated over two hundred years ago."

Both girls looked at the warmonger for several minutes without saying anything.

Finally, Sabrina asked, "So how did you become part of this group?"

Angelina got up to throw away the unwanted parts of the weeds she had been stripping and replied, "I am the person who killed him."

~*~

It had been several hours now, and Angelina still did not know where the old woman and Airus had gone or why they had not returned yet.

Haden's daughter no longer seemed so eager to ask questions. Sabrina had not spoken to her since she told her she was the one who killed her father.

Haden and the young dragon rider were still doing something with the dragons.

She watched as both dragons suddenly stood up and started looking toward the forest to the right of where she was sitting.

Anna quickly tried to get her dragon to sit back down, but there was little she could do to calm the creature. Although the girl seemed frustrated, Haden did not seem affected.

Angelina did not think much about what Haden and Anna were doing until the dragons started coming toward the camp and her nightmares began to come flashing back to her.

However, one word from Haden and both dragons stopped to wait for whatever it was approaching from the forest.

Likos, as he always did, showed up out of nowhere with his bow drawn to defend her from whatever was coming toward them.

Suddenly, a small herd of about ten deer ran out into the clearing where the dragons were standing.

Within seconds, the dragons managed to knock most of the deer to the ground, and each grabbed deer for themselves.

Angelina watched as Anna quickly pulled her dagger so that she could kill as many as possible before they started running back to the woods. She knew exactly where to strike the poor beasts and was able to kill three of them before they could get to their feet.

As the deer started to run past Haden, he grabbed a young buck and, in a single movement, broke its neck. He then used it to stop a larger buck and quickly grabbed the creature and put it out of its misery.

As the last two deer ran back to the forest, Likos was able to get a clean shot, and one more of the deer fell to the ground.

The old woman and Airus walked out of the forest with branches tied to them. Angelina could hardly tell who they were.

She looked once again toward the warmonger, who appeared to be looking at her. She knew without a doubt that this man was a natural-born killer, and if she did not do something, he would kill millions. She clenched her fist and thought, *I killed him once before. I can do it again.*

It had been several days since Airus and Pangaea had chased the deer into their camp, and once again, Angelina found herself alone and away from everyone. She did not understand why she felt like she needed to be alone, but there were just too many voices in the camp.

She had not meant to use her power to make the rocks dance, but she was bored. It started with one small, and now there were several dozen rocks bidding for her attention.

She could use her magic to force the rocks away, but for each one she pushed away, another was sure to follow.

With every wave of her hand, she would send another rock away, but it seemed as though the number of rocks was increasing every minute.

Suddenly, all the rocks stopped midair. She looked around but did not understand why the rocks were no longer coming for her. After a few seconds, she realized Haden was standing behind her.

Startled, she asked, "What are you doing?" but the large warmonger just stood as still as the rocks he had stopped midair.

After a few moments, she demanded, "Stop this right now." As she started to glow, Haden turned and began to walk away from her.

As soon as he took a step away, the rocks again began to dance and come toward her. With a wave of her hand, she sent the rocks flying through the air with much greater force than before. However, as the force at which she had sent the rocks away had increased, so did the intensity at which they returned. She waved her hands and yelled at the rocks, but the more she tried to stop them, the faster the rocks returned.

Finally, she could not take it anymore and cried out, "Help me, please!"

Out of nowhere, Haden reappeared, and once again, the rocks stopped midair.

After a few moments to catch her breath, Angelina said, "Thank you. Can you make them stop?"

For several seconds, Haden did not say anything, but finally he answered, "For you, I would do anything."

The rocks fell to the ground, and she could feel his power. For the first time in her life, she understood why she did not have any control over her power. She gasped as she realized with absolute certainty that this man would kill everyone for her, and there was nothing she could do to stop him. She wanted to get up and run, but she could not find the courage to move.

As Haden left, Angelina turned to watch him walk away from her.

## CHAPTER 32

# FADING HOPE

It had been two weeks since General Vanessa Virgo had led the raid on the small southern city of Hela, but she was just now starting to put all the pieces together. If she understood half of what had happened, she knew the information she had was valuable. She also understood that it meant betraying her friend.

She had tried to make her way out of the area, but now she found herself only a few leagues from Lord Scorpion's main army. She knew she could not stay where she was, but for the moment, she did not know where else to go.

She had found a place to hide in an animal shelter, but she needed to find something to eat. The last time she tried to find some food, she saw at least a dozen people who could identify her.

Suddenly, she heard someone else in the barn with her. She slowly put her hand on the small knife she found a few days ago.

She exhaled in relief and removed her hand from her weapon as a child came into view. She closed her eyes and waited for the child to leave.

She realized she was not as hidden as well as she thought when the child asked, "Why are you up there when your friends are outside?"

General Virgo quickly lifted herself up and asked, "Do they know that I am in here?"

The little girl shrugged her shoulders. "I don't know, but they all seem to be looking for you. Should I get them?"

Virgo swung down from the rafters, but by the time her feet hit the ground, the girl had opened the door and was talking to one of the guardsmen.

When four men walked into the building, she grabbed a long-handled tool and struck the first person to come close to her.

As she hit the second man with the butt of the tool, five additional men came rushing into the small building.

Although she was better skilled than most, it only took a few moments before they were able to overpower her.

By the time the last three men came in, she was already on her knees and had very little strength left to fight back.

The captain of the guard lifted her by her hair as two of the other guardsmen bound her hands behind her.

The captain of the guard spoke, "General Virgo, Lord Scorpion and Lord Taron would like to have a few words with you, if you do not mind."

It had been several hours since the guardsmen had captured her, but they still had not taken her in to see Lord Scorpion. Surprisingly, they had not been that rough, but she still did not know what she was going to tell the warmonger. General Virgo did not want to put her friend Airus at risk, but the truth of the matter was that they had not made any effort to hide themselves. As far as she was concerned, there was no reason she could not tell the warmonger everything she knew.

Finally, someone came to take her to see Lord Scorpion so that she could tell her secrets and maybe keep her life.

The guardsman told her, "The giant and his brother are ready to see you now, General."

She had never met the one called Taron the Destroyer, but she could not see how that changed anything. She got up, dusted herself off, and replied, "It is about time. I thought they were going to keep me waiting forever."

As she was being taken to meet with her master, the ground began trembling beneath her feet. Although she had felt the ground shake before, this was somehow different.

Once she saw the giant, she realized he was making the ground shake with his pacing back and forth.

She took a deep breath and tried to remain calm because she knew the stories about how this monster fed on fear. Even though she knew better, all she could think about was the extreme size of Taron the Destroyer. She needed to shake some sense back into her head, but all she could think about was this giant smashing her skull with his massive hands.

When the guard stopped ten cubits in front of the two warmongers and dropped to one knee, she was still thinking about the giant and almost forgot to bow. As she quickly dropped to one knee, she could no longer see the giant and his sorcerer brother, so she held her breath as the shadows flickered before her.

Lord Scorpion finally dismissed the guard and told her, "Rise, General Virgo, and tell me and my brother about your mission. Where are the thousand warriors that I gave you?"

She did not know why, but for a moment, she took her eyes off the sorcerer to glance at the giant. She immediately turned back toward her master and replied, "Master, I believe that they are all dead."

After a few moments, she added, "The witch of Hela used a tactic that I am still not sure I understand."

The giant grabbed a large chair that had been set up for him and flung it over fifty cubits through the back of the tent.

She could only watch as Lord Scorpion tried to calm his brother, but there was little he could do. She was not sure if this was just a tactic to scare her, but it definitely was working. The giant grabbed another chair and flung it in the same direction as the first.

Lord Taron grabbed his brother by the neck and demanded, "I want this witch, and I don't care if you have to send every person in this camp to get her."

She was sure Lord Taron was going to throw her master out too, but she did not move for fear that she would draw attention to herself. She suddenly remembered the rest of the information she needed to convey, but she was afraid to speak without permission.

After a few seconds, the giant let go of her master and screamed, "Do I make myself clear?"

Lord Scorpion picked himself up, looked at his brother, and replied, "I think that we should send a larger raiding party to drive the witch into a trap." He signaled to his generals to prepare the raiding party. He then turned toward his brother and waited.

The giant watched as people ran to prepare his brother's raiding party. He knew his brother was up to something, but he was not sure what it was yet.

General Virgo knew she needed to tell them the rest of her information, but she still had not been permitted to speak.

Lord Scorpion walked up to her and mumbled something in her ear, but she did not understand what he was telling her.

She did not want to ask her master to repeat himself, but she did not have any choice. As she started to speak, she realized her master was speaking to her again. She tried to make out the words, but there was something different about his voice. She thought Lord Scorpion was asking about the thousand dead warriors. Although this was what she heard, she somehow knew this was not what her master was saying. All at once, she fell to her knees, and she no longer had any control of her body.

For years, she had wondered why anyone would stand still and let the sorcerer cast a truth spell on them, but now she wished she did not know.

She was screaming with everything she had, "Haden is still alive!" but the only words that were coming out of her mouth were gibberish that she did not understand.

General Virgo could not determine how long she had been babbling, but at least the ground had stopped shaking for a while. She did not understand how she could be talking about her childhood and still be conscious of everything around her. She felt as if Lord Scorpion had somehow separated her body from her mind.

Not that it mattered now, but at least she would get to spend her last remaining days watching the bastard get what he deserved when they found out that Haden was still alive.

She noticed that a messenger had arrived and was talking to the warmongers. Although it was hard to hear the man over her own voice, she was able to tell that he had news about the witch of Hela.

The messenger reported, "We have found the witch and her companions. They are camped at the edge of a small forest just three days from here."

She could hear the warmongers discussing something but did not immediately understand what they were saying. Finally, she heard something about how the rebel dragon guilds had managed to capture one of Haden's dragons.

Lord Scorpion mumbled something about the north regrouping and another dragon, but for some reason, he was the hardest person to understand.

She could not tell what the giant was throwing this time, but she did hear him screaming, "I don't care about dragons or how many warmongers are heading this way!"

Finally, Lord Scorpion said, "There is no place for the witch to run now." He looked at his brother and asked, "Should we send another raiding party to bring this witch to justice?"

The giant turned toward his brother and, after a moment, replied, "I will take a raiding party and bring the witch back myself."

While Lord Taron's back was turned, Lord Scorpion smiled smugly and said something like, "I will have a thousand of my finest warriors ready within an hour."

Taron did not need to be told that his brother could not be trusted. However, he knew he did not have much of a choice with so many warmongers heading toward Utopia. Finally, he replied, "I will lead the raiding party myself."

The messenger indicated that there was more to his message, but Lord Scorpion held up his hand, signaling the messenger to wait.

As the giant started to turn back around, the sorcerer wiped all expression from his face and asked, "Are you sure? This witch killed our father and has already taken out one raiding party."

3However, Lord Taron did not respond as he stomped out.

General Virgo thought to herself that their plans would be over as soon as they found out who traveled with the witch.

When the giant was far enough away, Lord Scorpion turned to the messenger and demanded, "What other news do you have for me?"

The messenger replied, "Lord, we believe the witch has taken control of one of your father's dragons."

Scorpion stopped. "I want this dragon. When my brother has left the camp, I want every general to report to me."

General Virgo heard the conversation and wanted to smile, but her body was not her own, so she continued to talk about her first crush.

General Virgo knew she probably only had a day or two left because she had never seen anyone live beyond their last memory. Her pending death made sense because with the body and mind separated, once the last memory was reached, the body did not know what to do next.

As she watched the two lights in the distance, she thought, *At least, I will get to see Lord Scorpion get what he deserves.* She did not know how the sorcerer always seemed to have such great timing, but as she continued to watch the battle in the distance, she spoke about how she did not understand the lights.

Suddenly, she realized there was a chance she would tell her secret before Lord Scorpion was confronted by Haden. She could only guess she had about twenty minutes left before she revealed her secret.

She had not cried since she was ten years old, but if it were possible, she would have bawled her eyes out.

With little hope left, all she wanted was to die. However, she could not even do that.

She listened as a messenger reported, "Lord, we believe that your brother has been defeated."

Lord Scorpion smiled at the thought of his brother's defeat and then began ordering his troops to prepare for battle.

She looked down at the battlefield below, and the lights had gone out. The battle was over, and she would not see justice. She knew now that there was nothing she could do—the sorcerer was going to win after all.

As she lost all hope of seeing Lord Scorpion defeated, she heard herself tell the world that "Haden is still alive and with the Witch of Hela."

Lord Scorpion was not listening to her anymore, but the mere mention of his father's name made him stop what he was doing. He demanded the scripter tell him what the general had just said.

The scripter shook as he fumbled through his script but was finally able to read aloud, "Haden is still alive and with the Witch of Hela."

Suddenly, two dragons landed in the middle of the camp, and Haden stepped from the largest one.

General Virgo watched as a thousand people stood seemingly in shock and did nothing as the warmonger continued to walk toward the center of the camp.

Haden stopped and then demanded, "Do you not know how to bow down before your master?"

Instantly, people began to fall to their knees as the warmonger continued to walk toward his son.

Lord Scorpion quickly bowed as his father approached him.

General Virgo then noticed her old friend Airus, an old woman, and the giant walking toward her. She may not have been able to keep her secret, but at least the sorcerer did not win. She knew she only had a few minutes left to live, but she accepted the inevitable.

Airus stopped in front of her as Lord Taron continued to walk toward his father.

Airus said something to the old woman she did not understand, but that did not matter anymore.

She watched as the old woman pulled out a dagger. General Virgo wished she could talk to her friend, but she knew that this end was for the best as the old woman stabbed her with the dagger.

~*~

As General Virgo started to wake up, she was not sure where she was, but it did not take long for her to realize she was still alive. Every muscle in her body hurt, her throat was dry, her vision was still blurry, and there was an incredibly sharp pain going through her right shoulder.

Airus looked down and told her, "You should not move, or you could start bleeding again."

She slowly put her hand out to him and asked, "Why am I still alive?" Before he could answer, she asked, "Why does my shoulder hurt so much?"

He gently put his hands on her and replied, "You were stabbed with a dagger forged in dragon blood. It was the only way to save you."

She looked at Airus. "Why did Haden wait so long to return?"

He shook his head and replied, "It is a long story that I don't understand." After a few moments, he added, "Haden is not the person I thought he was—at least, I don't think that he is." He then told his friend to rest while he found someone to bring her some water.

# CHAPTER 33

# THE GATHERING OF FORCES

The north had built up their defensive positions along the foothills in the northern part of Utopia. It had been well over a full cycle of the moon since Haden had driven them out of the southern part of the kingdom, but they were starting to regroup and look like an army again.

General Hortz hated that they had to leave so much of the south behind, but they were overwhelmed so quickly that he was lucky to have an army left. He only wished that the warmonger Haden could have been defeated before he used his dragon to invade the southern part of Utopia.

He could see a messenger waiting for him, but he knew he did not have enough men to help whatever city had sent the man. He took a deep breath and started walking toward the messenger who had been patiently waiting for him.

The messenger snapped to attention as the general walked up. After the general acknowledged him, he relayed, "Sir, the city of Asmir has managed to capture one of Haden's dragons."

General Hortz asked, "What is the condition of this dragon?"

The messenger replied, "Although the creature destroyed half of the city, I believe that it is unharmed."

The general knew that most people would want to kill the monster so that it could not destroy another city. However, he understood that a weapon as powerful as one of Haden's dragons meant that they could use it to drive the other warmongers from Utopia.

After a moment, the messenger added, "Sir, the high council has requested that you send a representative to help determine what to do with the dragon."

General Hortz nodded his head and dismissed the messenger. He had taken command of the southern forces just a few hours after Hela fell to Haden's dragons, and as far as he knew, he was the last remaining general in the South.

It was true that Haden's forces were no longer advancing north, but they did control all the southern part of the kingdom. The only good news was that without the warmonger Haden leading the invasion, even the clashes were not as bad as they were when he was in charge.

It had been about a month since the northern cities had promised to send reinforcements, but now he was not sure they were coming. He believed that Utopia's force, divided among half a dozen cities, would be no match for the large army in the south even without Haden's dragons.

It had also been a month since he had sent guardsmen to find the witch of Hela, but he had not heard any news about her since she defeated the raiding party at Hela.

After a great deal of thought, he decided he had waited long enough and demanded a dozen messengers to report to his command center. He was going to go to Asmir himself and once again unite the forces of Utopia.

As the first six messengers reported, General Hortz told them, "Go to the large cities in the north and find out how long before they are ready to commit forces to this war."

The lead messenger asked, "What if they are not willing to leave their cities?"

He looked at the messenger for a few seconds and replied, "Tell them that if they cannot provide forces, then we can no longer patrol the border. Make sure that they know that the high council wants representatives from every city and every guild."

The messenger replied, "Yes, sir," and then directed the other five messengers to relay the same message.

Within a few moments, six more messengers showed up to receive orders.

The general sent the rest of the messengers to the east and the west to see what forces were gathering.

As the messengers were leaving, he emphasized, "I want to know where every warmonger is and how long before they arrive here."

The last messenger stopped and asked, "Should we see if the dragon guilds in Athena are willing to provide forces?"

General Hortz nodded replied, "An enemy of my enemy might be worth pursuing." He paused then added, "See what it would take for them to join us."

He thought to himself, *We are finally starting to look like an army again, and it is time we start acting like it.*

General Hortz did not know what had changed, but the enemy was not pushing north the same way they had just a few days ago. Normally, he would have taken this as a good sign, but he knew the enemy had no reason to stop or withdraw.

It had been days since he had sent the scouting parties south, but no one had returned yet. He needed to start heading north, but the lack of enemy aggression made him think that the warmongers in the south were preparing for a full-scale invasion.

He did not believe he would be gone for any longer than a week or two, but he did not like the idea of leaving his army. As he walked through the camp, he ordered all the captains to provide him with a count of all able-bodied warriors.

The captains had completed several drills in the last month, so it only took a few moments before the general was getting reports back from all operations.

Although they had been resupplying since they started fortifying the foothills, he sent out additional patrol teams to gather more supplies.

The camp was as busy as any city he had ever seen preparing for war. General Hortz looked around, and although it was not what he imagined a month ago, there was no doubt that they were starting to look like a real army.

From his current location, he could see that some of the messengers were returning. As he walked toward the messengers, General Hortz thought, *I think that we can maintain our positions until I get back with reinforcements.*

As he walked into the command center, he could tell that something was wrong because everyone was watching him.

He quickly demanded, "Tell me what news you have. I have a thousand things that I still need to do."

The first messengers said, "Sir, he is alive." When the general did not say anything, he added, "Sir, the warmonger Haden is alive and back in charge of the army in the south."

No one said a word as they waited for the general to issue instructions on their next course of action.

General Hortz knew they would not want to abandon their post especially after they had given so much to defend it. However, without reinforcements, he knew his forces would not stand a chance against the warmonger Haden and his army. He announced, "Prepare the troops to pull back to the north. We are going to Asmir."

For several seconds, everyone around him just stood there as if they expected him to say something else.

It had taken almost a day to pack up the camp and just over three days to get to Asmir. General Hortz had hoped to get some rest before meeting with the high council, but it had taken longer to bring everyone than he had hoped, so he only had about an hour.

He had also hoped to speak with the captain of the guard to negotiate a few patrol teams. However, he had been stopped by half a dozen messengers and now did not have time. He already understood he would have to make time after the meeting with the high council if he had any hope of getting additional patrol teams. He turned and told the young man appointed as his assistant, "See if you can set up a meeting with the captain of the city guard."

The young man wrote down a few notes and asked, "Sir, how soon do you want this meeting?"

He waved his hand and replied, "I would like to meet as soon as possible."

When he looked up, he saw that hundreds of people were waiting on him. He turned to one of his captains and asked, "Do you know what is going on here?"

The captain shook his head and replied, "I think that they believe that you are here to save them." The general nodded and waved to those who caught his attention as he made his way to the center of city.

A dozen council members came to meet him and his senior staff as they entered the building for the meeting.

It took about twenty minutes before the group settled down enough to start the meeting. As the speaker started the introductions, the general looked around and could not see very many military members and no other generals.

When he stood up, the speaker stopped and asked, "General Hortz, would you like to address the council?"

He looked around once more and then asked, "Should we not wait for some of the other generals to come here before we start?"

No one said anything for almost a minute until the speaker finally replied, "Sir, you are the last known general, unless you know of another."

He shook his head and sat back down to hear what else the council had to say.

The speaker nodded and then continued. "We have received word that the warmonger Haden is alive. The good news is that we believe that the witch of Hela was able to take out a significant chunk of his forces before she was captured or killed."

General Hortz stood up again and asked, "Do we have a status on his forces and where they are now?"

A captain not far from him stood up and replied, "Sir, with the damage the witch has inflicted and the number of deserters, we believe that he only has about twenty thousand warriors."

The general stood thinking about this for a moment. "Has he started his retreat to the west or the south?"

The captain replied, "For the last few days, he has continued his march north and appears to be heading for Asmir."

Someone yelled, "It is that damn dragon! Haden is after the dragon!"

Someone else added, "We should kill the monster, and then Haden will not have any reason to come this far north."

The speaker waved his hand. "What if he continues to come north even after the dragon is dead? I have heard that there are dozens of warmongers heading toward us, so even if this warmonger turns back, it will not matter because more will follow."

General Hortz put his hands out and demanded, "Listen to me. Like it or not, we are at war, and it is not going to get better anytime soon." He raised his voice and added, "This dragon may be our only hope, and I will not let you kill it."

The speaker asked, "What would you have us do—just give up and run?"

The general smiled and replied, "No, what I have planned is much worse. I want you to stand and fight. I want this council to declare martial law and put me in charge. Here is where we will make our stand."

It had been well over an hour since General Hortz had demanded to be put in charge, but he still had not heard anything from the high council. Regardless of what the council decided, he was still the senior-ranking military person.

While the council debated on whether or not to turn power over to him, he ordered that all messengers report to him or his senior staff. He also demanded a status report from all the military in and around the Asmir area.

One of his captains arrived with a messenger from the western city of Athena.

The messenger reported, "The dragon guilds have captured a dragon also."

General Hortz asked, "What do you know about this dragon, and do the guilds know how to control the beast?"

The messenger nodded his head. "It is the largest dragon that I have ever seen, but the guilds can feed it and move it to wherever they want."

The general told the messenger, "Go back to these dragon guilds and tell them that if they will join us, I will grant them the city of Athena, but I want that dragon."

The messenger nodded and left to return to Athena.

By this time, the high council was once again requesting his presence, but General Hortz already knew what their response would be.

He sent out orders to restock the city with as many supplies as they could find and for anyone who could not help to leave. He also dispatched messengers to the neighboring cities demanding that they send every able-bodied person to Asmir to prepare to defend the city and the dragon.

It had only been a few days since General Hortz had taken control of all operations in the Kingdom of Utopia, but already he had an army of almost fifty thousand. He also had every magic guild within 150 leagues under his control. Just a few hours ago, he received word from the dragon guilds of Athena that they agreed to join his stand against the warmonger and were on their way to Asmir.

His guards had captured a tall, skinny man hiding just outside the city in an abandoned farmhouse. The man was in very poor shape, but he claimed to be one of Haden's dragon riders who deserted when his master was killed. General Hortz did not trust the man and was not foolish enough to let him on the dragon. However, he was able to feed the beast and could direct it to do anything he wanted.

From the last report he had, the warmonger Haden and his twenty thousand warriors were still a week out. By most calculations, the dragon guilds and their dragons would arrive two days before the warmonger Haden and his army.

General Hortz would have liked to have more time to prepare, but with two master dragons, a hundred magic guilds, and an army almost twice that of Haden, he would take his chances. He also believed that if the warmongers behind Haden wanted to fight, he would be ready for them too.

## CHAPTER 34

# THE END GAME

It had been days since they started moving north, but Airus still did not understand why they did not head west or south to regroup.

From most of the intelligence he had received in the past few days, the north had regrouped and now controlled two of Haden's dragons. The other dragon was under the control of a lunatic from the east who also had a large army.

He was beginning to believe that Haden thought he could conquer the entire kingdom with just twenty thousand warriors and two dragons. However, he doubted they were ready to fight any of the armies, let alone any one of the larger armies heading toward them.

For the moment, his biggest problem was the witch they had picked up along the way. The young girl was out of control, and no one knew what to do with her. She was yelling and telling everyone they needed to leave, or Haden was going to kill them all.

He did not understand why Angelina did not just leave with the young man who was always trying to protect her. He thought, *Hell, I don't understand why any of these people stayed in this mess.*

As he stood listening to the young woman, he realized there were very few other people listening to her. He could see that Likos was trying to get her to calm down, but without the old woman, he was barely able to help her maintain control.

As she started to glow again, Airus knew that if he did not do something, she would tear the camp apart.

He walked up to her and asked, "Angelina, can I get you something to drink?"

She took a deep breath and replied, "You do not need to worry. I am not going to start destroying things."

He smiled and asked one of the guardsmen, "Can you get us something to sit on?"

Suddenly, the ground started shaking, and dozens of people fell to the ground, including Angelina and Airus.

When the shaking stopped, Angelina told him, "Your master is going to kill everyone in this army, Utopia, and all the armies on their way here if we do not do something."

Airus shook his head and asked, "Why would he do this?"

Angelina pulled back and wanted to say something, but she could not find the courage.

Finally, Airus held out his hand and added, "He is not who you think he is. I just can't believe that he would do such a thing."

As he helped her to her feet, he asked, "Why don't you leave if you think that he is going to do this?"

She looked at him for a second and then replied, "I wish that I could."

In the hours since he had talked to Angelina, Airus was still not convinced his master could kill so many people. He decided to walk around to see if he could clear his head, but he was surprised by Haden.

He seemed emotionless as he asked, "You have been looking for me?"

Airus looked at the warmonger for a few moments and then replied, "I just wanted to see if there is something I should be doing."

Haden replied, "Everything except one thing has been put into motion. Now all that we can do is wait."

Airus thought for a moment and then informed his master, "The scouts tell me that there are dozens of armies tracking us.

Haden looked at him, "I have counted forty-seven different groups with more coming."

Airus had no way of knowing if his master was just guessing or if he truly knew that, there were forty-seven different groups watching them. "Master, shouldn't we move somewhere safer or even pull back to the west or south so that we can regroup?"

Haden replied, "No, what must be done will be done. However, there is one more thing that I need. I would like you to go with me to talk to the dragon guilds."

As far as Airus knew, they did not have any dragon guilds other than the boy who had appointed himself as the guardian of the witch, but he replied, "Yes, Master."

They had managed to direct the dragon to go anywhere they wanted, but Alexander still did not think that moving the beast was a good idea. The dragon was big, and half the kingdom knew they were trying to move it to Asmir.

Several small raiding parties had hit them, but with their numbers in the thousands, they had been able to hold their own.

Maria and the other dirt masters had been demanding that they stop to rest for a while, but most of the elders wanted to push on to the safety of Asmir. Alexander also wanted to push on, but Maria had finally convinced him to stop, and since they controlled the dragon, everyone stopped when they stopped.

Alexander had given the order to start moving again, and the dirt master had already removed the dirt from the chains that bound the dragon.

Suddenly, they were once again being attacked by another raiding party.

The dragon was startled and caught half the area on fire, which made it very difficult to defend their position.

Maria had built a wall so that they had some cover, and every time someone came near, Alexander would bend the dragon's fire toward them. Most of the guilds were working well together, but they were overwhelmed and had no retreat options.

Out of nowhere, two additional dragons landed in front of them. Alexander watched as the smaller dragon's rider and one of the riders from the larger dragon started toward their dragon. Three warriors attacked the young girl on the smaller dragon. She kicked the first two in their faces and turned the dragon to knock the third off his feet.

The larger rider continued throwing the attackers around as if they were rag dolls while the smaller rider stayed with the larger dragon. Seconds later, the larger rider walked up to their dragon and released it from the chains that bound it.

Finally, the man turned toward them, so Maria once again built a wall to protect them, but he walked through it as if it was paper.

Alexander grabbed as much of the dragon fire as he could stand and sent it toward the dragon rider.

With a wave of his hand, the man sent the flame into a dozen attackers. Within a few seconds, the three dragons had killed hundreds of the raiding party and were chasing others away.

Haden ran his hand along the ground to bring the dragons back. He demanded, "Tell me, who is in charge here?"

Alexander looked around, but no one had the courage to step forward, so after a few seconds, he replied, "I am."

For the last hour, Angelina had been tearing the camp apart, and there was very little that old woman or anyone else could do to calm her down.

Finally, when a rock hit Likos, she decided to sit down and try to stop throwing things around before she destroyed the whole camp.

The old woman grabbed the first person she could find. "Get this girl something to drink and eat." She then ordered everyone who was watching them to find somethings else to do.

She appeared to have the situation under control, and no one wanted to deal the witch for moment, so few hesitated when they were told to leave.

The old woman walked over to Likos and pulled his hair up so she could see how much damage had been done. "Boy, I think that you are going to live, but you should know better by now."

He started to get up, but the old woman dug her bony little fingers into the cut on his head and told him, "Sit down, boy, before you hurt yourself."

Angelina tried to calm down before she hurt anyone else, but she could not see how she would be able to stop Haden when the time came. Finally, she looked at Likos. "Haden is going to kill everyone for me, and I do not understand why."

The old woman stopped cleaning Likos's wound when she heard the girl's words. Finally, after nearly a minute, she replied, "Girl, you don't know what you are talking about." She then smacked Likos's hand again when he tried to take the rag she was using to clean his wound.

Angelina said, "I thought that I could stop him like I did before. I just do not think that I can now, and I do not know why."

The old woman handed Likos the rag and started walking toward the young woman. She held out her hand and told her, "Of course, you don't, girl. You are still too young."

Unexpectedly, Taron the Destroyer walked up and stood behind Likos but did not say anything.

The ground had shaken so much in the last week that Likos did not realize the giant had walked up behind him until he was only a few cubits away. As soon as he realized the giant was there, he scrambled to get to his feet so that he could get between Angelina and the monster.

The old woman shook her head and walked around the boy to see what Lord Taron wanted. She spoke a few words with him and then turned to see if Angelina was okay. After a few seconds, she asked, "Are you going to be okay?"

Angelina nodded as the old woman was walking away. She then grabbed Likos's arm and asked, "Do you still think you can get me out of here?"

~*~

He had been riding for hours, and as he jumped off the horse Likos had supplied him, the poor beast stumbled and fell to the ground. The messenger tried to catch his breath and then demanded to speak to whoever was in charge.

Even from on top of the great wall, General Hortz could see that this man was one of his guardsmen.

As the general came into sight, the messenger exclaimed, "The witch of Hela has escaped from the warmonger Haden and is about fifty leagues south of the city!"

One of the senior captains reminded him that there were also dozens of large armies just south of the city.

Another of the general's captains laughed and added, "Maybe all these warmongers will kill each other, and we will not have to worry about this war."

General Hortz demanded, "Show some respect. The witch of Hela is in the middle of this mess, and she has done more for this kingdom than all the warriors and magic guilds combined. I will be damned if I let her die now."

He looked around and saw that there were hundreds of people just standing around waiting for him to tell them what to do.

Finally, General Hortz ordered, "Prepare the dragon. We are moving out." A few seconds later, he added, "I want all the magic guilds and every able body ready to go in the next ten minutes."

They had been running for what seemed like hours, but according to one of the guardsmen, they were only an hour or two away from Asmir. Angelina had never been so far north, but for some reason, the land looked familiar. As far as she could see, there were open fields that they would have to cross if they had any hope of getting away from Haden's army.

Suddenly she stopped, despite Likos urging her across the field.

Likos asked, "What is wrong?" When she did not answer, he added, "We cannot stay here."

She was already starting to glow when she replied, "You are right. We cannot stay here because this is the place where everyone dies."

When he looked around, he could see people coming over every horizon. Within a matter of minutes, there were thousands of people in the open field, and more continued to arrive every second. To make matters worse, a large dragon landed in front of them.

He knew he needed to get Angelina away from this area, but there were thousands of soldiers in every direction. He drew his bow because he had no doubt this is where they were going to have to make their stand.

At first, Angelina believed that Haden had finally caught up with them, but when the two dozen smaller dragons followed, she realized she did not know who this was.

She understood there was nothing she could do now. Therefore, she took a deep breath and closed her eyes to wait for the end.

As Xio and his dragon started toward the witch as he had been directed by his master, he realized that the hatchlings were not following him. The witches had convinced his master that this girl was the key to controlling everything Haden once owned. Once again, he directed his dragon toward the young witch, but to his surprise, the dragon hesitated. When the dragon could not be directed, he jumped off the beast and started walking toward the glowing witch. In a single motion, he knocked out the boy who was guarding her.

He grabbed Angelina and was about to kill her, as the witches were directing, when all his dragons took to the air.

He did not understand because a dragon would only leave its master for the alpha dragon or a higher dragon master. He could still hear Master Yang and the witches yelling, "Kill the witch!" When Haden, the four master dragons, and twenty-five smaller dragons landed in front of him, he released Angelina, dropped to his knees, and exclaimed, "Master Nedah, I thought you were dead."

As he looked at his master of so long ago, the image of Yang started to fade until he was no more.

Fearful of the dragons, the warmonger, magic guilds, and endless armies could only watch as more people poured into the battlefield.

As Angelina ran toward Haden to see what she could do to stop him from killing all these people, one of the two-faced witches grabbed her and stabbed her in the side.

As in her dream, she grabbed her side and fell to the ground.

Instantly, Haden also grabbed his side and fell to one knee.

The other two-faced witch giggled. "Kill her now and destroy the one who walks in Haden's place."

Before the two-faced witch kill Angelina, Sabrina came out of nowhere and stabbed her with Anna's dagger.

Jeannie screamed, "What have you done?" and ran to her sister.

Angelina realized she was bleeding from somewhere in her midsection. There was so much pain that she was not certain she could stand. When she looked up, she saw that Haden was on one knee.

As she was fading in and out of consciousness, Angelina heard Haden scream, "Enough!" She prayed that this was only a dream, but as his power once more rushed through her body, the ground began to quake and ripple.

She kept her eyes closed, but she could still feel the ground shaking beneath her. When she opened her eyes again, Haden was standing with his arms extended. As she was again fading out of consciousness, she saw that there were dead bodies everywhere and more people falling for as far as she could see. She cried, "Please don't."

When she awoke, Angelina could no longer see Haden or the dragons, but everyone else appeared to be dead. She thought, *All these people, dead in my name. How could he have done this?*

In the distance, she could see the old woman and the giant coming toward her. She sat up and realized she was still bleeding.

When the old woman got close enough, Angelina asked, "Do you know what happened here?"

The old woman replied, "As was foreseen, Nedah has returned the magic to the ground and kept the world from tearing apart."

Angelina cried, "Did he need to kill so many people?"

The old woman smiled and replied, "Child, these people are not dead. Their power has been taken, but it is the people who will decide what to do with them."

She looked up again and could see that a few people were starting to move. She could not help but wonder if she was the reason Haden had not killed all these people as she believed he would.

However, she could still feel the warmonger's power rushing through her body. Therefore, she knew Haden had not taken her power, but she was not sure if she should say anything.

Without thinking, she commanded a single rock to come to her and then stopped it midair. She now understood why she had never been able to control her power. It was never her power in the first place. It had always been Nedah's, but now it was hers to control.

The old woman smacked her in the back of the head, and when the rock fell, she directed, "Sit down so that I can look at your wound. You need to be careful. Magic might not be popular right now."

As Angelina did as she was told, Haden's son Taron came up and sat down next to them.

~*~

People soon realized that none of the hundreds of warmongers or magic guilds had any power left. They quickly turned on these people who had once enslaved them. The rumors soon spread that the witch alone had defeated Haden and had taken everyone's power.

General Hortz ordered that a tent be set up so that Angelina could rest, but it would still be a while before the structure was ready for her. However, there were already people demanding to speak to her.

General Hortz believed that all the warmongers and magic guild had been stripped of their power. However, he was hearing rumors that the dragon guilds might still have their power.

Angelina could see that Airus was waiting to speak to her. She was certain that Haden's general would know what was going on, so she signaled for him to come forward.

Airus, Alexander, and Maria walked up to her and bowed down.

She asked, "Why are you here, and do you know where Haden is?"

Airus looked up and replied, "Haden wanted me to bring the dragon guilds here to protect you, but I am afraid that I do not know where he has gone, my Queen."

She asked, "Is it true that the dragon guilds still have their power?"

Airus nodded.

## CHAPTER 35

# THE NEW PROPHECY

They had been traveling for weeks now, and Sabrina did not believe they would ever make to the Dark Lands.

For the moment, however, all she cared about was that the dragons were starting to descend, which meant that at least they would be able to rest for a while.

As they started to land on the cliffs overlooking a large body of water, she could tell that Anna was confused.

By the time Sabrina was able to get off the dragon and reach Anna, the young dragon rider was looking out over the water.

Anna explained, "This water was not here when I left, and I am afraid that my home is gone."

Sabrina looked at the ocean. "My father knows what he is doing, and besides, if the world was breaking apart, maybe your home drifted away from where it was."

Anna looked back at the dragon master for a few moments. She knew that if anyone could get her home, then he could. She took a deep breath and turned around so that she could help find food for the dragons.

As Sabrina walked away, she thought, *I wonder just how close the world was to being torn apart?*

~*~

They had been island jumping several weeks, but finally, Anna could see a large landmass in the distance. The only thing she could think of was that she would be able to get some real food and see her friend Gaho-Meda.

She had never seen her home in the light and could not believe it was already so green. She took a deep breath as she watched a squad of dragon riders take to the air to meet them.

The dragon riders did not make any effort to stop Nedah and his master dragon, but instead they fell in behind them.

Once on the ground, Anna looked at the dragon master to see if he had instructions for her, but if he had something, he wanted her to do, he did not indicate it.

As Sabrina slowly started climbing off the dragon, Anna ran toward her old friend.

Gaho-Meda gave her a hug, but he did not stop looking at Dragon Master Nedah.

After releasing the old woman, Anna told her, "I need to help put the dragons away, and then I have a thousand questions."

Gaho-Meda once more looked at the dragon master. "Child, there are plenty of people to take care of the dragons. Your parents are expecting you, and I need your help to get back to town."

Somehow, Sabrina found herself helping Anna with the old woman. She thought about how much this old woman looked like Pangaea who they had left six weeks ago. She could hear Anna talking about something, but to be honest, she was not really listening because the old woman kept looking at her.

Finally, Anna asked, "Gaho-Meda, you seem to be having trouble walking. Is your leg getting worse?"

The old woman waved her hand. "It is not anything that a little time will not help."

Sabrina smiled and whispered to herself, "Time is relevant if there is such a thing."

The old woman pointed her cane at her and asked, "What do you know of time?"

Sabrina shook her head and replied, "I am not sure that I know anything about time, but my instructor used to say that time is relevant to the observer."

The old woman slowly turned to ask Anna, "What do you know about this girl?"

As she listened to Anna explain how they met and that she was Dragon Master Nedah's youngest child, Sabrina felt as though she should be the person telling the story.

Gaho-Meda turned to look at Sabrina again and then asked her, "How long have you studied the laws of existence?"

Sabrina looked at the old woman for a few seconds. "My father made sure that I was being taught the laws of existence before I could walk."

Gaho-Meda continued "So what do you think you know about the laws of existence?"

Before Sabrina could answer, Anna was once again telling of all the things she had seen in the month since she had gotten lost.

Finally, the old woman put her hand on the young girl. "Child, your parents are waiting for you, and I am sure that the city has something planned for you by now. If you don't mind, I would like to talk to your friend for a while."

Anna looked at Sabrina. "Of course. I am sure that my parents are wondering where I am." She gave the old woman a hug. "I will talk to you later."

Gaho-Meda had been expecting this since she watched the dragons land, but now she did not understand why he was waiting. Finally, she took a deep breath. "Child, you don't have to hide. I know that you are there."

Haden stepped out of the dark and waited for the old woman to acknowledge him.

She reminded him, "Child, you know that you are not supposed to be this close to me."

He did not say anything for several seconds. "How did you know that I was here?"

She smiled and replied, "Every dragon for a thousand leagues knew that you were coming, but that is not why you have come here, despite me telling that you should not come here."

He looked at her for several seconds before replying, "I do not know what to do now."

While she waited for him to say more, Gaho-Meda adjusted her weight to relieve some of the pain in her leg. When she could not take enough of the pressure off her leg, she asked, "Has your power returned yet?"

Haden shook his head. "What if it does not return as you said it would?"

She finally found a place to sit down. "Why did you leave my daughter, Pangaea, behind? I have waited so long to see her again, and she has looked so long for you."

He replied, "I am sorry, Grandmother, but the girl needed her help, and I did not know what else to do."

She nodded her head and then asked, "I see. So why did you leave the giant behind?"

He almost smiled before answering, "Because Pangaea needs to be a mother, and I cannot be the child that she needs."

She smiled once again. "I know, my child, but you cannot stay here as you well know." For a moment, she caught a glimpse of his human side that she did not believe he was capable of having.

He hesitated and then asked, "What about this girl? I miss her more than anything I have ever known, and I know so little about her."

She nodded her head and softly whispered, "I know, my child, but she is not ready. First she must understand."

When he did not say anything, she asked, "Tell me of your daughter Sabrina."

He looked at her for a few moments. "She will serve you and the laws of existence well, but she can be a bit hardheaded at times."

She had come to believe she would never find someone to take her place, but she would never have guessed that Haden would be the one to provide her a replacement.

She thought, *Maybe there is hope for this man after all.* She nodded her head. "Thank you. Now that you are here despite my warnings, there is much that we need to discuss."

It had only been a week since her father had brought her to this place, but for some reason, Sabrina felt comfortable here.

The old woman whom everyone called Grandmother had given her some medicine to help with the pain in her leg, but she was still barely able to walk. A few days ago, Anna had given her a wooden cane that made it a little easier to get around, but she did not think she was ready to travel.

Gaho-Meda had asked her to stay, but the truth was she really had nowhere else to go. Therefore, she decided to stay with the old woman for a while.

They had both hobbled out to watch her father leave when they realized Anna and her family were leaving with him.

Although her father and his dragon were only moving fifty leagues to the south, Sabrina wished she had known that her friend was going with him before she agreed to stay.

She thought the old woman was going to try to stop Anna from leaving, but for some reason, she did not.

Gaho-Meda took a deep breath. "Child, we need to go because there is much that we need to discuss."

As they hobbled back toward the center of town, the old woman told her, "I fear that this world is still in great danger."

Sabrina laughed and thought to herself, *This woman sounds a lot like my instructor Pythagoras.*

The old woman smiled. "The laws of existence are not always so easy to believe in, but soon you will understand the obviousness of the truth. Now that your father has started time, what do you think will happen when the suns meet?"

Sabrina looked up at the suns and began to wonder what would happen if these two massive balls of energy met. She only had to understand the very basic rules of the laws of existence to realize that the collision could kill everything on the planet.

The old woman put her hand on her, "Yes, my dear, we still need your father and his monsters."

It had been two months since Haden had taken the power from the warmongers and magic guilds and returned it to the ground. Angelina expected the world to be better off by now. As far as she could tell, the only people who had any power were the dragon guilds that Haden had sent to protect her. However, no one in the dragon guilds had as much power as she did.

Even without the warmongers and magic guilds, in the last week alone, she had received word that five different kingdoms were already at war, and there was nothing anyone could do to stop them. In the last few days, hundreds of people had come to ask for her help, but she did not know what she could do.

To her surprise, Airus had stayed, and he was doing a great job controlling the dragon guilds.

Angelina wished she could go with Pangaea and Taron, but the old woman was probably right when she said that people would follow her to the ends of the world.

She watched as the old woman and the giant slowly disappeared over the distant horizon.

She did not know why, but she knew this would not be the last time she saw Pangaea. For the moment though, she had other things to worry about not the least of which was Likos.

Likos and the cocky young fire bender Alexander, who had somehow become her captain of the guard, could not agree on anything, and the only person who could keep either in line was Airus.

She had given up trying to convince people that she had not defeated Haden and his dragons. Still most people were convinced she had drove him away and defeated the other warmongers. She thought it was funny that the mothers of Athena were telling their children that if they did not behave, Haden would return and take them away.

What was left of Utopia still had a government, but they would not do anything without consulting with her, including the building of a library to house the scrolls about magic.

General Hortz, like most of her council, wanted to put the dragon guild in charge of the library. Angelina thought to herself, *At least then I could promote Likos to captain of the guard, and Alexander would not be tormenting him all the time.* As if she did not have enough to think about, the land between Athena and Asmir had started to flood.

It had been three months since his father had defeated the other warmongers. Lord Scorpion, however, was not yet willing to reveal he still had his power especially with the witch of Hela threatening to use her ever-growing army on anyone who invaded someone else's kingdom.

He had heard rumors that the Kingdom of Persha was building armies to rival any on the planet. He knew this kingdom was far enough away that it would be a while before the witch could find him especially with the great valley flooding.

He looked up and, with two suns in the sky, knew there were plenty of places he could hide until he had a chance to rebuild his army. He smiled as he turned and started toward the east.

It had only been a year, but Sabrina knew she had learned more than she thought was possible. She could now see that the suns were moving closer together, and it would only take about twenty years before they collided.

As she watched the old woman hobble around, she asked, "Gaho-Meda, is there anything I can do to help you?"

The old woman waved her hand and replied, "No, my dear, there is not much anyone can do to help me now. Time catches us all at some point."

Despite what the old woman said, Sabrina lifted the items she was trying to carry so that she could get around a little better. She worried that Gaho-Meda did not have much longer and was not sure if she would be able to figure everything out on her own. She now realized that her father was an instrument of the laws of existence, and this old woman was an architect of these same laws. She wondered if something happened to this woman if she would have the strength to help save the world. For as long as she could remember, she had wanted power, but she would give almost anything not to know what she knew.

Gaho-Meda laughed. "Child, you will not have to do this on your own because my daughter will be here soon."

Sabrina put her hand on the old woman. "I am afraid that without a dragon, there is no way that your daughter could make it here." As the words came out of her mouth, something in the distance caught her attention. She shook her head in disbelief as she watched Lord Taron, with Pangaea on his shoulders, walking over the hillside.

She just did not see how the old woman could have made it back to what used to be the Dark Lands without magic or dragons.

www.ingramcontent.com/pod-product-compliance
Lightning Source LLC
LaVergne TN
LVHW091719070526
838199LV00050B/2467